SCENES THAT ARE BRIGHTEST

"You're as old as you feel," it is said. If so, Frances, widow of Doughty Dormer, was, at moments only, as young as the grandson with whom she had come to live in her old age, even as young as his son and the other grandchildren who gathered in that hospitable house. But such an illusion of youth, woven out of memory, needs some accidental tweaking aside of the curtain of years that hides what we were from what we are today.

Such an accident occurred when, on an afternoon so wet that floods were rising and the storm-whipped tide was pounding the coast, one of the children idly strummed a refrain she, Frances, had once sung long ago. By the singing of it had been set in motion the train of events that had moulded her life and brought into being these young folk of hers by whom she is surrounded. Thus, old and bereaved, frail and dependent, she lives once again the scenes that are brightest, in her long memory, to the subdued accompaniment of the fury of natural forces, like those that had so often threatened her during her long and now apparently almost completed life.

R. H. MOTTRAM

has also written

THE WINDOW SEAT

BUXTON THE LIBERATOR

BOWLER HAT

THE SPANISH FARM

MISS LAVINGTON

THE GHOST AND THE MAIDEN

THE WORLD TURNS SLOWLY ROUND

THE CORBELLS AT WAR

VISIT OF THE PRINCESS

THE GENTLEMAN OF LEISURE

COME TO THE BOWER

ONE HUNDRED AND TWENTY-EIGHT WITNESSES

THE PART THAT IS MISSING

OVER THE WALL

ETC.

SCENES THAT ARE BRIGHTEST

R. H. MOTTRAM

LONDON

HUTCHINSON

Hutchinson & Co. (Publishers) Ltd.

178-202 Great Portland Street, London, W.1

London   Melbourne   Sydney   Auckland
Bombay Johannesburg New York Toronto

First published 1956

*Printed in Great Britain
by The Anchor Press, Ltd.,
Tiptree, Essex*

TO
MY GRANDCHILDREN

NOTE

Some of the characters have already appeared in *Our Mr. Dormer* and *Castle Island* but this narrative is complete in itself

CONTENTS

"TURN ON, OLD TIME!"

THE words, once so familiar, so long forgotten, came rippling through the light veil of her afternoon siesta. Remote, yet so poignant, the notes of the air might have been struck on the chords of her heart, rather than the wires of the upright grand. The precise voice, as of a singer not quite sure of himself, reading at sight, renewed an intimacy so old that she did not rouse herself until the four bars accompaniment heralded the second verse. She sensed some confusion or hesitating somewhere, exclamations:

"Now you!"

"I can't, it's too——"

Lest it should be missed, she herself took up the cue. Her quavering old voice at once shocked and amused her a little, but she knew the part so well that she got the lines out and heard the pianist, after an instant's astonishment, rally to her with careful compunction.

> "Stay, fleeting Time, thine hour-glass
> The tide of life, oh stay!
> Nor let the golden moments pass
> Like worthless sand away . . .
> Like sand aw . . . ay!"

The succeeding chords were drowned by a kind of collective gasp and respectful mock applause. They had all turned to her, and spoke in order of familiarity:

Victor's warm affection, "But, Gran'maman . . .!"

Emil, apologetic, "I beg pardon . . .!"

"Not at all, Emil, I asked you to play or sing something. It sends me off——"

"But, Gran'maman, you burst into song!"

"Nonsense, Victor. I happen to know that tune rather well, that's all!"

Nina Cresswell had come over and knelt down beside her and was drawing up the shawl that had slipped off her shoulders at the sudden gesture she had made to straighten up and sing. By now she was thoroughly awake, not even bemused by the music, and she was visited by that momentary irritation that besets infants and the elderly. She felt . . . not quite cross, they were all so kind . . . but she had caused silence to fall on the little group round the piano. There sat that little Jean, bolt upright and not saying a word, her hands on the keys. And the Palgrave children . . . er . . . young people, Barnard must be twenty-five . . . staring a little nonplussed. She nearly blurted out:

"I won't be an interruption. I'm not an invalid. I was so comfortable, listening to you all, just nodding off when I felt like it. Now you're all staring at me as if I were an exhibit. Well, I suppose I am, but I'm not going to admit it."

Carefully schooling her tone, she translated it into: "Thank you, dear, I'm quite warm. Go on, Jean, I was enjoying it so. I haven't heard it for years. Go on, Emil, there are some jolly solos, even if they are a bit old-fashioned. Don't Barnard . . . Barney and Jennifer sing? I know Jennifer does!"

That sent them back to the piano.

"It goes into a trio . . . you can't do that!" The authority of Jean! Was it because she was so sparing of words, that every one told, when she used it?

Victor was whipping over the pages in his summary way.

"What's it called?" demanded Barney.

" 'Maritana in the Moated Grange', I should think. That's what this house will be if the rain persists."

They turned to the window against which the sheets of water were flung as from a bucket.

"*Maritana!* Never heard of it!"

"I should think not. Have you, Emil?"

"No. It is not a serious opera, I think."

"Serious!" Victor had turned back to the "argument" on the next page to the title. "There's a gipsy . . . at least a Gitana, two Dons, the King and Queen of Spain . . . and a poor boy, who is mezzo-soprano. Were you a poor boy, Gran'maman?"

"I sang that part when we gave a concert performance."

"Good Lord!"

"When was that?"

"Eighteen eighty-four, Jean."

"My!"

" 'There is a flower that bloometh', let's try that."

"No. Here's one for Barney. 'Yes, let me like a soldier fall, upon some open plain.' Might be Salisbury Plain, mightn't it?"

"Sounds high-falutin to me."

"Is it high-falutin, Gran'maman?"

"H'm. I dare say it would be thought so now, my dear."

Then something rebelled in her. What business had these young things to be so superior? And in spite of her sedulous self-control she added:

"I'm not sure you haven't missed something, all the same!"

"Missed? I should think we have. You had two more numbers in your part, Gran'maman. ' 'Tis the Harp on the Air'. Did you have a property harp?"

"No, dear, besides, it was a concert performance. In those days the Institute Choral Society gave two concerts a year, for charity. At Easter it had to be *The Messiah*, of course! But in the autumn, as soon as the schools resumed, we had what the Dean used to allude to as our 'secular effort'. We gave an opera or cantata . . . non-sacred, you know."

They were all looking, too polite to titter. Of course they didn't realise the distinction that used to exist between sacred and profane musical composition. Nor did she intend to try to enlighten them.

"I expect you call it uplift and down drift"—she had the

words on the tip of her tongue—"but we got a lot of fun out of it all. I wonder if you ever have as much!" But she didn't say it.

"This is an inscribed copy," proclaimed Jean. "It's signed by the principal artists for you."

"Yes, I believe it is."

"Let's look!" Necks were craned and hands outstretched but Jean withdrew the old scarlet-covered golden-lettered score firmly.

"No, you can't finger it all over. It's valuable, and it's Gran'maman's. If I'd known what you'd got hold of I wouldn't have let you have it. There's plenty of stuff in the music waggon that doesn't matter, find something else."

"Oh, never mind, Jean dear"; she was touched.

"I do mind. They'll just waste it."

The young men good-temperedly rummaged amid the tattered and dog-eared leaves between the turned mahogany bars of the ancient piece of furniture.

"Look here. 'Ole Man River'. You can't sing that, Barney!"

"Go on, Barney. You can." His sister tried to make it easy for him.

But the mood had died out.

"Look, the sky's clearing. I thought the storm was too violent to last. I expect there's a great sea breaking over the groyne. Go and have a look!"

She guessed that Nina Cresswell was just getting them out of the way so that she, the precious grandmother of Victor and Jean, the hostess to the others, should have her afternoon sleep undisturbed. She resented this, she couldn't bear to be a spoil-sport. And she was reluctant to turn them out. Lately she had felt she couldn't have enough young people round her, she never knew when she would have them no more, at her age. But Nina Cresswell was too thoughtful to be contradicted, and she was just so much older than the rest, that they would accept her suggestion.

So the little party round the piano broke up. Jean put away the piano score of *Maritana* as if it were some precious document. It amused her to see how the girls went off with an air as if to say, "I don't want any young man to walk with me!"

It had been different in her time. And the boys made no fuss about walking with the girls nowadays. They trooped out and could be heard bickering good-humouredly about who had taken whose rubber boots. All pretence; she knew. Young people wanted to be with young people of the opposite sex. In spite of all the sorrows, disappointments and losses of a long life, her old heart warmed at the atmosphere that had invaded the house ever since she had suggested to her grandson that some gesture should be made towards the various descendants, the fourth generation of the family who happened to be in London for the Coronation. Her grandson had dutifully replied:

"You don't want a whole lot of kids makin' a row and upsetting you, do you, old lady?"

She could have sworn, if ladies of her generation had ever acquired the habit of swearing. She nearly burst out:

"I may never see them again, except perhaps your Steve, can't you realise what people feel at my age?"

She kept it back because Archie was, under his mask of imperviousness, a very sentimental fellow. Otherwise he'd never have made a home for her as he had. Whenever he was mentally reminded of her age he looked as doleful as anyone could wish. So she toned her feelings down into:

"I think we rather owe it to them, Archie."

"Very well. I don't know what Mrs. Kitchen will say."

"Mrs. Kitchen will be delighted and will show off her cooking. Could we have a goose, do you think?"

"Shouldn't wonder."

"There's a lot on it, and they won't often have tasted it. It will give Mrs. Kitchen a chance."

He had agreed, bless him, and she had written to her step-nephew Victor, if that was what you called him (she didn't). She called him a dear boy, so quick, so intelligent and so ready to show affection in his half-French way. He was her stepdaughter's grandson, after all, but her feelings about him had become even stronger since his father had been killed by the Nazis, and he, a mere schoolboy, had taken part in that awful, implacable Resistance Movement. It hadn't (miraculously) spoiled him and she was still his cherished "Gran'-maman".

Then she had written to her Canadian granddaughter and asked that her young Jean should be one of the party. She had never seen the child, who must be nearly twenty, and who, after taking a degree at some fabulously rich and remote university in that enormous country, was to come over for the Coronation and stay on to do some "course" or other. She found all this modern education a little difficult to follow. In her day ladies had been ladies, even if they had to work as she had. Now all women were just women and had to work all the harder. But when the child had turned up she had shown no trace of the Dormer stock, and little of her French Canadian father, save perhaps a neatness of movement and an endearing way of calling her "Gran'maman" also, when she heard Victor do so. All the rest was pure Scots.

And to play with those two, she had her "own boy" as she liked to think of him, though regretting that he went by the shortened form of his name, "Steve". Convenient, perhaps, for his father, who was an engineer and liked everything brief and clipped. When *he* heard the other two do so, *he* began calling her "Gran'maman" in mocking imitation, for he had some signs of the perverse irritability that had caused his mother to leave his father in that far-off New Zealand in which he had been born.

"You seem to have assembled a family from all quarters of the globe," Nina Cresswell, the schoolmistress, had laughed at her when, a habituée of the house, she had heard about this proposed post-Coronation gathering.

She had demurred. Victor had been born in France it was true, but had been to England several times in childhood, and now had a place of business in London, and might almost pass for an Englishman save that he had not much time for games. Jean was a Blomfield, and young Steve had left New Zealand as an infant.

"Most old families get spread out a bit," was all she had thought it necessary to reply.

So she had gathered them together, after the Coronation. There was plenty of room, thank goodness, in Cockle Hall. No one knew, and she didn't care, if it had received its name from the scallop shells carved in the corners of the great ruined gateway or because one of its proprietors had made a fortune out of the shellfish trade. Another had run a school, and rebuilt the ample rooms and the cell-like cubicles on the first floor, providing accommodation for young people who didn't mind roughing it. Since it was near enough to Archie Dormer's engineering job under the County Coast Erosion Authority, in a pleasant part of the coast, not too far removed from the facilities of Easthampton, she had come to live there because she would be cared for, and see people about her whom she loved; what else mattered at her age? So she had brought them together, and only now admitted to herself the real reason.

All those young things gave her the warmth, the feeling of creative attraction she craved. The death of her son, a casualty from damage done him in the first war, the death of her stepnephew in the second, the dispersal of the old family had weakened and saddened her. And now she was making a last effort to fight back.

Life! Life! More and more young life, to make up for all she and others had lost and been deprived of. That was why, when, on this wet afternoon, they had roused her from her nap with the strains of *Maritana*, she had felt that particular glow. *Maritana!* Sentimental! Victorian! A period piece! Of course it was. So was she. But the easy, sugary melodies, the wistful "poetic" words, the wild improbability of the plot, and gilded "romance" of the old opera had struck something in her old heart.

As Nina Cresswell went bustling off to see about tea, for

Mrs. Kitchen only "obliged" as late as washing-up after the midday dinner, she closed her eyes to resume her interrupted nap. And, half-remembering, half-dreaming, she went back over half a century, to the time when *Maritana*, of all things in the world, had been the beginning of it all. Yes, she could hardly forbear a sleepy chuckle. If it hadn't been for that long-ago "Concert Performance" the Choral Society had given, in the 'nineties, there might not have been any Jean, or Steve or Victor, to go walking together with their young friends, this wet summer day of Queen Elizabeth the Second's new reign.

She often found, now that she had passed her eightieth year, that she remembered what happened more than half a century ago, better than she did what had happened as recently as half a decade. A lot of the Second World War was just a dreary smudge of discomforts and alarms, that be-smirched what had, even then, seemed to her a time when she ought not to have been bothered by such things. But it had passed. She couldn't, now, have told with any accuracy, how many years it was that they had waited, hoping against hope, to have news of Victor's father, and of the child Victor had been then. And by the time the news came that one had been brutally done away with, and that the other had spent what were supposedly his formative years, a hunted fugitive, eye-witness of guerilla warfare and savage reprisal, she had become so numb that it had been an effort to show the joy she felt that her stepgrandson had escaped. She had seen the other grandson, the Blomfield boy who was a member of one of the Canadian divisions, for a few hours. A fine young man, if shy. He had been killed in . . . what was it . . . ? Ah, the landing in Normandy. H'm. Her memory was better than she thought, or was it the strangeness of a British and American Army landing in Normandy, of all places, that made some impression. But none of it stood out with the clarity of the figures, the scenes, the very words of the 'eighties, when she had first come to Easthampton.

It had been the doing of the friend of her schooldays, Hannah Scrivener. Hannah had started a school for "the daughters of gentlemen" and had written to her to come and take charge of the Art side, music and drawing. She had accepted with alacrity. At the age of twenty-one, she had already been earning her living for two years, but only just. A "music connexion" in the West End in those days meant earning a guinea an hour a week, in the houses to which she was "recommended", in which she was treated no better than the upper servants. None of her "clientèle" (one mustn't call them "customers") ever thought of enquiring if the young woman who came to teach the piano to the daughters of the house were hungry or tired or sick of it, or wet to the skin, or brokenhearted about her old parents, down in the home counties, or if she proposed to go on teaching music for as long as she kept her health and looks. She was a convenient way of acquiring a small grace that added something to the daughters' marriageable qualities, she soon found. She could be kept waiting, dismissed, forgotten about, sometimes not even paid what she had been promised. Even if she was paid at most of the houses she attended, fairly punctually and sometimes with good grace, half of the money went in paying for the lodgings, that were "respectable", which meant that she was watched all the time, in procuring "transport" as they called it nowadays, in dressing herself in such a way as to keep her connexion and in feeding herself where she could, during the working hours, lest she faint.

"If you didn't like it, why did you adopt it as a profession?" she had asked herself, knowing well enough the response if she had complained. There was no one to complain to, and when, in the off seasons, the families whose homes she visited were away (and sometimes forgot to tell her when they were going so that she went to houses that were closed, or at which the servants were familiar towards her) he went back to her half-paralysed father and her step-ther, down in Wiltshire, she received an answer that was enough:

ell, my dear," the old man quavered from the invalid which too much sherry and too many optimistically purchased horses had reduced him, "how long are you staying?" It meant how long would she read the paper to him, help her stepmother to feed him and clear up the small messes he made.

"Well, Frances, how long are you staying?" her stepmother would ask, a bleak smile barely concealing the thought that Mary Jane, the maid, could be released for springcleaning or other duties.

"Well, Fan, how long are you staying?" from brother Edward, meaning how long had he got to try to borrow money from her. Not that they were not affectionate. They were all fond of her in their way, fond as self-indulgent, or self-righteous, or self-satisfied people can be of the member of the family with enough brains and energy to launch out and bring back more than she consumed.

So, for two years, she had left them and gone back as soon as she could to her lodgings and her London "connexion". And all the time she had been conscious of the great roaring river of human vitality, of animal reproduction, along the bank of which she walked, an attractive young woman, a possible victim, if her foot slipped or her eye strayed. It began in the morning when she hastened, wet or fine, to the cabrank. She had to take a four-wheeler. Hansoms were not respectable. Omnibuses were impossibly full of grumpy old men who wouldn't make room for her, and she couldn't climb up on to the roof without exposing herself to the salacious jeers of the "cad" who collected the fares, or the males who happened to be within sight. Even a four-wheeler was no protection. Flashily dressed men would range up and she knew their approach by heart, "Where might you be going, all alone?"

Sometimes she wondered if the beery cabmen were in league with such characters. She grew adept at nipping into the cab and closing the door in the face and sometimes on the fingers of such adventurers and calling out her destinatio through the opposite window. She did her best to dre discreetly and had disciplined her glance sternly to pavement immediately before her feet. The fact remained that, while she would have scornfully rejected any suggestion that she was good-looking, she could not help the fact that she was, apparently, attractive and she was alone. That made her fair game. She was not even safe, always, from the males of the family, when she arrived at her destination and had to cultivate a second sense that told her when a door behind her was opened with a caution that was not the caution of a servant. "Thank you so much, I am just going. I wonder if I might trouble you to call me a cab?" she would say to the son of the house, or some other male creature, in her iciest manner. The elderly ones were more trouble. "And how is my daughter getting on?" "As well as can be expected!" she would shoot at the greasy, flushed face, pushed much too unnecessarily near hers, as she wrenched her hand free, grabbed her portfolio and moved near the bell. She sometimes enjoyed a sardonic smile over the fact that she did not lose appointments by a tart and frigid rejection of these advances. Presumably they were too scared even to disparage her to their wives.

By midday, or later, if her appointments fell awkwardly, she would have to seek some place of refreshment. There was Gunters in Berkeley Square. There was the Metropole. There were various "pastry cooks" to which she could drive (another shilling). She learned by hard experience, in which of them she would be surveyed, appraised, and finally accosted, with a polite remark about the weather, an enquiry:

"Would you mind if I shared your table?" or an invented acquaintance, a bow and a smile:

"How nice you are looking this morning!"

She developed what she hoped was a devastating stare and a turn of the head which she hoped conveyed that she regarded the intrusion as if she had stepped over one of those patches of horse dung with which the streets of those days were so profusely littered. It took some firmness. They looked such fools, and her natural warmth of heart responded to the fact that, after all, even such outrages were a tribute to something in her which could not be entirely her accessibility. But only for a moment. She prized her independence. She would have admitted that, in those mid-Victorian days, she was a menace to the male, taking a job he might conceivably have undertaken, at a lower price than a male music and drawing master would have accepted. She read in the papers that she was unsexed, debasing her woman's prestige, betraying the sacred purpose for which Almighty Providence had created her.

"I only wish I was, I only wish I had!" she would apostrophise the print in which she saw such sentiments. But she knew she didn't mean it. For somewhere amid the boisterous menacing billows of that flood of sex was the master-wave to which she would willingly surrender. The very completeness of that foreseen immolation of herself was the very thing that made her tread the brink with such circumspection.

Then Hannah's offer had come and she had accepted jubilantly, by return of post, with youthful and happy impulsiveness. To live with people who liked and wanted her, instead of in those grim and expensive lodgings; to have professional status in a school, instead of clinging to the skirts of people who only cared for art as they cared for conventional ornament; to teach girls who wanted to learn (or whose parents wanted them to learn) instead of visiting young débutantes-to-be, who fitted her in between visits to dressmakers and social calls which they regarded as more important. That would be life indeed.

She had advertised and handed over her "connexion" for what it was worth, and blissfully disregarded the injured tone of clients who seemed to think they should have said when they could dispense with her, and not she with them. She gave notice to her landlady and was amused at the incredulity with which her disclaimers were received.

"What? Not going to get married? What are you going to do, then, miss? Better think twice. It looks easy and pleasant, but it's the road to everlasting torment. Here, read this!" She was handed a tract. She burst out laughing, pushed past the hands raised in sanctimonious horror, and pursued her final round of farewell engagements.

The Easthampton to which she had come in the 'seventies was an old provincial capital and cathedral city, in which industry, seeking cheap land and labour, had created a rising middle class, the members of which had no intention of remaining in the moribund and precarious situation in which they had been born. One of the means of escape was education. It was, just then, being given for the first time wholesale, on a national basis, to the entire population. But the set in which Hannah Scrivener and all her circle moved, had far more ambitious views. Hannah, who, she well remembered, combined a semi-invalid body with a masculine brain, and a thin religious aspiration with a sound sense of business, had felt, rather than seen, all around her, the demand of the professional class for an outlet for its daughters, immeasurably wider and more stable than matrimony. The school, housed in a great mansion which a wealthy manufacturer had vacated to occupy a "Hall" in the county outside, had already attracted a hundred day pupils, as well as a score of boarders. She was greeted with something more than affection.

"Now, Frances," Hannah had taken her up to the elegant and comfortable bedroom, with its draped dressing-table, business-like desk littered with books of account and prospectuses, its gas-fire burning amid asbestos coals of the period, that looked like miniature human sculls, "let me show you your time-table. We are so glad to have you, my dear, the visiting mistresses were so unsatisfactory and unreliable. The only thing to be said for them is that they were better than the men with whom we had to start our Art side. They were extortionate. Look here!"

Hannah unfolded a large double sheet that might have been a map, but which proved to be ruled in columns, the left-hand one giving the hours of the day. "This is where you fit in," said Hannah, patting her affectionately on the shoulder and tracing a number of entries with her finger.

This was something new, and she did not at first grasp the allocation of her time, from seven o'clock until . . . could it be? Nine at night? Hannah enlightened her.

"We share invigilation at evening preparation and discipline at drill. Thus you have two evenings a week entirely free, and alternate Saturdays and Sundays. Do you see?"

She looked, but did not really see, until she had followed the routine so meticulously laid down for her for nearly half a term. By that time, although the warmth of Hannah's feelings was still expressed whenever (not often) there was an opportunity, she had noticed certain things about her sometime schoolfellow, who was now, apparently, her employer, while remaining (of course) her friend. Hannah knew that her own precarious health might end the career she had made for herself at any moment and would certainly prevent her ever contemplating marriage. So the high if thin and intermittent vitality that might have gone to attract and content a husband, control a home and bear and rear children, was poured into the school. To invade what had been so largely man's domain, Hannah had adopted, as far as she could, a male attitude. She cared nothing for winning parents by airs and graces. Dressed so plainly that her clothes had rather the air of a monastic uniform, she told parents and members of the public generally their duty towards daughters. The rising semi-professional classes were impressed with this new attitude. The school motto:

> In the shadow will we work,
> And mould the woman to the fuller day,

might be from Lord Tennyson's poem "The Princess". A few years earlier, it would have been scorned as "poetry", and "putting ideas into women's heads". In the 'seventies, however, to those who meant to get on in this world and the next, it sounded like a secular hymn, promising more intelligent factory hands (Easthampton employed a good deal of female labour) and more devoted shop assistants (the old county capital was the centre of the distributing trade for miles around) for the middle class to exploit. Perhaps many parents only noticed that it was something new. That was what they were looking for. So they sent their daughters. Hannah was a born teacher, a predestined elder sister (she had brought up a motherless family of younger sisters), a good organiser and took after her father's habit of mind (he was chief clerk of the biggest insurance office in the city).

All this Frances had admired and supported. She liked her work, liked children, felt that she had something to give them, both musically and in the visual arts. Hannah backed her up, encouraged singing in class, and the learning of brief, suitable cantatas for performance before parents at end of term. When the Banly estates went into Chancery and much of the statuary was sold locally at derisory prices, Hannah bought several lots including a stucco Victory of Samothrace and plaster copies of Venus de Milo, reduced replicas of Praxitiles, tiny votive figurines, and distributed them on brackets and mantelpieces, from which they could be fetched for Drawing class. "There, my dear, you are set up now!" she said cheerfully. "We might have an exhibition of the girls' work perhaps."

Again: "I've been dreaming of the day when we could go outside, hire a medium-sized hall and give a concert, charging for admission. I don't know much about it. There's this Choral Society at the Institute. Don't you think it would be a good thing if you joined, and acquired some idea how such things are run, and got to know the sort of people who would be useful? It meets on Wednesday, that's your free night."

Hannah was full of ideas, never spared herself, or anyone else, and was usually in a state bordering on collapse by the end of the week, spending Saturday in bed. The staff admired her, commiserated with her, pleaded with her to fall back on them and bravely faced the extra turns of duty her falling back entailed, for the new ideas came to Hannah just as rapidly and in as large numbers when she was on her back as when she was erect. No one was so churlish as to say in so many words that they all meant more work for the same money. Any member of the staff who felt so, resigned and went elsewhere. But the waiting list of pupils seeking admission grew and grew.

"I have written to the officer commanding at the depôt of the regiment, asking for the services of a drill-sergeant. If one is available, I think we might circularise the parents and offer drill on Saturday mornings. It would have to be an extra, of course, but I think the parents might like it if it improved the carriage of the girls."

And yet again: "Miss Potts, Mrs. Slokum was saying how nice it would be if Kathleen's little brother Edward could come with her, while he's so tiny. You could manage with a few small boys among your little ones, couldn't you? I'll tell Mrs. Slokum to tell the Stokesbys . . . and any others you can think of who have little brothers. I'll put it on the board in the lobby."

So on Saturday mornings a fine-looking sergeant with a beautiful flaxen moustache and immaculate scarlet tunic arrived, clicked his shining boots and made the girls, in the suavest of military language, march about the wide gravelled paths of the old garden, expanding their young bosoms, making their cheeks flush and their ankles firm and holding their heads high. On other mornings, little boys began to appear, in the first form, and even to wear smart little caps, and find out how much slower they were in learning than their young sisters. But perhaps the most pregnant idea of all those that Hannah enunciated was that she, Frances, should join the Choral Society. She filled up the proper forms, submitted to the examination of a sub-committee of rather snuffy old gentlemen, duly sang a small portion of the chorus of an oratorio, and was admitted to membership.

She found herself seated on the lowest row on the right or contralto side of the raised tiers of seats in the Institute Hall, in which the Society met. She had been confronted by a gentleman of good figure and presence, whose sandy whiskers and sparse hair were going grey, who greeted her with a slight bow, and consulted a roster in his hand, saying in an assured voice, "A new member, I believe, Miss——?"

"Reeson."

"Thank you." He put a tick against her name, and conducted her to her place.

"Who is that?" she asked of the nearest woman member.

"That's Mr. Doughty Dormer, from the Bank."

"Is he the——" she nearly said master, for there was something about him of authority.

"He's the registrar and secretary . . . and nearly everything else except conductor and accompanist. He sings in the basses, arranges for the hall; a most pleasant and capable person."

So she discovered. He passed along, handing out copies of the vocal score of *Maritana*. He gave her a smile as well. When they were all distributed he looked at his watch, glanced at the door, waited a moment as if listening. Then suddenly he clapped his hands three times and made a sign at which all members of the chorus rose to their feet. The door opened and in came a person who, in an instant, by no apparent effort, made the whole room and everyone in it appear very English, and somehow very ordinary. He seemed to walk as in a dream, his dark eyes fixed on something invisible to others, his sallow cheeks indrawn, pendulous lips red and moist, a hint of blissful carelessness about his clothes, not so much dowdiness, as the habit of wearing . . . would it be a leopard skin and sandals? Mr. Dormer shepherded him into his conductor's box and indicated the copy, open on the desk, the baton laid beside it, and turning, motioned them to be seated.

"Radolin, the conductor," her neighbour whispered.

She had heard of him, of course, a good deal about his consummate ability in giving a new rendering to pieces that were old established, and introducing new pieces that became established through his rendering. People sometimes shook their heads, lowered their voices and left sentences unfinished, concerning his private life. Well, it was no business of hers. And usual enough, she ought to know.

The conductor seemed suddenly to realise where he was, shook his dark ringlets and said: "Good evening, ladies and gentlemen. The piece we are going to put in rehearsal is called *Maritana*. . . ."

With a few masterly sentences in English, which he spoke, not so much with an accent, as with elaborate care not to betray one, he gave the main dramatic points of the story, touched on the important solos, indicated briefly the chorus responsibilities. He had a way of looking at the piano accompanist and the ranks of the chorus as if they were parts of a mechanism into which he had, by effort that was almost pugnacious, to breathe the spirit of what they were doing. She responded from a feeling that if she and all the others didn't he might dwindle and fail. The number came to an end, and a sudden smile rounded and humanised that face too like a waxen model.

"Poor Wallace," he lamented, "how he must be suffering if he can hear you." He rapped the desk. "Ladies and gentlemen, for the moment you are not citizens of this prosperous city. You are handsome Spaniards regarding a wonderful wild gitana or gipsy who is inexpress . . . essibly beautiful. You don't feel like Spaniards, do you? No!" (He made it Noh!) "You have never seen a gitana, have you? No! You don't believe the King in disguise is hiding among you, no! Then we may as well go home and play cricket!" Into that word he put an edge of contempt that would have cut a wooden dummy to the core. Then, as if feeling he had gone too far, he wreathed them in a seductive smile, continuing:

"But you will not go home and play cricket. You will try to be what you are not, you will impart passion you do not feel, you will make the audience laugh and cry. I am not being sargustic. . . . I speak from a broken heart!" He placed his hand on his lapel with a leer.

Thus exhorting them he raised his baton, the pianist struck the opening chords.

She, Frances, at least, had done her very best, not so much from the inspiration of the music, or the words, as from a

eeling of compunction. Suppose he did really double up
rom a broken heart, or broken spring, for sometimes he
ooked like a clockwork figure.

He became suddenly benevolent as if he were the kind-
nearted uncle of all of them.

"Very good! You can, you see, feel excited if you wish!"
He whipped over the pages to the next concerted number.

And so it had gone on. By the end of the summer term the
chorus had a fair knowledge of their parts. They would
return after the holidays to begin the serious rehearsals with
the principals.

Signor Radolin bade them a stage farewell. "Do not quite
forget me, while you see me no more!"

"As if we were likely to," she heard her nearest companion mutter. They all rose as Monsieur Radolin, with a
gesture that was only just not a kiss of the hand, wafted to
them, took his leave. She found herself delivering up her copy
to Mr. Dormer of the bank. She gave him a brief glance of
complicity. He smiled down at her. How refreshingly real
and honest and everyday he was, after the inflated atmosphere
of the opera. All very well in its place, but its place was in an
unreal existence.

That was the year when she had felt "on top of the world"
as people called it. In her half-dozing state she smiled to
herself. Youthful vigour, pretty good health, a career opening
before her, modest but suitable, the sense of being wanted,
being in the movement of the time. No wonder *Maritana*
became indelibly imprinted on her memory.

"Frances, how would you like to join us? We are going to
a pension in the Swiss Alps for three weeks." That indefatig-
able woman, Hannah, who never knew from one week to
another when she might have an "attack" as it was called, and
never knew if it might be fatal, was proposing to travel, by
rail of those days, by paddle-wheel steamer across the
Channel, and to sit up all night in a second-class carriage to
Basle, and there change and go on to Steig. There would be
the young Scrivener sister and a friend, four of them, in stout

boots and skirts that barely touched the ground, special cap
with ear-protectors, that tied under the chin. They had
passports, golden sovereigns fixed in special belts, and stick
with spiked ferrules. Off they went. She had not been abroad
since schooldays at Suresnes, nearly ten years before, and ten
years then was like a century.

Once more she smiled. Odd they must have looked. Odd
Hannah looked like death several times, but didn't have an
attack, or if she did, mastered it by sheer will-power. And the
little pension, high up on a shoulder of the Alps, had been
clean, cheap and efficient, although on wet days, completely
enveloped in cloud. They were so happy there, Hannah
reading long extracts from Goethe as they sat in the flower-
starred grass and stared at the formidable shapes, where the
Oberland tapered up into fastnesses of snow, gleaming in the
sunshine, and if possible, even more beautiful by moonlight.
The days soon passed. They felt quite wistful about returning
home, loaded with pressed edelweiss, carved wooden nick-
nacks for Christmas presents, bursting with health (even
Hannah had a tinge of colour in her parchment cheeks),
change of food, air and scene.

"Heigho!" she muttered to herself, "a long time ago. I
wouldn't do it again for a fortune. The hard wooden seats
made weals in one's . . . person. One would have endured
more, for the sake of the experience then!" She remembered
the qualm she felt as they, on their return journey, sped
through the awful outskirts of London. The wretched people
in those deplorable streets. H'm. Rather creditable, on the
whole. A generous impulse! And finally the towers and trees
and roofs of old Easthampton. As they rattled back to the
school in a four-wheeler (over cobbles in the less modish
streets) she had felt that there was just nothing she was not
equal to:

> In the shadow will we work,
> And mould the woman to the fuller day.

It would be luminous, delightful shadow. She then saw ahead

of her years and years of three terms each, across which she would skim, faster than the paddle-steamer from Dover to Calais. She saw generations of girls, whom she would rescue from the sort of servitude and dependence she herself had emerged from, and they would all-together dance out into the sunshine of . . .

Her head fell forward abruptly and she woke, hastily recovering her poise, touching her dry old lips with the tip of her tongue, and stretching her fingers which had stiffened. She hoped she hadn't snored. Not that it mattered, there was no one in the room, which was filled with the pale straw-coloured light of an afternoon in which storm-clouds were breaking up and dispersing. The young people hadn't returned. It was still too wet underfoot for her to go the few yards of which she was capable to meet them. She didn't really want to, but they were such nice children, and she could not bear to be out of things, not able to show an interest in their affairs. But wet grass and damp sand were excuse enough. And somewhere in the extensive, tile-floored kitchen regions of the inconvenient old house, she could hear someone getting out the tea-things. So she might be excused.

She folded her hands again and the golden glow of the brightening afternoon gilded the opposite wall, as her eye-lids drooped, and she recovered the impression that had been interrupted by her awakening, of something golden in motion, that enveloped her. Her old mind took up again the memories of her youthful, active years.

"The evenings are beginning to draw in," someone said as, on their return from their Swiss trip, they had reopened the school, prepared for the return of the boarders, drawn up the time-tables for the five forms, into which her Music and Art periods fitted.

"Yes, aren't they," she assented brightly. Autumn had no languid depression for her. The Choral Society opened in the last week of September. They would have to rehearse by artificial light. In those days it made not the slightest difference

to her. There was zest and anticipation in her quick firm footsteps through the mild dusk of the evenings, when the lamp-
lighter was going round with his long pole, poking into
luminousness the yellow flickering gas-lamps, that hardly
overcame the obscurity of the narrow and tortuous streets of
old Easthampton of that day. The working population had
withdrawn to its rookeries and hovels in the hundreds of
yards and courts near the river. Only a great lumbering old
waggon or two, or an occasional smart gig passed her as she
hastened to the old building in the wall of the Close. She
vaguely knew it was part of what had been the monastery.
But it was only interesting to her because she would be taking
part in the singing, meeting people of similar tastes, admiring
Mr. Dormer, for his admirable management, admiring Signor
Radolin, in a different way, for his conducting of the opera.

"No, it was more. He inspired the very ordinary chorus
we were. We should never have given more than the average
church choir performance if it hadn't been for the devastating
things he said." In her doze, she smiled tartly to herself. It
was difficult now to credit that she could have been such a
little ninny, so easily impressed, so directly moved, by the
lightly "cultured" set of a provincial town, and the sort of
harrying they deserved and got from the kind of professional
conductor they could afford to employ.

"I don't know," she told herself. "It was innocent. I may
smile at it now. So much has happened since that I can hardly
credit that I ever was that jejune young person, in those
obstructing clothes, taking so mediocre an affair so seriously.
But I won't apologise. It was fun. I loved it. Why not?" Why
not indeed?

There started up before her long-sighted memory of old
age, as if she saw them in a marionette theatre, the little
figures of that first full rehearsal. She could not restrain a
chuckle over their clothes, so admirably cut to conceal the
human form that it was a wonder Dr. Darwin's remarkable
theories about the origin of human species had ever made
any headway among people so habited. And it wasn't only

he clothes. There was a sort of . . . would it be unkind to call
t pretentiousness? The one or two women who were there
before her, were not quite sure if they were a fraction above,
or a fraction below her in the social scale. She hadn't fought
her way up step by step, out of the bucolic Wiltshire in which
she had been born to be stopped by such nonsense. "Good
evening," she bade them, in a voice too decided to be ignored,
"what a lovely day it has been. I hope you've enjoyed some
pleasant holiday trips since we last met."

There was a general murmur of response from the throats
of half a dozen females, not quite prepared to snub, and not
quite certain if they ought to encourage such an opening.
One old enough not to mind, and assured enough not to feel
that it mattered, replied, "Why, where have you been?"

"Steig! In the Oberland, you know." They didn't, of
course, so she kept up the pressure. "It was lovely. The great
peaks covered with eternal snow!" The word "eternal" was a
great help. It had religious connotations and maintained one's
thoughts at a high level. So much so that there was malice in
the query:

"Did you go alone?"

"No." She looked the speaker in the eye. "Miss Hannah
made up a party." That did it. A party was respectable.

Thus established as a young woman who would have to be
noticed, she was admitted to the desultory conversation of
those who, increasing in number as new arrivals joined them,
fidgeted a little at the delay in beginning. Characteristically,
it had been the men who expressed the impatience they all
felt. The men of those days! Black-coated and top-hatted,
they twirled long drooping moustaches, or tugged at whiskers
that swept the lapels of their frock-coats. "I sa-ay," she could
hear still, across more than half a century, the drawl cultivated
by young Chenery the auctioneer, "what are they doing in
the-ar?" as he glanced towards the firmly closed door of the
committee room, from which a dull rumble of voices could
be heard. No one answered for no one knew, and it was
nearly fifteen minutes after the time for which they had been

summoned, when that door was opened and the voices suddenly grew loud and near, evidently bringing to a summary conclusion a discussion which had become a dispute.

The committee, in those days exclusively male, filed out and its members fell silent in the presence of the accumulated members of the chorus. These latter had just time to notice that Signor Radolin was livid green with suppressed fury while that Mr. Vizer, the "contractor" as he was called though she had no clear notion as to what that might signify, was very pink about the cheeks and bright blue in the eye. She didn't like him, he was inclined to be familiar, but he carried a good deal of weight in the Society.

"He's so energetic . . . and he goes to London more than most of them, and gets to know things!"

She still felt a little on the defensive when he spoke to her. While what he said was perfectly decorous there was a slight over-emphasis, as if he meant to infer that he was making . . . er . . . advances. Her bitter experiences in London had taught her to class him among the numerous men with whom one had to be careful.

There had supervened a moment of uncertainty and confusion. The woman next her, whom she rather avoided as a rule, sensing a tendency to repeat gossip and impute motives to which the comparatively idle middle-class women of that date were all too prone, nudged her and glanced meaningfully at Radolin and Vizer and back to Radolin.

What a relief it had been to hear Doughty Dormer's voice, loud and decisive, calling them to order. "Come, we mustn't waste time like this. We're all behind. Signor Radolin, are you ready? Where's the pianist? Librarian! Copies out. Look sharp!"

It was like a breath of fresh air. Dear Doughty. The short-sighted pianist with thick-lensed glasses scurried like an insect to his place, the librarian, Doughty's somewhat over-kind description of the cross-eyed lawyer's clerk who took care of the vocal scores, band parts, etc., hurried. They all shuffled into their places.

"The pianist is ready. The librarian is ready," exclaimed Signor Radolin, with deadly intonation as if, she thought, he had been uttering a curse. These foreigners, really!

"Very well." Doughty Dormer evidently didn't intend to be intimidated. "Where do we start?"

"We start at the beginning!"

Once more, Doughty, with admirable good temper, she thought, evaded what was plainly meant for a challenge.

"Very well, then. Opening chorus. Give us the beat, Signor. Last line, page thirteen, ready!" And they swung in on the words:

> "Sing, pretty maiden, sing,
> Sing that lovely song again."

Even now, across the years, the simple sugary notes came ringing back to her. What was it she had said to the young people?

"You have missed something!" Yes, it was all past and dead and gone, along with the people who sang it and the people who listened to it, but it had had its day, its life once. And she had tasted the innocent exuberance of it all:

> "Sing, pretty maiden, sing!"

Nowadays they wouldn't put it like that. The boys would say: "Warble, old funny face, warble!" or something slighting, and the girls were just as bad. They wouldn't thank you to call them "pretty maidens" or ask them to "Sing that song again!" They would say in reply, "Come off it", or some equally undignified slang. Well, they must go their own way to find out.

It had been a very different thing, sixty years ago. It was true of course, that, at the time of which she was thinking, women had already been allowed control of their own property, had secured, even if it were grudgingly, an entry into some professions, a footing in education. She herself was evidence of that. But there had lingered, to the end of the

c

century and in odd holes and corners even longer, a kind of hang-over from Victorian prudishness and condescension towards "the weaker sex", the "fair and frail". Even now her lips hardened in a sardonic grin at the memory.

The rehearsal had come to an end as even rehearsals must. There were the usual repeats and criticisms. It had to be said for Signor Radolin, that, once engrossed in his job, whatever difficulty he might have been raising with the Committee, whatever temper he might have been showing, whatever it was between him and Vizer, were all ignored. He was an artist, and let nothing interfere with his art. Among the growing number of conductors she had worked under or listened to, he bore no insignificant place. For his attitude, even towards an amateur choir in a provincial city, was just as painstaking as if he were engaged with one of the leading professional choruses. He *made* one sing. She enjoyed it.

"Do you think he'll blow us a kiss, one of these days, when he looks so angelic?" a stupid girl had asked her. She had thought fit to reply, "I can't believe he'd do anything so unutterably foolish!"

At the conclusion, the ladies left in twos and threes so as not to appear to be inviting escort. She had fallen into the habit of walking home with a Mrs. Cavendish, who lived not far from the school, not from any great feeling of regard for her, but in order to conform to a standard of conduct which, while she despised it, must be observed so as not to bring the faintest tinge of irregularity on Hannah and her establishment. Mrs. Cavendish was fussy, and her fussiness took the form of disliking a chorus part which had a broken back and slightly torn cover. She went over to the book store and pestered the librarian for another. This meant waiting for her, or appearing abrupt, and this again meant that most of the chorus left, Signor Radolin with bows and smiles hiding whatever might be his thoughts, and the room was fast emptying. As she waited voices could be heard from the committee room, the door of which was open. Mister Dormer, as she then thought of him . . . odd now to reflect that she

ever had . . . was restating with emphasis something he had
stated before. Years later, when she had been married to him
long enough to have learned his habit of mind, she knew
better than to try to change his sensible if superficial and
purely practical judgment. But on that evening he had been
trying to overcome some opposition from Vizer.

"I can't believe it!" Doughty declared, the soul of honesty
and open fair dealing as he always was.

"Very well. We shall see!" She didn't like Mr. Vizer. She
had nothing against him except his way of looking, which
made her feel less completely clothed than she knew she was,
and a tone as if he knew things he had no business to know.

She leaned forward and stretched this way and that. One
of the penalties of old age was that one couldn't even sit in
one's accustomed chair for an hour without becoming
cramped. She'd be glad when the young people returned and
they had tea. But it was early yet, and she'd better not interfere. Nina Cresswell would rather do it herself. Having eased
the ache in her bones, she folded her hands again and sat
back, allowing her eyes to close. There wasn't much else she
could do, at her age, and the train of thought that had been
started by the children . . . no, no, she must remember, the
young people . . . carried her on again, into the ever-circling
orbit of memory. It was pleasant, not that one wanted old
times back. That was nonsense. One wanted to warm oneself
at the memory of fires long ago extinct. It gave a sort of glow
the present couldn't emulate. For it was real. It had happened.
That was the only reality. The Present was never here, it was
the future one moment, and the next moment it had become
the past. As for the Future . . . well, she hadn't much. And
she sank gratefully back into memory.

The thing which had caused the dispute between Doughty
Dormer and Vizer, the thing which had drawn out the
committee meeting, and made them late at that first rehearsal
after the holidays, became plain. They all attended the

second rehearsal, very punctual, very alert, for it had become known that some of the principals would be present. And sure enough, when they all trooped into the monastery building, there, sitting just below Signor Radolin's "pulpit" was a young woman who stuck out from the surroundings, the hall, the members of the chorus, the committee men, just as the new fruit, tomatoes and bananas, on the greengrocers' stalls in the market, where they were just beginning to appear, stuck out from the grey and green vegetables of a northern clime. "Exotic!" someone said, and the word was apt. It was not that she was beautiful, or well dressed, and certainly not that she looked "distinguished". No. She looked professional. Features and frock, carriage of the head, expression of the face all had a hard-worked, adept air. The impression was heightened when they reached Lazarillo's first solo, and she took it without the slightest hesitation. "Alas, those chimes!" In a moment it was evident what made her so different. That was her life, the life of the boards, of dressing-up and acting what could never be real, but which had to be accepted for the purposes of the performance. She sang well, correctly, with expression and finish.

But Frances, watching her with the attention trained by watching a class, noted that she wasn't really thinking about the words or the music. She had been drilled to sing the words in conjunction with certain notes. At the end of her solo, she gave Radolin a glance of complicity, closed her copy, and appeared to be engrossed in the stitching of a pair of well-darned gloves, over which she frowned with more concentration than the music had caused.

"Now, let us have the chorus, 'Oh, what pleasure'!" Mr. Radolin, tapping smartly on the ledge of the desk, called out, "Chorus!" She could hear it, as if it had been spoken yesterday, and the way Doughty took it up. "Page 172, fifteen bars!" He kept them up to it, knowledgable, serviceable, and well able to account for the minor part of the King, for the Choral Society could only afford four professional fees, and these had to go to Maritana and Lazarillo, Don Caesar and

Don Jose. Vizer sang the "Captain of the Guard" with very fair competence, the "Marquis and the Alcade" were given to two of the basses from the cathedral, while the Marchioness, who had only one entry, in the quartet, was sung by Mrs. Pardon, who was said to have had "professional experience" though no one seemed to know quite what. A big handsome woman with a fine figure, she advanced one foot when it was necessary to take a note at the extremity of her register.

"My dear, that's how all the great prima donnas do, haven't you noticed?" little Mrs. Cavendish added spitefully. She needn't have made such a remark, it only looked as if she thought she ought to be singing the part, which goodness knew, she never could.

It must have been after that rehearsal, that she had offered to sew up the backs of some of the more tattered copies they were using, and the librarian, with the fussiness of his kind, made all sorts of difficulties.

"You must ask the secketery!" he kept repeating. "I haven't no authority to let you have 'em out. My business is to lock 'em up. If you want 'em out, you must ask the secketery!"

Outraged by this specimen of male obstructiveness, she had replied tartly, "Very well, I will!" and turned on her heel, going to the committee room where, she knew well enough, Doughty and Vizer and other members of the committee would be settling up matters of detail.

On the threshold she stopped, forbidden to interrupt an altercation, by the tone of the voices.

"Of course he sees her home to her lodgings. I told you so. And stays as long as he likes, on the grounds that he's got something to talk over about the part. She don't mind. Girls like that have to keep in with the conductor if they want the job!"

"Even if you're right, I can't see it's any business of yours!" Doughty was making the best of what he evidently considered a bad job.

"It'll be our business when it gets about the town that we pay a fee to one of Radolin's fancy women!"

"It's a monstrous suggestion, and there's no proof."

"A lot that'll matter. We ought never to have allowed Radolin to engage her. I said so at the time."

"We must have professional voices for the leads. What you say may be equally true of Signora Torticelli, but who else could sing 'Maritana'?"

"Quite true. But she goes to the Lamb, and everyone knows who she is and why she's there, not to some obscure lodgings, where no one knows what goes on!"

Horrified at being an unintentional eavesdropper, she had moved away. The old librarian was waiting for her.

"Well, what does he say?" was the sardonic query. She hadn't known what to reply. Voices in hasty altercation could be heard from the committee room.

The old man fidgeted and began to whine: "I can't stay here all night. You'll have to come again." But before he could put his threat into force, there were footsteps, Doughty and Vizer came out of the committee room, saw her, and suddenly stopped.

"Well, ask her!" Vizer insisted. "Here she is."

Doughty Dormer, commanding and decisive, crossed the floor of the hall to where she waited by the librarian's wicket and hatch. He gave one of those important coughs that were at once a challenge and a warning, and that she was to know so well.

"Miss Reeson." He made her a little bow. "I want to ask you something in confidence. May I be assured of your discretion?"

She tried to rise to what she felt to be the level of the occasion. "I hope I shall always be discreet, Mr. Dormer, but it would be easier if I might know in what particular the assurance is required."

Vizer moved up and the two men stood regarding her.

"This is the point," Doughty laid the index finger of his right hand in the palm of his left, as if telling off the facts with which he was dealing, "we may have to discontinue employing Miss Mardicras. If that should be the case, would you be willing to undertake her part?"

She had been at once dumbfounded, flattered and even slightly amused. Men! The circuitous formality of it all.

"I . . . I think I could try . . . if it is really necessary."

"Time is getting short, and Mr. Vizer and I are responsible, together with Signor Radolin, for the casting. He will have to consent of course. But I don't think he will oppose us." He looked at Vizer who smirked unpleasantly.

"Not when we've said to him what we're going to say."

Doughty waved his insinuation aside.

"It will demand some extra rehearsal, but we believe you are capable of doing it. May we put forward your name to the committee?"

She looked him straight in the eye, and at that moment some other feeling, something far deeper and stronger than anything she had ever felt about her career, or the school, about the position of woman, and "in the shadow will we work, and mould . . ." and all that, something that was to alter the whole course of her life, invaded her as she said, "Very well, then, I will!" and did not know if she were more thrilled by the look of admiration and . . . something else, Doughty Dormer gave her, or disgusted by the smile on Vizer's face, or embarrassed by the open-mouthed stare of the librarian, who had heard, she felt sure, every word.

There was noise, movement, a jerk on her old consciousness, and she began laboriously to climb up out of her dreaming of those long-ago days, into the reality of the year nineteen fifty-three and her eighty years.

"What is it? Who is that?" She restrained herself with the disciplined habit of one who must always be a dearly loved Gran'maman, and never exhibit ordinary human weakness. It was the young people, back from a belated walk on a wet afternoon, and she must look as if she welcomed them. What were grandmothers for, except to say:

"Well, my dear. I hope you've had a nice walk!"

"Lovely, thank you, Gran'maman! But what a gale!"

"A high wind, a high tide." Young Emil's expressive face lent emphasis to the somewhat restricted vocabulary.

"You'll want your tea. I expect Nina is nearly ready."

Jennifer stepped forward, sweeping aside the strands of pretty light brown hair that had blown into her eyes.

"I'm not sure that I ought to stay. Barney wants to see some of the men about the cattle on the marshes."

"Barney can wait half an hour for a cup of tea!"

Young Steve broke in: "I'm not so sure, Gran'maman. The chaps on the lighthouse have sent out a flood warning. It's the spring tide pushed up by the wind."

"I thought we were safe with the new groyne."

"We're safe enough, if the water doesn't come over the top. They say this combination of wind and tide only happens once a century, but it's happening now."

"Your father won't be pleased, my dear Steve."

"Here's Barney. Don't bother to change, Barney, if you really must go. But there's time just to give you a cup of tea, and a piece in your hand, as Jean says."

"Indeed, I haven't opened my mouth," the firm little voice chided him, but the eyes were not unfriendly, only lit with that perpetual challenge.

"Now, Victor, we know you're Gran'maman's spoiled boy, but I can't see what you want with another jam when there's plum out already!" Nina was trying to be firm, but Victor knew he was privileged.

"Gran'maman, tell her I like greengage. Gran'maman, you know I like greengage *pour goûter*!"

"My dear, we give Nina all the trouble——"

"Not in the least, Gran'maman. I'll get it in a moment if you say so. It's your jam."

They clustered round the table and brought her over her tea to her chair. Soon, the room that had been so empty and quiet, was full of the laughter and chatter of half a dozen happy hearty young people on a holiday. She was where she liked best to be, just outside the circle, able to hear most of what was said, if not able to catch the allusions and share the jokes. It was nice to see them all so happy and jolly together. Even when Barney and Jennifer insisted that they must go, and a shade of anxiety tinged young Barney's blunt, good-humoured features, the merriment of the other four did not slacken, and Nina kept them well supplied. Then Emil felt it was time he was getting back to his camp, and she roused herself.

"I think it is time I had my constitutional. The sky's clear enough. Let's take Emil as far as the cross-roads."

"The wind's pretty high, Gran'maman, sure you can stand it?"

"If I can't, I shall come and lean on you, my dear Victor."

"*Enchanté*, my dear——"

"I'll give you an arm," put in young Steve, as if to say, "we mustn't let these foreign cousins have all the credit."

"I shan't be a moment." She feared she belied the words, by the way she hobbled to the door, as her old legs resumed their function. But she waved them away. She could still find her own cloak and her bedroom was on the ground floor.

As the little party emerged under the great stone arch which still surmounted the entry to the enclosed yard before the house, Steve was explaining to Emil who, with the thirst for information of the well-educated European, was completely nonplussed, as well he might be, by the peculiarities of Easthamptonshire nomenclature.

"Nobody knows exactly why it's called Cockle Hall."

"But there must be good reason, I suppose?"

"It don't follow. In this country places get called names for reasons someone's forgotten, or for a joke, or to save trouble, and not waste words. Cockle Hall is short enough, everyone who wants to come here knows where it is. What more do you want?"

"But still . . ." the young German's eyebrows were climbing his forehead in mystification.

"My dad thought he ought to know, when we came here. But all he could find out was that some folk said it was because of that shell carved in the corner of the arch."

"What shell is that?"

"Look, up there."

"But that is not a cockle—it is an oyster shell."

"Well, Emil, that's how folk are round here. They call a place what they like, not what they ought."

"It is funny!"

"Yes it is. If that's too funny, there are other people who say that the old chap who owned it before it was a school, before it was a boarding-house, made a fortune out of selling shellfish. So it got called Cockle Hall. . . ."

The two young men, engaged in close argument, drew ahead rather faster than she cared to walk, even with the assistance of Victor's arm. Jean and Nina Cresswell were engaged in conversation. As they mounted the slight rise from the cross-roads at which Emil would have only a mile or so to his camp, the low-lying marshes that stretched away to Seaton, south-eastward, came into view.

"Look, Gran'maman, the water is over the dykes already!"

"Shall we be flooded, Gran'maman?"

"I don't think so, dear. Your Uncle Archie always says that Cockle Hall and the church are built on a 'tump', whatever he means by that. It's a slight rise, in the contour, but it lifts those few acres just above the submersible line, as they call it. No, you can't see distinctly from here, too many trees. But there are the dunes on one side, and the water has to come up the dyke on the other. So we shall be safe."

There were murmurs and questions, and they peered between the hedgerows, and Emil, suitably directed, went on his way.

But she stood a little apart, glad to regain her breath, as they paused, and to gaze, with long-sighted eyes, over that wide expanse, the rather higher ground, to the north, the great semicircle of sea, east and south, the marshes, where unusual gleams of mounting waters, lined and divided the lower pastures, away westward to the well-wooded heights towards the centre of the county. Below them, the grey walls, red chimney-stacks and nondescript buildings of Cockle Hall, formed the edge of the picture.

"That's how I've always been," a sudden thought struck her. "The flood all round, but never quite fatal to me. I wonder why?" No use asking any of these young things about her. They had still their long journey to make. She had not far to go.

Yet somehow she found herself not depressed as she might have been by such thoughts. Somehow, for no good reason, her old vitality began to mount again, and she found herself humming an air ... What was it?

She replied absent-mindedly, chasing through her musical memory, which contained, goodness knew, enough odds and ends of tunes she had sung, played, listened to and taught. What could it be? "Turn on, turn on, old time, thine hourglass!" That was it! The other verse of the aria the young people had roused her with in the afternoon. Why that? Why now? Was it just that they had turned after taking leave of Emil and were now descending slightly, on their return to Cockle Hall, and it was easier on her old lungs and heart? Or was it that, somehow, the channels into which one's vitality had once flowed, were always ready to receive it again, just as the ancient dykes of the marshland below there, half full of sluggish water for most of the year, and controlled by sluices and embankments in any case, would receive the flood again, once it rose above the artificial barriers made to restrain it?

She didn't know, but she hummed to herself, "The sands of Time, oh stay!"

CHAPTER II

"THE HARP ON THE AIR"

WHEN they arrived back at Cockle Hall, however, she had other things to think about.

"Look," Nina exclaimed vexedly, "there's Mr. Dormer's car. He'll have had to get his own supper," and hurried forward.

She herself followed at a calmer pace, partly because she couldn't hurry now without making her heart pump, partly because she smirked a little to herself over Nina Cresswell, who in her view rather limited in scope in a village school in a place like Summerscale, and an admirable lodger for one of the several unoccupied rooms at Cockle Hall, would make an admirable wife for Archie even yet. The arrangement was that, once Mrs. Kitchen had completed what she considered a fair day's work, she departed, leaving the tea and supper, such as it was, to be provided by those who consumed it. She had no doubt whatever in her own mind that Archie, most independent of men, and well used to fending for himself when the necessities of his job made his hours quite unpredictable, had got what he needed from the larder, and helped himself. But men in her experience were usually the better (less grumpy) for a little cosseting, so she didn't hinder Nina, but arriving, at her slower gait, in the big living-room and finding Archie as she expected with a plate before him and his mouth full, merely greeted him as any affectionate grandma' might.

"Well, my dear boy. You've had a long worrying day, I'm afraid."

Archie gave her a glance, not without affection, but only grunted. She knew better than to make a man talk until his hunger was satisfied, and moved out again into the yard, to

44

ntercept the young people who had lingered a little, fortu-
ately, discussing someone or other of the odd things that
eemed to interest young people nowadays, girls as much as
ooys.

She longed to say to them, laughingly:

"There, there, it all sounds very important, but you
wouldn't think it so if it weren't that you're all young
together and are vaguely and mutually attracted."

She hadn't been able to make out yet if that little Jean were
leaning slightly more towards her cousin Steve, or her rather
more "removed" cousin Victor, but time would show. Jean
wouldn't, until it suited her, the self-possessed little creature!

Instead of which she said to Steve: "Dear, do tell me again
what you were saying to Emil about Cockle Hall. I never
get it right!"

As she expected Steve, always a boy readier with his
fingers than his lips, gave that little throat-clearing cough
which meant that he was arranging his thoughts, and the
others, how far really interested and how far just being nice
to her she couldn't tell, waited to hear.

"Miss Cresswell knows it all. This was an old Abbey, and
some of the Friars went to the Holy Land . . . Palestine, that
is. When they came back they brought shells with them.
Some say cockle shells. And when they built this gate new,
they put the shells in the corner there to show."

"Oh, I see, how interesting."

Steve gave her his tight-lipped grin.

"That's what everyone says!" He gazed up at the scallops
that adorned the corners about the broken arch of what had
been the great gateway. "But some say it isn't that at all, but
an old fellow who lived here in the old days and sold cockles
and shellfish and made a pile doing it!"

"That sounds to me quite as likely. I must remember."

They all laughed and she laughed with them although she
had heard the story, she didn't know how often.

"Whichever way it was, the friars, or the shellfish
merchant left us a lot of room."

"Miss Cresswell says this is only the entrance and the forecourt, and the upstairs landing over the kitchen is part of the cloister."

He ran his eye along the line of grey flint and freestone, into which patches of later brickwork had been introduced, and in which modern sash-windows had been inserted.

"Gran'maman," cried Victor, "isn't there a ghost? I thought all respectable abbeys had a ghost."

"I've never heard of one. Do you know, Steve?"

"I know what Miss Cresswell says."

"And what is that, pray?"

"She says the village people in a place like Foreshore will believe anything!"

"Nina has lived in the big city too long!"

"Not longer than you did, Gran'maman."

"No, but I don't count, dear!"

There was a general chorus of disclaimer. It was really rather pleasant, the affection of the young things. But Victor had all the pertinacity of his French parent and wanted to know.

"But what exactly do they believe?"

Steve paused a moment, but overcame his inbred taciturnity. Could it be that he liked to be the centre of information in front of Jean?

"She says when she first came here, before we took Cockle Hall, she lodged with old Mrs. Mantrip."

"Not the old woman we saw on the sand-hills, who looked like a witch?"

"That's the one. She told Miss Cresswell not to go out at nights, or she might meet something she didn't bargain for."

"What did she mean by that?"

Steve laughed. "No one would tell her, but she wormed it out of the children after a time." He paused, as people will who are not confident of the value of words, but resumed: "It seems there's a legend of a big dog without a head, with two great fiery eyes, which wanders about the lanes at night. To meet it is bad luck."

"I should think it might be." Young Jean allowed him her are smile. Victor folded his arms across his chest and faced teve, with one of the few noticeably French gestures he had etained.

"This is ridiculous. A dog with no head can't have one, or wo, or any eyes, fiery or not!"

"Just as you like. That's what the children have been old!" Steve was slightly huffy.

She interposed to maintain the good temper that had pre-ailed among them all so far: "You mustn't expect the villagers to be logical about it, Victor. It's an old legend, I have heard it."

"That's right, Gran'maman. Miss Cresswell traced it to ome Norwegian folklore, or what's it!"

"You asked for a ghost, Victor, and that's it!" young Jean out in.

"But it is preposterous!"

"Of course it is, my dear boy. I was always told it was kept alive by smugglers, who didn't want odd visitors poking about the lanes when they were busy."

Victor however was obstinate and well informed. "But there's been no smuggling here for a century."

"I'm not so sure. Even if it wasn't smuggling, there were still plenty of poachers about, with the same reason for wanting to have the lanes to themselves after dark."

"Ah! That I can well believe. These village people!"

Oddly enough that tone stung her slightly. "Not worse than you would find in Brittany, I suppose?"

Victor's drawn-down brows smoothed out. "Why no, of course, Gran'maman. These peasants!"

She did not engage in the eternal argument that arose if she tried to explain that there weren't any peasants, as he under-stood the word, in Easthamptonshire. She shrewdly judged that, by now, Archie would have appeased his hunger, and they might all go in and get their own supper. She led the way in.

As they entered the big living-room it became evident that

they had moved into a different atmosphere. Here was n
light-hearted banter of young people enjoying the aftermat
of a Coronation holiday. Archie was speaking to Nin
Cresswell with the assured intimacy of an equal in a
emergency. Yet he turned with a smile to her. It wa
brief.

"I've just been explaining that you mustn't mind if w
have a disturbed night. If the wind holds, and the tide make
as it looks, at the moment, we shall have to evacuate th
farms on the marsh, and it may be, part of the village that lie
on the lower road. You young men might keep your clothe
handy. I may want you to take messages."

She could not repress a slight thrill. The two boys . .
she begged their pardon . . . young men seemed to stiffe
automatically.

"I can use Nina's bike, or drive a car." They had no
noticed young Jean, but she stood forward with a determine
air.

"That's fine. But I thought perhaps you'd help Mis
Cresswell if we have to open her school as an emergency
centre." He gave a circular glance over the group, an
seemed to feel almost apologetic. "Always provided nothin
changes between now and ten o'clock. Don't say I panicke
if nothing happens. I don't mean to be caught unprepared
that's all."

They silently dispersed.

She had a horror of getting in the way of busy people,
dislike of being told, "No, Gran'maman, I can do it, you g
and sit down," coupled with a small doubt that they might b
right. It was no good her bustling about, and then having t
stop because her breath was so short. So she reinstated hersel
beside the electric fire Nina had pushed into the grate, and
took up her knitting. She soon regained her composure tha
had been slightly ruffled by Archie's warning, and let them
bring her a tray with her Ovaltine. She was less bother lik
that, and supper at Cockle Hall was never a formal meal. She
did not even ask where they were all going as, their appetites

satisfied, the young men followed Archie out, and Jean went with Nina Cresswell, presumably to wash-up, for in that sort of home, in nineteen fifty-three, nothing must be left over to give Mrs. Kitchen a bad impression in the morning.

Alone by the silent glow of the electric fire it happened to her, as it does to people of her age, that the present, once its urgency had receded and its decisions had been taken from her hands, ceased to be as real to her as the past in which she had been a dominant figure. She did not muse, as she sat there, on the possible commotion that might be caused by some awkward combination of wind and tide to the coast nearby. Her mind ranged back to the vicissitudes of her own early life, her memory of once-familiar airs that the young people had stirred up that day. How nice they had been, not laughing at her for ever having taken part in such a now unimaginable production as a "Concert Performance" of an opera of which they had never heard.

She sighed, ceased knitting for a moment and closed her eyes, and into her ears crept the sound of the chords struck in the orchestra, and a voice, her voice, coming in, with meticulous exactitude, "'Tis the harp on the air!" She could hardly have blamed them all if they had giggled a bit. She could see plainly enough that the incident of her past they had so accidentally unearthed was, by the standards of nineteen fifty-three, comic enough.

"Ah, my dear, you little know!" she murmured to herself, half inclined to smile with them. The fuss created, the passions aroused by her simple willingness to step into a gap left by a series of events of which she had, beforehand, no exact knowledge. It was only later that she had discovered, little by little, why Miss Mardicras, brought down from London to sing the part of Lazarillo, had been discarded, and why she had thus been thrust into the vacancy.

The ill-suppressed fury of Signor Radolin, the cautious and at first decorous triumph of Mr. Vizer, above all the fact that she did pretty well, and saved the committee, the Choral Society, the whole then narrowed and specialised "cultured"

D

musical class and public of Easthampton from blatant sensation and crying scandal, were all dead and gone and forgotten. The thing that remained was that she had, innocently enough, fascinated the middle-aged widower Doughty Dormer, so that, after refusal and long postponement, she had eventually married him. And here were her grandson, her great-grandson, her stepnephew (did they call it?) to show, as the result.

"So that's how things come about," she told herself. "Who on earth could tell where it was all leading?"

The more she thought of it, the queerer it seemed, in the light of nineteen fifty-three. Here was Archie, preparing for the possibility of a flood that, more than anything else, was an Act of God. Here were these young people, preparing themselves, during years, for some hypothetical job they might take. Here was Victor running a business that, a few years ago, was threatened with imminent extinction just as he, that same Victor, had been threatened during the years of his youth and young manhood. Here was Nina Cresswell, a whole national educational system behind her, teaching the young of yet one more generation, so that they might be prepared for a way of life that might never be, and was utterly unpredictable anyhow, and there were Emil the German boy, and Barney and Jennifer that she needn't account for. And if anyone asked her how these people came together in Cockle Hall, at this particular moment, the answer was, "Because I sang Lazarillo in eighteen-ninety, and Doughty Dormer was captivated."

It just didn't fit, but that was what had happened.

Then, for a moment, there did seem to be a kind of correspondence between that great stream of life that had washed them upon its shores at this moment, and the great ocean, faintly audible, pounding against the sand-hills that protected the marsh. It was that great pulse of life that had made Signor Radolin desire the girl Mardicras with such passionate longing of a southern nature, easily kindled perhaps. It was the same pulse that made Vizer, perversely perhaps, jealous.

Finally it was the same basic urge, in a different form, in so different a person, that had awakened the latent philoprogenitiveness, the sentimental middle-aged family feeling, of her long-dead husband, Doughty Dormer. He had been left, by the death of his first wife, with two daughters, no son. So far as she had been able to discover afterwards, he felt Providence had treated him unfairly. He could never feel for her, a second wife so much younger, so utterly different in outlook and upbringing, what he had felt for his girls' departed mother. But she had been a justification of himself, and of Providence, in his eyes, when she had borne a son. The great flood that moved all humanity, without which humanity would cease, had been dammed, and confined, with sluice-gates and locks called "holy matrimony", "family life", "respectability", and "good middle-class Victorian habit". And here she was, watching the fourth generation, the result of it all.

"I suppose it really matters?" she said to herself. She could not even tell if she had spoken aloud, the question gave her a mild shock and she opened her eyes to make sure no one had heard. No, it was all right. The room was empty, in the failing light. The sky had clouded over after sunset. Was the wind rising? What did that portend? Well, she was safe anyhow, well looked after. Perhaps that was why she now found herself harbouring these somewhat indecorous ideas. As if the decencies of civilised life didn't really matter as much as she once thought they had. There must be so many millions of people who never had enough money, and good regular situations, like Doughty's, and the prestige and authority of a bank manager's wife which she had had, and the chance of a good education and assured prospects, as her children and grandchildren had had. Were they, those others, the outclassed and unclassed, the helpless and the ill-provided any less precious in the sight of God? Of course not!

"And after all, my son has been dead these thirty years, my husband forty. Well, this remains." She glanced round the comfortably if sparsely furnished room in the home Archie

had made for her. It was getting too dark to see, and perhaps
easier for her to perceive the visages that started up, on the
inside of her eyelids, than the world visible to sight. She saw,
once again, as she had seen from the side door by which the
orchestra and chorus entered, the Institute Assembly Room,
the platform with its plants and empty chairs in the gas-
light, heard once more the rumour of the audience, noisily
filling every seat, the subdued tootling of the band, even the
odour of concert hall, dust and disinfectant, humanity and
hired furniture. She could almost feel, down her spine,
Doughty's authoritative voice:

"Now then, chorus."

They had all come trooping past, in the evening dress of
the eighteen-nineties, the more dashing of the men with a
coloured handkerchief tucked into the edge of the waistcoat,
as the fashion then was, the ladies in white, sopranos with a
blue sash, contraltos with a pink one. It seemed an age before
they were all seated and Doughty commanded:

"Are you ready, Signor? Principals!"

Signor Radolin, all smiles and electric glances, his bald
head shining between its fringe of ringlets, advanced, holding
by the tips of his fingers, the tips of the fingers of Signora
Torticelli who was singing "Maritana". Applause! Bow and
curtsey! Then the men. Modified applause. Finally, the
amateurs who took the minor parts, led by her ice-cold,
almost delirious self. Nothing but sheer will-power and
perhaps Doughty's, by that time, adoring smile set her in
motion. But it did. She took her place. No applause, a titter,
perhaps. Lazarillo was a minor part. There she remained,
numb but alert, until the quartet. How appropriate! Her first
words were: "Mercy! Mercy!"

Once she had uttered them her feelings subsided, her
courage returned, she seemed to communicate her desire to
do her best, to acquit herself in a fashion worthy of the trust
imposed in her, to the audience. There was a slight stir in the
packed seats, not exactly applause, which would have been an
interruption, but as if so many of the good citizens, who

might have known her by sight or reputation as the new young music mistress at Miss Scrivener's, were agreeably surprised.

"H'm," she could almost hear the mutters of approval. "Not bad. We must take this young thing under our wing!"

It hardly needed that to make her do her very best. She sang with a kind of devotion, as if she could not throw herself completely enough into the romantic sentimentalities of the opera.

When they all trooped out for what, she remembered, that Mr. Vizer described as "a breather", at the end of the first Act, she was the recipient of kindly if rather condescending smiles from Signora Torticelli, even a patronising, slightly interested glance from the men. "Very good, very good!" from the Don Caesar of that long-ago evening. She had bowed, silently, respectfully, and she hoped sufficiently frigidly to forestall any attempt at dalliance. Had she been wrong? If she had smirked and responded, would Doughty have been alienated? Well, he wasn't. He had pressed her hand and said so nicely:

"Admirable, Miss Reeson. I'll say no more now."

Ought she to have been warned? Well, she wasn't. She had smiled back and when he took out his gold watch, replaced it, and clapped his hands three times, returned, with the others, in her proper minor place.

"Now, ladies and gentlemen, please. Act Two."

She put all she could into the one or two minor numbers that fell to her part, with spartan restraint and conscientious accuracy. She had seen the great danger that she, an amateur, so far as a teacher of music could be, would run, if she tried to outsing the important rôles and drew upon herself attention that those who filled them would naturally expect. So she did no harm, the performance was a great success, everyone was nice to her, in the over-generous, loud-spoken way of professional people who know they have amply earned their fees. Just because she had the sense to behave so, she set in train a whole cycle of events far more permanent than the applause and congratulations of an amateur choral society in a provincial city. To her astonishment, she found she had become a person with a public character. It is true that the paragraph in the Easthampton *Gazette* was almost wholly devoted to the singing of the principals, the skill of the conductor, the correctness and enthusiasm of the chorus, the painstaking work of the band, even the decoration of the hall by a local contractor. She was given a scant line recording the fact that "Miss Reeson acquitted herself suitably as Lazarillo." The principals were news, and went back to London; the band and chorus had many friends among the readers of the *Gazette*, the contractor was an advertiser. But she was a private individual, an assistant mistress at Miss Scrivener's, and one line was more publicity than she had ever received before. Hannah could not attend an evening performance, but she was plainly impressed by what she read in the *Gazette*. Favourably, oh yes, for Hannah was never ungenerous, but there was just a note in her voice as if she were wondering how her friend and music teacher's success would affect the school. Naturally enough, the school was Hannah's life. She had no other life.

"My dear, I hear all sorts of complimentary things said about you."

"Far more than I deserve. I just did what I could."

"Oh, I think you're too modest. I hope you will follow up this success. I almost foresaw it, didn't I, when I suggested that you should join the Choral Society, though I must say I didn't quite picture you taking so prominent a part. Now I wonder, can the school give a public performance, do you think?"

And so on. They had discussed the idea, always, so far as Hannah was concerned, as something affecting the school. But Hannah had induced consequences she certainly had not bargained for.

She received a letter on the superior turkey mill paper of Doughty's Bank, from no other than Doughty Dormer.

Punctiliously polite and sedulously noncommittal, it made her heart beat.

Dear Miss Reeson,

May I ask if I may call on you, on any afternoon in the near future when you will be at liberty to receive me? Perhaps you will appoint the time that suits you best.

Being merely a member of the resident staff, however much a friend of the Headmistress, she felt thankfully obliged to show it to Hannah. She could not have said if she hoped Hannah would say it was inconvenient, or unbecoming, or what. But Hannah didn't. Her thoughts were otherwise.

"Oh, my dear, some new part they want you to take. We shall have you appearing in *Messiah* at Easter, I can see that. By all means invite Mr. Dormer to call on . . . Thursday will be best, will it not?"

Still, with an odd reluctance, she had written in reply to say that she would be pleased to see Mr. Dormer on Thursday next, at three-thirty.

Fateful words! She kept telling herself that it was all nonsense. Hannah was probably right, he and Vizer and the rest found her sufficiently reliable to be given a small part in some forthcoming concert, and cheaper than a professional, she reflected grimly. But there remained a flutter in her breast. When summoned by the maid to the study at the appointed time . . . and Doughty, she noticed then, was exactitude personified . . . she took herself firmly in hand, and entered the room called "the study" but used for interviews, outwardly self-possessed.

Doughty Dormer was, at least by Easthampton standards, an imposing figure. Tall, and holding himself well when away from his desk, he carried the black cutaway coat, black made-up tie, Gladstonian collar and grey mixture trousers with a certain distinction. His sparse hair and well-kept whiskers were turning grey from sandy. But most of all, the attraction lay in the almost boyish simplicity of an utterly honest and fearless nature. She had heard him reprove some gloomy prophet of disaster at the Choral Society with a loud, assured: "Pooh! If you work hard at it, and really mean to do it, and try to think what the part is about, you'll manage it." That had been his simple and sufficient creed and he looked as if he thrived on it.

He took her hand, lingered a little over it as he handed her to a chair.

"Won't you be seated," she proffered, but he remained standing, plainly full of what he had to say.

"I think you know the position I occupy in this City. It is a comfortable one. In my leisure I have certain tastes, which I know you share." He made her a little bow and she returned it. She noticed the slight fullness of the red lips, between the natural unshaven hairs that surrounded them. "You have probably heard me well spoken of. I hope so. You will perhaps have difficulty in believing what a broken heart I carry about with me!"

She fumbled for some such words as might suit such a confession. . . . "I am sorry!" she could, she ought, to say. And she felt inclined to add, "But why are you confiding in me?" She failed to get it out and indeed she rather felt he would have continued saying what he wanted to, in any case.

Not deeply experienced in the habit of the male mind, she was a little startled by the innocent directness of it, rather like an animal pushing at a gate. Then she was shocked. Good gracious, the tears started from his eyes, he spoke hoarsely, gazing over her head out of the window at the autumnal garden.

"I lost my dear wife . . ." he choked slightly, ". . . we had not been married ten years . . . she left me with my two little daughters!" He whipped out a handkerchief, a nice clean ample one, she noted with approval, sobbed heartbreakingly into it, blew his nose with a high efficient trumpeting and regained control of his voice, and replaced the handkerchief in his breast pocket. Suddenly he lowered his glance to her, in a mixture of command and appeal. "Miss Reeson ... dear, dear Frances ... you are the only person who can replace her. Oh, do come to me, heal my broken heart and care for my motherless girls!"

Things happened so quickly that she had no chance to avoid what she had never for an instant anticipated. With a convulsive movement he flung himself on his knees beside the chair she occupied, reached for her hands and buried his face on her shoulder in a paroxysm of sobs. She was enveloped in the contact of a heavy bony man's body, an odour of lavender water and healthy male. The physical shock galvanised her to instant action. She levered herself to her feet, the chair toppled backwards, she caught his hands to support herself, and managed to gasp: "Mr. Dormer ... what can you mean. ... No!"

That word, emphatic enough, seemed to affect him as much as the firm resistance of her body to his unheralded embrace. He rose with agility creditable for his years, and still holding her hands, confronted her with what seemed mainly astonishment.

"What, you won't?"

Made thus plainly to consider her words, she saw in a flash that what she had meant by "No!" was not really a direct negative to the appeal he had made. She was deeply touched by the confidence so unexpectedly reposed in her, moved by his complete sincerity, his childish need to tell where and how gravely he had been hurt.

She had really meant: "Not here. Not in the study. Not with the imminent possibility that a maid or a pupil might knock at the door, that Hannah or one of her colleagues might enter without knocking!" It was due more to her sense of privacy and decorum, than any lack of sympathy. Faced now with an equally immature consternation, as of a child denied a remedy for an abrased knee, she temporised:

"Mr. Dormer, be sensible. How could I know what you were going to say? You should really have given me some

warning. One doesn't answer such a question on the spur of
the moment!"

He swallowed, his tear-bright eyes searching her face, his
mind unused to the emotion he had allowed to obscure it,
trying to grasp and appreciate her words.

"You won't really refuse? You'll think it over, won't
you?" His expression calmed and his face brightened. He
gently relinquished her hands, used his handkerchief again
and seemed to regain his poise, as a swimmer emerges from
deep water into which he has dived. "You are quite right.
Forgive me. I ought to have written. I considered it, but
somehow I thought . . ."

Evidently he had not contemplated refusal. Accustomed to
use his judgment successfully in practical affairs, he had made
up his mind and it had only remained for her to drop into
her destined place. Yet she was oddly flattered by his evident
high opinion of her, touched by his admiration, so different
from the kind of approach she had repelled with distaste from so
many men. And his attitude to his daughters was persuasive.
He picked up the chair.

"Would a week be sufficient time for you to give me an
answer?"

A week! To make up her mind to say what he plainly
expected her to say, or to refuse? It wasn't much. But did she
want this sort of decision hanging over her? No. She knew
she didn't.

"Yes. I will give you an answer in a week."

He was staring at her. That was what was meant by
"devouring with his eyes". That, and the short physical
contact she had suffered made her feel, what . . . she wasn't
quite sure, but something she hadn't felt about any man
before. At the same time she wondered at herself, at her not
having said:

"No, I'll have nothing to do with you. Go away!"

With an instinct that at all costs she must bring this interview to a close, she moved over to the bell beside the fire-
place. He took up his hat and gloves and umbrella. The maid

appeared. He followed the girl out like a good obedient boy. She flung herself into the chair and covered her face with her hands.

H'm. How emotional one was in those old days! One little knew what was coming to one. She had sat there as if flung on to a stone beach by a rising tide. Ridiculous! She was excited, rather pleased, had not been ill-used in any way. He had behaved nicely and gone away before she felt she couldn't stand any more. No, it wasn't Doughty Dormer . . . that was how she would think of him now, not as Mister Dormer from the Bank, the Secretary of the Choral Society, the father of two girls. . . . No, it was something bigger, something that had lashed at her before, an elemental force trying to engulf her, and hurry her, immersed but floating to some fate she couldn't foresee. It was something that had no place inside the great old house that contained Hannah's school, a kind of Protestant lay convent where girls were shielded from such exposure.

> In the shadow will we work,
> And mould the woman to the fuller day.

The school motto didn't say anything about women being bound to men, and then used by nature . . . or was it Providence? . . . for ends that couldn't be assessed, but only roughly provided against in summary fashion. Marriage . . . for there could be no other outcome to Doughty Dormer's proposal . . . seemed a flimsy and insufficient precaution against . . . against something she had felt at work within herself, something that wasn't taught in class, and that she couldn't tell Hannah about, though plainly, in the next few hours, she reflected she would have to tell Hannah something. Or, if not, to thrust the whole thing away from her, sadden and she feared annoy Doughty Dormer, who was obviously capable of emotion she hadn't suspected, draw her feet, her skirts away from the threatening element and dedicate herself to teaching, to celibacy, to a sort of vow. Was that what she wanted? She didn't know.

All very odd now, very distant, more than half a century away, across two world wars, and a peaceful social revolution that had so changed life even in slowly moving English provinces, where emotion was well under control.

"I should never have thought of it now, if I hadn't felt something of the same sort, working in all these young folk, if I hadn't felt this atmosphere of elemental forces, of flood waters liable to be let loose. I might never have remembered any of it, if, on a wet afternoon, they hadn't turned up the old score of *Maritana* and brought it all back!"

Queer, that was how things happened. Years might pass, the whole aspect of human life might change, but things once felt, and said and done, scored a groove, in which long subsequent happenings to a generation unborn, would run. She could see herself, a diminutive distant figure in unbelievable clothes, sitting huddled in a chair, and galvanised to life by the sound of movement in the busy school; classes changing over, people running up and downstairs, the aura as it were that impregnated the thick walls and long corridors of the spacious solid old house, emanating from all the vitality of a hundred young bodies.

She had roused herself, given a hasty glance in the great, gilt-framed mirror over the mantelpiece, that in all such rooms, in all such houses, caught and concentrated the light of a waning autumn day, filtering in between great heavy repp curtains, and through the lighter lace ones that completed the air of privacy then so essential. What a passion that age had for covering things up! Nothing like it nowadays. The girls and Nina Cresswell, if some physical emergency arose out of this flood warning, would go about with the men, calling them by nickname, wading in water, driving vehicles, behaving as if there were no difference between the sexes, seeing all sorts of indecorous and frightening sights!

"It's all very well, but as I told them, they've missed something. Gentleness! Or was it merely gentility? Respect! Or was it merely kindly contempt? It had all been very different, all those years ago."

Reassured that she showed no trace of disorder, she had left the study and hurried to the great board showing "Time Table for Today", in the wide hall nearly as busy as a street-crossing, with various streams of traffic, bevies of girls going here, coming from there, mistresses passing with pre-occupied air from one duty to another, or to the sparse relaxation that was all Hannah's time-table permitted.

"I needn't have been so careful. No one was thinking of me and my small affairs. No one but Hannah, and perhaps the maid if she ever reflected upon her duties, even knew I had received a caller, and neither of them had any suspicion of the purpose of his call. Hannah had a completely wrong notion of it, and the maid . . . I can't remember even her name . . . took it all as part of her day's work!"

Still, something had to be done, and when she had taken her turn at overseeing the evening meal and the evening task and all was prepared and given out for the morrow, she had taken her courage in both hands, and instead of going to her bed in the cubicle in the middle dormitory, she turned off along the main first-floor passage and tapped at Hannah's door.

"Come in."

She went in. Hannah was busy at her desk. What devotion was signalled by that bowed, round-shouldered back. Did the woman never rest? Silence.

Hannah finished whatever it was that so engrossed her, and suddenly sat up and swivelled round in her chair.

"Yes, what is it?" Dawning consciousness as it were of something unusual. "Frances, whatever——?"

"Hannah, something has happened. I must tell you."

"Sit down, my dear Frances, and tell me."

Hannah indicated the rather less comfortable chair on the other side of the sizzling gas-fire. It struck her with almost comic irrelevance that Hannah thought she had come to report some misbehaviour on the part of one of the girls, or some *contretemps* with one of her colleagues on the staff.

"Hannah, Mr. Doughty Dormer called this afternoon."

She could see Hannah sorting out the memory that she had

authorised the call and preparing to hear in what way it would advantage the school.

"He asked me to become the second Mrs. Dormer."

She could never think why she put it that way, but that was how the words came rushing out, half-defensively as if with pre-knowledge that Hannah would not approve and would not understand.

The strong features opposite her, features that expressed the empire of an iron will over a frail body, became ominously composed. Silence. Then :

"Well, Frances, and what answer did you make?"

"That I wanted a week to think it over."

Something like a bleak smile twitched the corners of the colourless lips.

"Why a week, Frances?"

"I wanted to consider——"

"But you've made up your mind."

"I wanted to tell you."

"I can't advise you. No one can, in such a matter."

Of course it was true. Of course Hannah was right. No one could advise her. She must go her way alone.

They stared at each other, and when Hannah spoke next the atmosphere, so exalted with momentous decision, had descended to detail that sounded trivial.

"I must advertise . . . as soon as you have communicated with Mr. Dormer."

"There's no hurry!" Why did she say that?

"My dear Frances, you can hardly keep a gentleman waiting longer than the end of the term!"

It was sound sense. Yet she lingered a little, hoping for what? Hannah did not encourage this. She rose and took her hands.

"I'm sure I hope you will be very happy. Your intended has the highest character. His two girls are thoroughly nice, sweet-natured young creatures. They have been admirably cared for by a devoted aunt since their mother died. You will have an exacting but precious duty towards them."

"I shall do my best."

"I'm sure you will." Pause, then:

"Now, I think we'd better get all the rest we can. Will you
eep, do you think?"

"I hope so."

"If you don't, let me know, I have something."

That wasn't what she wanted. She got it out:

"Hannah, give me your blessing."

Hannah, looking like someone out of an early Italian
ainting, kissed her gently on the forehead, opened the door,
d her out, and closed it upon her.

She sighed, and stretched, and smiled. It was all so long
go. Now the urgency it had once meant came flooding back,
s the water outside was flooding back into the channels it
ad long forsaken and which had become dry. She could feel
gain the odd, scaring, pleasurable excitement of the next
w weeks.

In spite of Hannah's doubts she slept excellently. Next day
he had to carry her secret about with her. She avoided
Iannah's eye, not from any feeling of estrangement, but from
ne that told her she would have all the disturbance she
eeded, without that which must occur between a woman
vho had yielded, or was in process of yielding herself, and
ne like Hannah who never would. But as regards the rest of
he staff, and the girls, she had that rather cosy enjoyment of
he fact that she knew something they didn't, and would
ave the advantage of letting them into her secret when she
vished. She took the chance of a short break of leisure that
fternoon to write to Doughty. She felt somehow she owed
to Hannah not to delay. "Doughty," she must call him, as
Doughty she must think of him. She still had odd quirks and
ualms, found herself saying to herself:

"Not yet. Not just yet."

The odd reflection that from the end of the term certainly,
he would no longer be a member of the staff, made her
autious. She must show no sign. So it was not in the study,

used as a kind of common room, but in a remote, outlying class
room, far over the kitchen wing looking into the garden, tha
she went to write the letter that was to seal her fate. "What
stupid expression," she caught herself thinking, "as if I wer
going to be hung, drawn and quartered, instead of bein
given love and affection, comfort and position no poo
schoolmistress ever had, not even very dedicated an
successful ones like Hannah."

She chose so well that, on entering, she fell over the char
woman of those days, and had to pretend she had com
searching for books. The poor sniffing, bowed creatur
mumbled some abject apology, hurriedly wiped up an
departed, still sniffing.

She sat down at the teaching-desk on its little dais, an
wrote on a piece of school paper: *The answer is in th
affirmative. Frances Reeson*, dated, sealed and addressed i

"Come to think of it," she now reflected, "it was an od
missive. It had to be. What else could I say? What did
know?"

Once again, watching the little figures, dwarfed to mari
onettes in the distance of over half a century, she could no
withhold an affectionate giggle. Could she ever have bee
that Victorian miss, so blissfully ignorant, so well meanin
and correct? Well, she had been. At any moment, the proo
the direct result of what she had been, might come bouncing
back from fighting the North Sea, "depriving it of its prey"
one might say, if one used such phrases. One used to, all thos
years ago. Not now, perhaps. Anyway she had done what sh
had done, and confronted with the consequences, Archie an
Steve, Jean and Victor, she was not apologetic. No. She wa
proud.

At the time, however, her main feeling had been pur
astonishment. How should it be otherwise? How could
Victorian schoolmistress know much of the utterly differen
life of matrimony, possible maternity (though that ha
hardly occurred to her), the social responsibilities, the daily

intimacies, into all of which she had consented to plunge. Hannah's school was "advanced" to the verge of scandal, with its wide curriculum, its physical drill, its "science", its assault upon Shakespeare and the Classic authors, both of whom said things most girls of that period were not supposed to hear. But, as yet, even Hannah could offer no preparation for the course on which she, Frances, had embarked. There was not even the faintest suggestion of teaching housewifery, not to mention hygiene, the care of children, or the political responsibilities so stringently denied to the whole female sex. It might be so enlightened a school as to be unrecognisable for the conventual establishment that most girls' school were, but the taboos, social and moral, of the age were as many and as binding as the rules of any professedly religious house.

"I was a little ninny, and considering all things, Doughty and Lois were very nice to me and gave me my chance. I hope now that they felt I was grateful. I think they did. But it all got smothered by what happened later and I've hardly wondered, all these years."

The immediate consequence of her bare, prim little note of acquiescence, for it was nothing more, how could it be? came by what seemed return of post. And it was double. One note came from Doughty Dormer:

My dearest, I cannot tell you how delighted I am. I do hope you can come to tea on Thursday as Lois says. Then we can talk. Could anything breathe more affection?

The other was in a good sloping Italian hand:

Dear Frances,

I think it is more sensible to address you so at once, though we only know each other by sight. Will you come to tea at five on Thursday, make my better acquaintance, know the girls, and give Doughty much pleasure? You may like to see the house. May I say I feel confident that he has made a wise and delightful choice.

Yours affec.,
Lois Marston.

E

She replied at once to her "dear Lois", accepting. But when not actively engaged in class, she found her mind returning to these missives. She "delighted" Doughty, he said. Did she? That was nice. She admired, respected, and for the moment when he had allowed himself that embarrassing exhibition of feelings in the study, had pitied him. It was a shame to leave him with two young girls, and he as utterly innocent, as all men, of how girls should be brought up and educated. Well, not quite, from what little she had seen of him at the Choral, and that in public, he was himself well educated and not without a certain discrimination in behaviour, and good taste in music. But delighted? Was that what she felt about him? Not quite. Almost anything else but delight! No, she was pleased, flattered, grateful, she wanted to help him, to mother his girls, and to join in as many musical performances as time and circumstance permitted.

She turned to Mrs. Marston's note of invitation. No, it was not merely that, it was her prospective sister-in-law asking her round to tea, to hand over the house and the young girls to her. And Doughty had made a "wise choice".

"Is that what he's done!" something rose rebellious in her breast. The courage that had been her stay for half a dozen lonely years, motherless save for a stepmother who liked her better the less frequently she saw her, fathered by an amiable weak man who was sentimental about her, but incapable of being of any use, was her own possession. She had fought her way up, among men and in spite of them, and had won the spartan privilege of being her own mistress, like Hannah, like all the few women who were making a new place in the world for a new sort of woman. And now she was a man's choice!

For a moment she had heard a voice . . . was it the Devil? . . . in her ear. They still believed in the Devil in the village from which she came, the parson still preached as if he might meet his Satanic Majesty anywhere between the White Horse, where the men went, and Hangman's Lane, where the girls went hoping the men would come. Was it the Devil?

"Give it up. Write to Doughty Dormer and Mrs. Marston

and say there's been a mistake. Do it now! Do it before anyone else knows!"

But when she faced the alternative, she knew better. She had repulsed several men in her time, because they had plainly wanted of her little more than animal satisfaction. That wasn't enough. She wouldn't be that, for any man. Here was Doughty Dormer offering her everything else, home, children, position, affection. If she refused all that, she didn't deserve to have it offered. She deserved to lead the rest of her life like Hannah. But she hadn't Hannah's devotion, or the blend of ill-health and high aspiration that demanded it. No, she would go on, and perhaps things would become clearer. Then, with what suddenness, matters had been taken out of her hands, even before she went to tea at the Bank House.

She had had to check one or two girls for talking in class, would hardly have noticed except that she prided herself on interesting her pupils and had little recourse to measures of discipline to make them attend. It just did not occur to her that she could be the subject of their conversation and covert look. Then, at the common table, at the wholesome substantial midday dinner, the new French mistress Hannah had recently added to the staff made her a little bow.

"Oh-oh! I hear we are to have a marriage in the school!"

She just couldn't think for the moment what the words meant, and might not have applied them to herself, had she not found half a dozen pairs of eyes considering her. Fortunately she did not blush easily, but she found no words to say.

"When do we congratulate you?"

The direct question suddenly condensed her wits.

"Thank you. You're very kind."

There was a moment's silence. Why did people all open their mouths when they wanted to listen? Gaping idiots. She hadn't bargained for this.

"Frances!" The younger Scrivener sister, Miss Flora, spoke reproachfully. "You might have told us."

"I haven't had much chance. How did you find out?"

"It's all over the school."

"Really. Some people haven't enough to do."

"But you are engaged, aren't you? They say it's Mr. Dormer, at the Bank. Do tell?"

"I expect it will appear in the *Gazette* before long."

"You are a little secret puss, aren't you!"

"Mr. Dormer! But he's . . ." The voice died away. The words which would have followed could only be "old, and has girls nearly grown up".

That was how it struck them. They were all baying at her like a ladylike pack of hounds.

"How long has this been going on?"

"Shall we all be invited?"

"So that's why you joined the Choral!"

It was fortunate that she had had so searching a training in keeping her temper and controlling her expression, one thing she had learned, ever since she had first determined to fling out of the village life of her childhood and become a lone professional woman. "Keep your temper and sooner or later you will have revealed to you the real motive which prompts people." She saw that behind this curiosity, these semi-jocular inferences, lay envy, not very spiteful, and half-willing admiration. In fact, what they really meant was that they wished they were in her shoes. She sweetened her smile.

"You would have heard all about it quite soon. But since you have found out, thank you all very much for your good wishes."

Silence. She attacked her dinner.

Thursday came. She had only one best frock, suitable for the occasion. She spruced herself and walked, careful where she put her feet in the dirty streets of those days, to the Bank House. Odd, now she came to think of it, how all the life of the place then centred in a few big houses in the main street.

Doughty's Bank was housed in a great old Georgian house with, it seemed to her, rows of windows, stretching on each side of imposing double doors that led into the Bank office along the north and eastern front. Its southern side looked out over what had been a big garden, stretching to the railings of Easthampton's famous Cattle Market, but now partly built over, with two or three small villas in gardens, some of which she knew, because the girls came to school, were inhabited by members of the staff of the Bank. The property ran westward and diminished into stables and dependencies that huddled under the great mound on which the Castle stood, from which they were only divided by tree-lined lanes. It had often struck her that Easthampton, in spite of its long and proud history, and its considerable size and importance, was really nothing more than a big, prosperous village, full of country people, with a few coteries of professional classes, clergy, law, banking, administration. It was bigger and more imposing, but not really different in kind from the village in which she had been born.

In the high wall that ran from the house was a door, with a wicket gate, admitting to the garden. On the brass plate above, polished nearly out of legibility, were the words, "Bank House". Entering here, and passing along a stone corridor, open to the garden, but sheltered by a veranda, she came to a wide handsome door, at which she knocked. It was opened by a red-cheeked girl, in the immaculate uniform of those days, who seemed to expect her, smiling as if she, too, knew the cause of this visit, and led her up a flight of wide stairs with a handsome banister that climbed three sides of the great well of the house. At the top, or rather summit, as she felt it to be, she sensed directly that she was in a different atmosphere. She had just time to notice below two other formidable doors, which could hardly lead anywhere but to the kitchen and offices in one direction, and into the Bank office in the other.

But here, on the first floor, were several other doors, and more than that, the feeling not of old, well-established business premises, but of someone's home, not without justified pretensions to a certain culture and style.

The maid knocked at the farther door, opened and announced her. She entered, and found herself facing Doughty Dormer, Mrs. Marston, and the two girls.

He came forward with that impetuosity that sat so surprisingly on a man of his age and position, taking her hand in both of his.

"My dear . . ." Whether he was going to say "Miss Reeson" or "Frances" never transpired. She hastened to release her hand and offer it to her hostess who took it, saying pleasantly and correctly:

"I am so glad you were able to come," and turned to the two girls who, becomingly shy, gave their young hands in turn, the elder, rather darker and taller, the younger, fairer and plumper with pretty frank smiles.

Considering how sternly she had armoured herself for so critical a moment, she had an immediate feeling of relief, gratitude and pleasure. Doughty . . . how well she was to grow to know that nature . . . might have been embarrassing with his straightforward, open emotions, but allowed himself to be steered by his sister-in-law.

It was Mrs. Marston whose attitude she had feared and doubted, quite unnecessarily, it now seemed. True, Mrs. Marston had a home and family of her own, and might well be glad to have her brother-in-law suitably settled, and the girls off her hands. But she, Frances, saw clearly enough that Mrs. Marston, who had been the close friend, she had learned (from Mrs. Cavendish's loose gossip, of all sources) of the first Mrs. Dormer, might well resent an interloper, possibly critical of what she had done in the running of the house, in time she could ill spare, and the care and affection she had lavished on motherless nieces, who returned that affection. Mrs. Marston was a sensible woman, rather older than herself, who from the first made no bones about the fact that she was handing over Doughty Dormer, his bereaved home, and the two young daughters to the care of the newcomer, without any attempt to advise or control. It had been charming.

At first, as the fine old teacups and cake-plates passed from hand to hand, the firelight winking on well-kept silver, the conversation had been merely friendly.

"The girls will want you to sing them some of the numbers they heard you give at the Choral."

"Do you find the pupils at Miss Scrivener's attentive?"

"Where did you study, at Suresnes, was it?"

Easy and pleasant, and Doughty, all devotion, interposing his plain statements, and the young girls, all eyes, but evidently attached. It was, indeed, a new view of life for her. Neither the village at home, certainly not her London lodgings, not even Hannah's school, had been the least like it.

Tea over, and the tea-things removed, Mrs. Marston had said, "You will like to see something of the house," and preceded her, Doughty and the girls dancing attendance.

If anything had been needed to win her, it would have been the well-meant, forlorn, unhandy companionship he was plainly trying to offer, had had to offer, for years, to two young girls.

The house, or at least the two floors she saw, was not so unlike the other mansion that contained Hannah's school. The difference was that it had never occurred to her to picture that busy and crammed to overflowing place as the domestic dwelling of a family. Now the Bank House, with its equally large rooms looking out over the garden, on the other side over Bishopgate, the main street, its seemingly mile-long corridors, its flights of stairs and cavernous cupboards, held only four people with, she judged, four others, shut far away in the remote kitchen, or equally far in skyscraping attics briefly indicated to her as "the servants' floor". That was it! All this carpet, all this paintwork, thickets of stair rail, great vaults of ceiling, all kept clean and serviceable for so small a party. There should be scope here for some little social life, but, so far as she had learned, the absence of its legitimate mistress, the limitations of its master, had never invested it with the usage it deserved. When she said, admiring the great landing:

"What a lovely place for a dance!"

Mrs. Marston had replied equably, "Yes, it hasn't the use it deserves!"

She saw the girls regarding her with interested, could it be adoring, eyes?

Finally, when they returned to the first floor, Mrs. Marston drew the girls aside. "Now Doughty is anxious to show you his special domain. We mustn't intrude!"

Before she could expostulate or enquire, Doughty had taken her arm and led her away from the wide stairhead from whence the door to the main living-rooms opened, and turned into another passage leading westward, saying:

"Lois is joking. But come and see!"

He led first to a pleasant room whose windows overlooked the garden, and away, beyond office outbuildings, to the great Cattle Market beneath the Castle.

"We call it the schoolroom because the girls do their lessons and keep their things here. So much handier than the old nursery in the servants' wing, Lois found."

She registered yet another degree, by no means the last, for the judgment and devotion of Mrs. Marston. He led on. When she halted at the next door, "a retiring room", he dismissed it like all his generation, "very convenient while the children were young. I used it myself when I was a young man. I was born and brought up here, you know!"

She hadn't known, but the fact that he was the second generation explained the air he had, as if he were conducting her round an ancestral domain, instead of his employers' premises. But he had passed on, and was holding open yet another door, with a naïve touch of ceremony.

"They call this my study," he announced.

He evidently was acting modesty, and expected her to be impressed. She was, if not quite as he thought. The room was roughly square, with one window only looking also partially over the garden, but partly eastwards where Bishopgate trended off to the railway and the Moor beyond the limits of Easthampton in that direction. But the room was not chosen

for its view. On either side of that window, on either side of
the fire-place on her right, and covering the whole wall
opposite, and again, as she turned her head, filling the wall
around the door, solid handsome book-cases stood, reaching
from floor to ceiling. On the top of them, between and
around the big desk that filled the window, stood boxes
and cases of all sorts, labelled as in a lawyer's office ("Mr.
(Somebody's) Trust", "The (Somewhere) Committee",
"The (number and crest) Volunteers", "The (. . . ological)
Society".

The sheer mass of custodianship and responsibility
squeezed out of her a little gasp. That evidently pleased him,
and he said with boyish pride, "The firm's affairs!"

Could he mean that all the great parchment-covered books
on all these shelves concerned the Bank? She hadn't time to
ask.

"The Choral Society!" Again he waved at what appeared
to be a complete library, surely, every musical score ever
written! She was moved to say:

"What an admirable collection!"

With a touch on a key, evidently kept well oiled, he turned
back the great glass door and exhibited all those gilt-lettered
spines.

"I hope you'll play many of them to me. They will recall
the pleasant evenings at the Choral, especially that on which
we met." He gave a little bow. She rewarded him with a smile,
reflecting that with the other duties she was undertaking, she
would have a full life. Her vitality, so long starved of outside
contacts, so long stunted within her by the lonely circumstances of her life, rose to meet this new vocation, and a little
bemused by what was happening to her, she missed the
precise nature of his other activities, whose records filled the
other cases, and whose titles he recited. He did not seem to
notice, and as he concluded he handed her to a chair with his
slightly formal charming manner, that of a gentleman of the
old school, to whom a lady is a fragile object only to be
touched with circumspection. Then his manner changed

abruptly, and he flung himself on his knees beside her, clasping her in his arms.

"Frances! When is it to be?"

She had to take hold of herself and remind herself of what he must be speaking. He was asking her to "name the day", as they said in novels.

In spite of admiration, gratitude, growing affection and a strong inclination to seize the opportunity of leading what seemed so much wider, fuller a life than school teaching could ever offer, she drew back from the finality, perhaps the inevitability of it.

"Not yet!" was all she could get out.

Strong, conflicting, hurriedly succeeding emotions chased each other across the features of that honest, not uncomely but unsubtle face.

"Why . . . what . . . when . . ." he stammered.

She determined, then and there, on a line of conduct, a relationship that was to last until his death. If he wanted her so much he must understand on what terms she came. She was no innocent miss waiting to fall fainting into eager arms stretched out. That was why she had left home and led the life she had. He was not going to be the only person in her life, any more than she was in his. It was going to be a partnership, not an ownership.

"I couldn't leave Hannah Scrivener in the lurch. It must be after the end of term. I will speak to her and let you know."

She rose with decision, gently putting aside his embrace. If she had not felt the lifelong importance of the moment she might have smiled at the result of her words. He did not attempt to detain her against her will. He even remained kneeling, his empty arms hanging for a moment. Then he got up, saying with resignation that was endearing in its simplicity and consideration for her, "Very well." The very picture of the good boy who is told that he can't have the piece of toffee until he has washed his hands.

Then, with comic anxiety, "You won't keep me waiting long, will you?"

She could have laughed at the image of herself as a piece of toffee or otherwise desired treat, if she had not felt a gust of warmth, of a rather different character welling up in her. Life had been hard, her own family well meaning but useless, she had been lonely. To be wanted, to have it in her power to give happiness, suddenly melted something in her.

"Not many hours, Doughty dear!" she had replied, a little surprised at the words that came out.

Unused to flirtation, to trifling with such matters, she wanted to confirm the strange thing she had said. She extended her hand to him, in unaccustomed warmth. He took it, and bowing over it, touched it with his lips in a gesture which was pretty, but sat a little oddly on his prosaic nineteenth-century clothes and whiskers.

"I think I will go now. Let me take my leave of Mrs. Marston and the girls."

He ushered her out and they regained the drawing-room where they were plainly expected. Mrs. Marston was working at embroidery, the elder girl reading, the younger sewing, but it was evident enough they were just waiting, and with cordial formalities they watched her being conducted down the great stairs by the maid.

She noticed little enough of the appearance of Easthampton on that drab day, autumn lingering a little before the approach of winter. She took an early opportunity of seeing Hannah. As she entered that spartan retreat where Hannah's private life was combined with her business, her necessary care of her febrile body, with her high dedication to the cause of womanhood ennobled, so that it was at once a shrine, but set up in an office, a cell which was nearly a sick-room, she knew she had travelled miles since the morning, and lived already in a different world. Hannah seemed aware of it.

"Sit down, Frances, and tell me."

"I have accepted Mr. Dormer's offer."

Hannah nodded. It was as if she had said, "So I see."

But the words were: "I congratulate you. I hope you will be very happy. We shall miss you."

Somehow it sounded as if she were being let off on account of extenuating circumstances.

"I'm not going far. We shall meet, I hope, often. I shall see very little of him during office hours, and you will always be welcome."

"I know, my dear. I shall come, once you are settled in. But you will no longer be a member of the staff, and we shall regret that."

"Oh, Hannah, I told him it couldn't be until the end of term, I wouldn't dream of upsetting you," she went on impulsively, because Hannah was already turning away to her desk. "I could even stay another term if you wish."

Hannah didn't look as if she believed her, and in fact she was relieved to hear:

"It's very generous of you, Frances. But no. It would not be fair to Mr. Dormer, or to you, or to the school. You will feel that, I'm afraid, during the classes you take in the weeks that are left. Girls are very . . ." (she seemed about to say "queer" or some word of such inference, but changed it) ". . . interested in such events. But thank you. I will accept your offer to stay on, and write to the agencies at once. So consider yourself free as soon as we have broken up, as you like. A Christmas wedding would be rather striking!" Hannah was smiling, but it was a smile of dismissal.

She couldn't quarrel with the fact. She was no longer a member of the spearhead of devoted women who were going to change the whole outlook of a sex that included more than half the population. She was going to be a married woman, a very fortunate one, but such would be her status. She would no longer be an isolated female, but the female half of a union. She would be mistress of a great, well-furnished, prominently situated house. Not her own, it was true, not even Doughty's, but the house in which he lived as part of his work in life. Still, she would have the considerable social position that belonged. She was going to be a mother. Or at least, a stepmother; she shied away from other possibilities.

Hannah was quite right about the difficulty of remaining

on the staff now that her decision was known. There was an air of furtive curiosity everywhere. Not only among the staff. "Well, Frances, when is it to be?" Or the girls, "Miss Reeson, the Sixth Form would like to offer you their congratulations on your forthcoming marriage," the head girl addressed her, with near-comic solemnity. The maids eyed her, as they never had before, with ill-suppressed smiles, part rather pleasant envy and approbation, she knew well enough what village girls such as they thought about marriage. Part, she felt rather than saw or heard, was salacious giggling behind doors and in passages after she had passed.

"There's this little old book," the fat-faced cook said to her, as she went to give the word for the school dinners on her duty morning, "I thought you might like. It was my old mother's, but I ha' done with it."

A marble-covered penny account book full of hand-scrawled recipes was proffered by a hand that had been ceremoniously wiped on the apron.

"My, ain't that nice!" the housemaid, a cheeky girl, had added. "You look at the end, miss, there's a lot of things you'll want to know, if you haven't found 'em out already!"

Realising that she was being presented with her first wedding gift, she had thanked the donor in her best manner, and hurried on to her duties. When, later in the day, in the privacy of her cubicle she had leisure to examine the book, she was glad this was so. After the kitchen information came home-made remedies, old country saws and sayings, information about babies, and hints about health which made her frown and put it away. She had been reared in a village and knew more than the housemaid thought.

All that was perhaps natural, excusable if not likable. What spurred her on to action was the circulars she received from tradespeople. How had they got to know? Was everyone in Easthampton inquisitive about the private affairs of the Art Mistress at Miss Scrivener's? The answer was, "Yes, they were!" Or at least, they were smirkingly curious about the young woman who was going to be the second wife of the well-known manager of the Bank, and confidential man of the wealthy and prominent partners, and who lived in the house. She wasn't going to be made an object of gossip, a kind of spectacle for the patronage of the class conscious, the tittle-tattle of the low-minded. She spent some harrassed and perplexing hours discovering all this and making up her mind what to do, and was deeply grateful to her "intended" (as she supposed she must call Doughty, he was hardly her "young man", and "affianced" or "betrothed" sounded affected) when another summons to take tea with him, Mrs. Marston and the girls reached her. She went with alacrity, and didn't care who saw her.

This time Doughty, loud-voiced and important, led her away to his study, produced from a little morocco leather box a handsome ring and slipped it on her outstretched finger.

Then she could not but tell him, what he was patently waiting to hear, and she kept strictly to facts and dates, realising how much these meant to him, her reasons for postponing their wedding day. They were: the end of term; her old parent and stepmother, with whom, in all decency, she could hardly do less than spend Christmas, probably his last, certainly her last in that village.

"Oh, my dear," Doughty had cried, with a real distress that warmed her heart, "you do try me hard!"

"And then"—she halted a moment on the words, to emphasise the gravity of her surrender—"when I come back, you may put up the banns." She even gave him the date. Seeing that he was liable to become too enthusiastic, she proffered her cheek, holding his two hands in hers when he had kissed her vehemently.

"We are keeping Mrs. Marston and the girls from tea," and she led him along the reaches of the first-floor passages.

Like a boy, he blurted it all out, and she noted the complicity of Mrs. Marston with her, and the delightful excitement of the girls who on this occasion came and sat on either side of her.

She noted with compunction and sympathy that there
were tears in his eyes as they discussed the "quiet" nature of
the ceremony. Nor did she grudge him the soreness that
remained, ever since the blow Fate had dealt him. It was
becoming. She could never be what that other had been, but
she could be a comfort, and she would. More vital was the
fact that she had gained the affection of the girls.

Then Mrs. Marston said, "Now that we have arranged so
far, I think you had better see what you will be undertaking,"
led her downstairs, and opened the door to the kitchen wing.

They engaged in a wide passage, floored with great flags,
on one side of which a dark cavernous set of steps led down
into remote cellars, no doubt, and others, of scrubbed wood,
up by the back stairs to the first floor. On the other side were
the biggest pantry she had ever seen, its window defended by
heavy bars, and finally a great hall, in which five women and
a youth rose from around a great table, over which was
suspended a great two-nib flaring gas-jet, that winter dusk.
By the huge range, with its armoury of spits and implements,
sat an old old woman, introduced as "Mrs. Bumphrey", who
peered at her and then seemed to resign herself to some
impending change. Mrs. Marston bade the others be seated,
and passed on with the elder maid, Wellowes, to a labyrinth
of larders, outhouses, laundry, bakery, brewery, with
glimpses of the remainder of the garden that had not yet been
built upon, and the side passages to the street, and great
yawning, vaulted places that might once have been part of the
stables. As they returned by some other route to the main
corridor, they ran into a man who touched his forelock and
another who wore a kind of livery.

"The bank porter, and the man who looks after the gas.
You'll have to see, my dear. When Mrs. Bumphrey goes, and
I expect she'll take the chance now that her grandson is
settled at Hoake, I don't know if you'll like to have the men
about with a kitchen full of young girls."

"Were there three besides Wellowes?"

"Yes. Each has ten pounds a year, a length of print, and

free beer. It's a fortune for them. They get married early of course. You'll never have any difficulty in replacing them except perhaps in finding a good cook. It's a heavy task she has."

So she thought. And with memories of that Dickensian scene, of something that had gone on for over half a century and that she would have to master and control, she had returned to her last weeks at Hannah's school.

A movement somewhere aroused her from her reveries. Good gracious, it was nearly dark, she ought to be going up to her room. Where could they all be? Alert enough, when she had something to take her mind off her age and make her forget the doctor's warning, she got to her feet, and stepped briskly across to the door into the passage, switching on the light. Not many steps took her to the old-fashioned kitchen that Archie had revolutionised with all the modern "gadgets" as the young people called them, until he had won the loyalty of Mrs. Kitchen and the thanks of all the other female members of the "family".

"It seems to me that all you have to do, nowadays, is to turn a few knobs, and the housekeeping is done," she had remarked to Archie jocularly one day. "But what happens when the electricity goes wrong?"

"It doesn't, Gran'maman," he had answered, laughing. "That's what we pay all these merchants at the grid all this money for."

She wasn't quite convinced, belonging as she did to a generation in which, if people such as she hadn't looked after the butcher, the baker, the candlestick-maker, Mister Well beloved, the bank porter and Mr. Bradford the gas man, the Bank House would have ceased to have its beds made, its slops emptied, meals cooked, not to mention the sinister things that might well have happened. She never went into the modernised kitchen at Cockle Hall without seeing in her mind's eye, the utter difference in the way Mrs. Kitchen, Nina Cresswell, or the girls turned on this, adjusted the regulator of that, plugged in the one, and turned off the current in the other.

In her early days at the Bank House, she had been confronted by a rather apologetic Doughty.

"My dear, Mrs. Bumphrey wants to go. She's over seventy, been here since she was seventeen in my grandfather's day. No doubt you'll say something appreciative."

"Of course. She's been a marvel, I can see." She could. The place had been run on a sort of dumb unimaginative loyalty. Already she had had to stop the girls from emptying slops down a noisome pipe in the cupboard under the stairs, which smelt as if it connected direct with the sewer and probably did.

So she said: "I'll hear when she wants to go, and see about engaging a new cook. Wellowes can manage meanwhile. At least I hope so."

"Oh, my dear, if you tell Wellows to cook, she'll cook, or I'll know the reason why!" he added gallantly. She had given him her best smile.

Wellowes had done indifferently, Doughty had put up with what she produced with stoic but obvious patience. She herself had received calls from a number of women anxious to be taken on at the Bank House. She had been shocked by a touch of servility, by patent attempts to deceive, with untruthfulness that she didn't even trouble to point out. When at length she had engaged the more responsible sort of person, not without grave qualms, the household routine had run on precariously for a few weeks. The new cook was too loquacious sometimes, too subdued at others, not capable of writing down intelligibly what she had bought, or of planning a week ahead. Finally one morning, Doughty, an early riser, had gone along to the servants' wing shouting in his stentorian fashion:

"Now then, together, it's six o'clock!" and gone down to his study.

A little later Wellowes had appeared, mysterious.

"Please, ma'am, I can't wake cook!"

Dressing in summary fashion, she had penetrated the narrow, oilcloth-lined passage where the maids' rooms stood ranked like cells. The larger one at the end was cook's. There, on the "truckle" bed of half a century earlier, lay cook, and dishevelled and snoring, the utter animal coarseness of that flushed bloated face, the stench of alcohol filling the little apartment like thick choking matter, told their tale.

She shook the woman, quite ineffectively. Her foot struck against something. It rolled out. A brandy bottle, nearly empty. Turning on her heel, she bade Wellowes prepare the breakfast. Later, there had been scenes, protestations, threats of suicide, symptoms of D.T., she thought, but she had been firm, and Doughty had supported her. The woman had gone, without a character, tearful, abusive, and imploring by turns. Luckily holidays were impending, the family went to the seaside, Doughty to the club, the maids on to board wages, Wellowes to Mrs. Marston to learn her job. It had been an early "major operation" she thought they called it nowadays, of her time at the Bank House.

There was nothing at all like it in this year of 1953 in the kitchen at Cockle Hall. Nina, Jean, young Jennifer, Mrs. Kitchen, and one or two women she hardly knew by sight were setting the old long table, boiling things, taking great packages from a man in Red Cross uniform at the door, sorting, arranging, preparing.

"Want your hot-water bottle, Gran'maman?" Nina called above the scurry and din. She reacted instantly.

"I can do that, dear, and I'd better do the others while I'm about it."

"Oh, no, Gran'maman——"

"Oh, yes, Nina, I was drowsing, I only heard——"

"I'm afraid so, though we did try to minimise the clatter. We shall have all the men and boys in, I expect, all soaked, and an unknown number of refugees from the marsh. The school's been got ready for the women and children, Archie thought the men could have the big loft. . . . Yes, yes, I'm

coming . . . that telephone hasn't ceased since eight . . . but do
go to bed, Gran'maman——"

"I'll do the household bottles, then I'll get out of your
way!"

"You're a duck. No offence meant!" and Nina kissed her
across an armful of blankets and socks.

"None took. Off you go!"

It heartened her. She wasn't so helpless after all, under the
spell of an emergency, though she must be getting dreadfully
deaf to have dozed among her memories, with all this going
on at the other end of the house. The walls were thick of
course, and they'd tried to be quiet no doubt, and vehicles on
the road didn't make much clatter, the surface was so wet.

Threading her way with a push and a smile among the
busy toilers, she got the rubber bottles and the stone ones,
filled them at the great electric copper in what had once been
the scullery, when there had been scullions, and took them in
her arms, two at a time along the passage and up the stairs, in
two journeys. There was Nina's, the well-furnished room of a
woman with a rich slice of human experience, a room full of
photographs of people and places, with good clothes hung up
and books about; Jean's, the ultra neat room of a girl who
meant to give nothing away; the spare room which Jennifer
would certainly need, her own, with the two windows
looking south down the coast, a room suitable to the old
ancestor she was. Not sorry to pause a moment before
drawing the curtains, she gazed down the long vista of the
coast that was her view from that, the best room in the house.
It was still light enough for her to make out the dim outline
to the left of the sand-hills, a confused network of hedgerow
trees; to the right, and far across the marsh, familiar beams of
lighthouses and utterly unfamiliar ones of flares and search-
lights being used in all sorts of places, as the whole farming
community set itself to secure as much stock and provender
as might be possible from the imminent threat.

"Whatever would the doctor say?" she grinned to herself
now that she had recovered her breath. She went down again,

to retrieve the remaining bottles, and found Archie, worn but triumphant.

"My dear boy," she touched his hand, "have you a moment for some food?"

"Had it!" He frowned over the paper he was signing for which a despatch rider was waiting in his soiled kit, gulping cocoa. "There. We shall do now. 'Night, Gran'maman. See you in the morning, if we're not afloat!"

He cocked his head with a boyish smirk and followed the man out, with a word to Nina. The girls were lifting a gallon container of something into a barrow or cart. She touched Nina's shoulder and left them to it, reassured by the answering pressure. Something romantic, something ridiculous, something out of the long-dead past that somehow mocked the raw present made her hum to herself as she went upstairs:

> "Come, let me like a soldier fall,
> Upon some fatal field!"

CHAPTER III

"IT WAS A KNIGHT"

SHE slept better than she deserved, considering the outrage she had committed on the orders of her doctor about undue excitement, unaccustomed effort and all the rest. But like most elderly people, she could hardly expect to sleep the clock round, and she awoke with the utter emptiness that lurks around the hour of dawn. By long practice she knew that this meant that her old body had slept all the sleep it could compass at one stretch, and needed a fresh start, as it were, to finish the night's rest effectively.

She rose, cautiously, drew on the thick fur-lined bootees one set of children had given her, pushed her arms into the quilted dressing-gown that was a present from others, draped her grey hairs with an ice-wool shawl Nina had presented to her last Christmas, and the mittens Mrs. Kitchen had knitted for her, a rare mark of approbation from such a quarter. Opening the door, she glanced along the passage. All the doors closed.

"That means Archie has made the girls take a rest," she reassured herself.

Still curious, she tiptoed down the stairs, which luckily were built of solid timbers, not mere treads, and made no noise. Once on the flags of the ground floor, she stayed a moment to see how many caps and coats hung by the big door into the forecourt. Several, but no telling, so many people went about bareheaded nowadays. Gingerly she turned the knob of the living-room door and peeped in. Archie was sound asleep in the big chair in front of the radiator, but still wore his waders and mackintosh, ready for instant action. From the other big chair in "her" corner a lithe figure rose and confronted her. It was Victor. He motioned her back and followed her out, closing the door behind him.

"My darling Gran'maman, what are you doing at this time of night, out of your bed?"

"Just seeing how you were all getting on."

He took her hand and kissed it, French fashion.

"You spoil us, Gran'maman. Uncle Archie is asleep as you see. I am listening in case the telephone should ring. Steve and Barney are out with the men, swimming the cattle across the dykes, if they can't be got into the old ferry boat."

"The girls are all abed, I hope!"

"I hope so, Gran'maman, but I would not be so indelicate as to go and look."

She made a motion as if to box his ears, but she could not forbear to smile. "Are we harbouring any visitors, do you know?"

"The big loft at the end of the passage Uncle Archie threw open to the men, but I think most of them went back to help with the boats when they had had . . . what shall we call it?"

"Supper, you mean?"

"Supfast would be more exact. It was after midnight."

"I never heard a sound."

"We are so glad. The further door opens outwards, so there is no need for them to come through the kitchen."

"You haven't mentioned yourself, Victor."

"Why, Gran'maman, I said I was listening for the telephone. But I have a little friend to help me."

He made a movement of the left arm, which had been plunged into the pocket of his waterproof, she had wondered why. Peering at this invitation she saw something drab and white, with darker patches. Suddenly two little liquid spots twinkled in it, a patch of pink appeared. Victor lifted the object out, and set it on the flags by her feet.

"Uncle Archie found it squealing on a wall. Its mother had swum with the others, one by one, in her mouth. But this one she forgot, or couldn't reach."

How like a bitch, and how like Archie. The little creature attacked the toe of her bootee and had to be forcibly restrained. No one could call it a beauty, nor vouch for its species. Yet there was an endearing courage and likability in its unprivileged mongrel vulgarity that touched her.

"Poor little thing. Take care of it."

"No need, Gran'maman. It chased Clifford's big sheep-dog away from the electric fire, ate Solomon's breakfast. . . . I have never seen a cat so completely cowed . . . and began to make such a noise that we feared it would wake you. Now it will sleep."

He scooped it up and dropped it back into his capacious pocket, stuffed with noisome newspapers, in which it turned round three times and composed itself amid the wetness it had made.

"Well, that's a good example. I'll go back to bed. You try to get forty winks, until your precious telephone begins again!"

"Mine are more likely to be forty snores."

"Never mind. *A bientôt*"

"Good night, Gran'maman, or rather good morning. Sleep well."

She gave him what she hoped was an affectionate and cherishing farewell look. A dear boy! Once again he blew her a kiss, one of the few mannerisms that betrayed his mixed national inheritance. And how nice! Hadn't the English always been the better for what they derived from France?

Upstairs she found, as she always did, that her brief excursion had readjusted her mood. She yawned slightly. It was broad daylight now, glittering rather on the storm-blown, rain-drenched coast. She hoped that not many wretched obstinate sheep, helpless calves, cumbersome pigs and frightened horses had been lost.

"The perversity of creatures, when their best friends are doing the very best for them!"

Slipping into bed, discarding dressing-gown and bootees, pushing down the hot-water bottle, she suddenly remembered why that thought had struck her.

The night of the great fire in Middens Lane, when the Bank had nearly been burnt, and her husband had received the injuries from which he never completely recovered, and which had begun the long decline that led to his death; the terrible task of getting the horses out of the stables of the old George Inn. If it hadn't been for that, her husband might not have been standing where the great brick chimney-stack fell. But his devotion to the business, to the very house beneath whose roof it was conducted, was such that it was bound to have engulfed him sooner or later.

"Captured and eventually engulfed by what we care for most, as we all are," she told herself sleepily. "Why, the Bank not only absorbed him. It absorbed me!" Indeed it had!

That was what she had discovered when, having left Hannah's school in a shower of "good-bye" presents, wistful, envious, some slightly jealous good wishes, she had embarked on her new life.

Hannah had made a nice little speech at the Prize Day, something about: "We so much regret that we are losing Miss Reeson, but she will reappear as Mrs. Doughty Dormer. We congratulate her, assure her of our best wishes and hope we may sometimes see her on these occasions." And then everyone had clapped, even some of the rather formidable mothers of elder girls, who let it be unmistakably understood: "You're too young, and not of the right class to be the mistress of the Bank House. If you can, why not my girl so-and-so? She's nearly your age, much better looking, and comes of decent folk. No one knows where you come from except that you taught Art. That's a bad beginning. 'In the shadow will we work' indeed! There is something shady about the way you've got on!"

She had heeded little enough at the time, bemused by the strangeness of a new outlook, pleased by the evident affection lavished on her. She had had nothing like it in all her life, as she felt, all the more strongly during the week she passed with her old father, and at best tolerant stepmother, who was plainly glad to have her settled and at a good distance. She took note, for, after all, she herself was now going to be a stepmother. Well, she would put a lot more into her duties as such, than she had ever received, as a stepdaughter. She had left her father with no more than sentimental regrets. It was easy for him to say, tears in his eyes:

"Why, my dear, I may never see you again!"

"Oh, yes, Father, Doughty and I will come this way as soon as his duties permit. He's a busy man."

She did not attach undue importance to his protestations for, although not unfilial, she had long made up her mind that, good-natured and well-meaning, he found it difficult to think about much except his own comfort.

So back to the school, empty save for Hannah and her sister Flora, two servants not on visits to parents, and several charwomen scrubbing the whole of that great mansion, as big in its way as the Bank House, acres of floor, furlongs of passage, flights of stairs.

"No wonder there's no domestic service left nowadays," she thought. Not that it had mattered much, then. Hannah, while friendly enough, had left her rather ostentatiously alone. Doughty, on the other hand, could hardly be restrained from having her round to tea more than the once a week she thought seemly. She compromised by inducing Hannah to let her invite him, with Mrs. Marston of course, and the girls, to tea in the study. After all, there wasn't long to go. The banns were up, the day was fixed, and anyhow, once the school reopened she couldn't entertain her family-to-be in that busy pupil-and-mistress-haunted establishment. The time soon went. Flora Scrivener derived a good deal of entertainment from helping her with her small preparations. Luckily it must in any case be a "quiet" wedding. She could spend her last quarter's salary, she would never have to fend for herself again. She had made her father a present, handsome by her standards . . . in cash.

Hannah's attitude she couldn't quite fathom. Was there just a hint of censure? Did Hannah feel that she, Frances, was not quite doing her utmost to "mould the woman to the fuller day" by getting married to a middle-aged widower? Perish the thought! Poor Hannah was incapable, no doubt, of doing so, and just didn't understand how one felt when a man offered one what Doughty offered her.

But all such thoughts were cut short by the march of time. The day had come, and accompanied by Hannah and Flora, she had walked, in her simple travelling-dress, to the church of St. George's by the Bridewell, to which she had marched the boarders on so many Sundays of term-time. There they had been joined by Mr. Cavendish, who did so much of Hannah's business and who was impressed to give her away. She was not nervous, nor too deeply moved by the solemn verbiage of the service. "After all, I had made up my mind first, hadn't I? It was rather late to be told all the things the parson read out so nicely and gravely."

It had been otherwise with Doughty, who, conducting himself with impeccable, almost military precision throughout the ceremony, when they arrived in the vestry, to sign the register, sobbed uncontrollably. If she had had any doubts about what she was doing, that would have dispelled them. There was the proof, if any were needed, that the death of his wife had broken his heart and she was given the opportunity of . . . hardly mending it, but patching it perhaps, and supplying something the girls had lacked, however good and conscientious Mrs. Marston had been. And further, there was the great opportunity her new position would afford. She would shew Hannah something about "In the shadow will we work . . ." yet, and in broad daylight too, not "in the shadow".

So with the organ pealing, the sexton and pew-opener bowing low, they had "repaired" . . . was that the word? . . . to the pastry cooks in Bishopgate where, in the back room, dedicated to such occasions, Hannah gave the wedding "breakfast" as it was stupidly called. With the girls, the Marstons, the Cavendishes, the parson and his wife, they made up a dozen, and she thought it was generous of Hannah to provide champagne.

It had been a great day, her day, a kind of day of emancipation for her, that she would have found it difficult, and certainly distasteful, to explain to Hannah. They were all very

ice to her, and she tried to show her gratitude. Once again
he had that feeling, something like compunction, at being so
ortunate. Good-bye servitude, however lady-like! Good-
bye penury, and watching every shilling, nay every penny.
Farewell dependence, obscurity, the penurious labour of
teaching other people's children what they didn't, in many
cases, really want to learn. She was going to have position,
the impregnable position of the wife of a man who commanded confidence and attention. She was going to have
money to handle. She was going to have a ready-made
family of her own. The young girls were treasures, intelligent
nd affectionate. She would do her very best for them. That
vould indeed be to "mould the woman to the fuller day".

Their discreet middle-aged honeymoon was planned for
the Riviera. Discreet because, not being a bride of social
pretensions, she had not had to satisfy prying curiosity about
t, and in marrying Doughty Dormer she had, as it were,
dopted his mature age and distinguished local position. She
vas agreeably surprised at his proposing it. Schooldays at
Suresnes had given her a taste, a gusto for French life, but no
opportunity of going so far south, to what had become
ashionable places. She had always despised what little she
had seen of the departure of bridal couples. The silly horseplay, the improper allusions, the air of furtiveness found out.
he and Doughty were spared all that, and left by the midday
rain, with affectionate but entirely dignified farewells.

"Good-bye, Hannah!" she had cried to that heroic,
doomed-looking figure, erect and withdrawn. "Good-bye,
Mrs. Marston, take care of the girls until we return." Silly!
Mrs. Marson had cared for them excellently for several years.
But she seemed to take it in good part. "Good-bye, Flora . . .
Mr. Marston. Thank you so much, Mr. Cavendish." Really,
he Cavendish couple had exceeded expectations. "Good-
bye, Sydney darling, good-bye, Evelyn darling!" The last
glimpse she had through the smoke had been of those two
ager, loving young faces.

Once out of sight she had turned to her . . . bridegroom

. . . no, he was something better than all the rather silly youn
men she had from time to time seen going off with equall
inexperienced, rather vapid young women. He was a ma
worth having, even if he did become rather exuberan
in the reserved compartment he had taken for them
Well, it must be a very moving day for him, if in
different way from what it was for her. She suffered caresse
she had so strongly resisted on several occasions, until sh
felt she must make herself understood to a degree she had no
yet attempted. He was just a little . . . a little . . .

"There, dear, that will do for just now! Help me, before i
all goes out of my head, to jot down the people who must b
written to. Get me down my little travelling-case, will you
The one the girls gave me."

That was the line! When one got tired of that kind o
contact, sooner than men, she opined, the kind thing was t
find them something to hold in their hands, then the
couldn't hold her! He was obedient, kind, even thoughtfu
for her, within the capacity of the man he was.

"Now, my dear," he said on arrival, "we'll drive across an
have a good dinner, that'll settle you for the crossing."

She rather wondered if it would, but there could be n
mistaking his intention. He had a gusto for good food an
drink she could not but admire, and indeed, in her presen
mood, share.

It was a change! The simple food at home! Th
monotonous food at a French boarding-school! The spartan
stodgy, good-for-growing-girls diet Hannah laboriousl
worked out for the school, subsisting herself on biscuits an
milk, magnesia and soda-water.

"What a treat Doughty gave me! All the better for it
being a treat for himself too."

And his way with waiters and servants, cabmen and railwa
folk. She chuckled triumphantly at the memory across th
years. Nothing like it nowadays!

"Good morning!" with that stentorian cough of his tha
brought *maîtres d'hôtel*, station-masters and all the rest t

attention while he was yards away. "Show the lady to the retiring-room, Mary." How did he know that all chamber-maids were called Mary, or at least appeared delighted to be so hailed when he hailed them. All the waiters were William, and sprang to his side. The more exalted people touched their hats and chivvied the underlings.

She had been doubly proud when, later that night, they had boarded the packet ". . . the old paddle-wheel packet, dear me, what a period-piece I am getting!" Proud because, though glad to avail herself of the cabin he took for her, she hadn't been seasick. She was almost equally proud of him, tramping about the pitching decks, demanding brandy and water of stewards who ran to fetch it, and coming to see how she was far too often, had it not been that the effort to smile presentably and reassure him had kept her in control of queasy feelings until they reached Calais. There, mounting into the wide first-class coach, she had been proudest of all. Doughty's French was not even First Form, not Infants' Department. She deftly assumed command over some detail of the disposal of luggage and glowed when, as the train moved out of the Maritime station and they settled down, he said admiringly:

"My dear, what a linguist you are!"

She smiled sleepily. Yes, she could speak French. But far more important was the look in his eyes, the utterly frank satisfaction and gratitude of a man incapable of simulating feelings that did not possess him, and contemptuous of suppressing feelings that must be honourable, or they would not occur to him. After that, she had slept, worn out by the ardours of the day. No doubt he did too, but she couldn't have told. The next thing she knew, they were halted at a wayside station in a *bistre*, dark green, blue and violet land-scape, of a wide plain between mountains, of a France she had never seen. A plump, blank-faced woman in a kind of peasant's dress was selling coarse mugs of coffee and fresh rolls. She leaned out and demanded two of each, and threw a two-franc piece on the tray. The woman fumbled for change.

"Tu peux le garder . . ." she uttered. Why?

"*Mais . . . mais . . . c'est trop . . . pourquoi?*" The woman made it "*pour-quoye*". But she knew now.

"*Parceque je suis heureuse!*"

Blank stare!

"*Sois heureuse!*" she called as the train moved. The expression, or lack of it, on that peasant face altered as the coins were tucked away. She must have been potty! Sleep! Excitement! The incident was quite incredible, but it stood out in her memory like some well-preserved, long-forgotten "view" found up in an old album, and suddenly recognised.

So, by the time they reached Bordighera of those days, they had lost none of the impetus, or whatever it was, that led people to get married. She had watched as many young couples, as most people, presumably had wondered at her own father and why he had married again, a woman he couldn't in the nature of things love as much as he must have loved the first one he married, who had been her mother. What made them do it? Foolishness, was the first answer. Not altogether, though. Divine Providence, the Church said, had ordained it. That was true enough in a certain sense, but it made marriage a sort of *pis-aller*, something that was to be excused because men couldn't help being animals. Surely it was better than that?

Well, it was going to be, for her and Doughty Dormer. They were neither ignorant youngsters, or farmyard creatures, nor were they enticed by gain, or other motive. He wanted, needed, demanded what she could give, love, cherishing, protection, honour. She admired and wished to be all that to him. She didn't love him, in the sense that ludicrous Valentines lent the word. Only, that sensible view left nothing to help her get over the momentary awkwardness of the fact that she had never shared a room, much less a bed, with a male before. He was experienced, but that didn't help. Probably most men knew, by marriage or less honest means, what to expect. Few women could. They must be surprised, and the very silliness of most young couples somehow muffled that surprise. Once that moment was over, it didn't matter. But

her particular case she just couldn't pretend. She was going
to be surprised.

"How lovely Bordighera was," she thought with a sigh.
I'm happy enough here and admire the coast. But that early
spring along the Riviera. The mild sunshine, brilliant colours,
banks of flowers, charming simple peasant people. I must
have been half asleep, and had eaten too much, and drunk far
more than I was used to. I believe we dozed all the afternoon
on that lovely terrace, until the sun went down in the sea and
it grew chilly, and we went in."

So at length the time had come. Doughty had been considerate. He had a dressing-room and didn't mind that she
had put out the light.

It was quite true. She had been surprised. But not in the
least as she had anticipated rather than actually feared, but for
which she had armoured herself with rigid stoicism. Not in
the least! It was not he who had surprised her. It was she who
had surprised herself. She had never had, up to that instant,
any inkling of the depth of tenderness, sympathy, immolation
of which she was capable. Had she, indeed, been capable of it
before? Had she not, brusquely and clear-headed, refused and
repulsed plenty of advances in her time? Had she not restrained his endearments in the train? Now, at the far more
critical moment it was she, apparently, who could not have
enough! Ashamed! The very reverse. Here she was, half a
century later, as a result of that surprise, cared for and loved.
It was to that long-ago ephemeral moment that she owed
Archie's father, Archie himself and now Steve, Jean and
Victor. So it must be Divine Providence after all, as the
Church said, only it seemed to put it all the wrong way
round. She hardly recognised herself in the words of the
marriage service. She had no doubt about the reality of her
marriage with Doughty Dormer.

"How easy it was, and how pleasant after that," she mused,
as the warmth of the bed-clothes settled round her, and the
stillness of the house enclosed her in a kind of vacuum. "How
lovely the country was. How nice Doughty tried to be!"

For what she discovered was, that by being so surprised b
herself, she had discarded an inhibition. She was on bette
terms with life. She could afford to indulge Doughty hence
forward, secure in the fact that he was naïve as she had neve
been, could be led, and at need, just commanded. Odd t
think she had gained all that by giving away what wa
supposed to be her most precious possession. It had half
dozen names, designed to cloak its nature. Virtue, good name
modesty, maidenhead all meaning that its value lay in giving i
away. Who made all those rules about human conduct? Wel
she knew which must be kept, now!

"I didn't have to give much away. Doughty had so simpl
and direct a nature, like a well-brought-up boy. Grateful as
child given a treat, reassured like a patient after an illness. An
we were both on holiday. He never took more than a fort
night, because he could not bear to be away from the busines
of the Bank. I had never had a holiday like it, and its necessary
brevity made it all the more precious to both of us."

It had not taken her long to see through the lives of mos
of the people in the hotel and the surrounding villas. The
were not on holiday. They were either invalids, or wer
working harder than even she and Doughty had ever worked
at pleasure. It was a bond between her and her new husban
that they joined in despising benevolently most of th
querulous, febrile crowd.

"What do they do, all the time, do you suppose?" she ha
asked him.

"Mostly what they shouldn't, and don't enjoy it," he ha
answered, shrewdly enough.

"Where do they get the money?" for she had never see
so much wealth squandered with so little result.

"Friends and relatives in the background somewhere.
can't think why. I wouldn't lend most of 'em a fiver, as
matter of business."

"That lady, Bamburg . . . if that's her name . . . who wa
talking to me in the lounge while you were ordering the carri
age, seemed to think it odd we hadn't been to the Casino."

"She's a——" He decorously restrained his verdict. "They're all hanging on until the first of the month when they get their remittances. Then they go to lose it, at the tables."

A thought struck her. "I should like to see these rooms where they go."

He looked at her, but only for a moment.

"Very well. We'll go round after dinner."

They did. She was touched by his acquiescence, his apparently implicit confidence in her. She justified it. He gave her his arm and they entered the establishment and passed through the gaudy, over-heated apartments that were so strange a land to both of them. She had never forgotten it. Not that they were molested. None of the frantic, bewitched crowd that, eyeing each other, pushed, round the squares of coloured cloth, the glittering little spinning wheels, had time or interest to resent their intrusion. They made the circuit and passed out.

"Pah!" she exclaimed. "If it wasn't for all the scent and essences they daub themselves with, I should say it smelled like the zoo!"

He chuckled. His imagination wasn't very active and he hadn't thought of that one. "They certainly did look like birds of prey," he agreed, always factual, and squeezed her arm.

"But it seems to go on and on. Some of the people from our hotel go every night."

"You'd know better if you stayed here longer. That chap I talked to in the lounge says they mostly shoot themselves!"

"Good gracious! Isn't there a fearful scandal?"

"Hushed up. Bury 'em in the gardens somewhere. Too much money involved to have a fuss!"

"What about their wretched relatives?"

"Equally anxious not to have a fuss . . . if there are any relatives. That lot didn't look as if anyone cared for them, or they for anyone."

It was true enough, and a rare flight of imagination for him. He and she were out of place in that company. That, and

G

the fact that, to such as they, the essence of a holiday was its half-wistful brevity, the fact that it was a holiday, a brief interlude in something deeper and more satisfying, united and reconciled them. They left the lovely place with a contented sigh. It had been an unforgettable moment. They would now return to something longer and stronger, and theirs. It hadn't mattered, therefore, that old Easthampton indeed had looked rather grey and dowdy, with thawing snow, fog, and finally fitful sunshine.

She had set about her new rôle as mistress of the Bank House with verve. They had been greeted with friendly smiles from Mrs. Marston, affectionate clinging of the two girls, the dutiful glances of the maids.

That was the order in which she saw her future. Doughty must come first. It was his life, his home, that he had asked her to share, that made it all possible. Then there were the girls, who must be set on the path of free, independent and happy life. Finally, there were the domestic surroundings of them all, in that great old fortress-like place, hub of the business life of Easthampton, that had lacked its real mistress so long.

She waited a week to see how things turned out, but on the second Sunday evening after their return, feeling she knew what to say, she sought him in his "study". Service in the morning, a walk in the afternoon, a long evening drowsing, she suspected, over books, for it was only on Sunday evenings that his various meetings, trusts, committees, the Choral or the Subscription Library were not accessible.

"Doughty, can I come and talk to you?"

He roused himself and pushed forward a chair.

"Why, of course, my darling. Give me a kiss first."

She gave him a very brief one.

"Doughty, a lot of people have been calling. Some are old friends of yours, and the girls' mother's. Some are just busybodies who come out of curiosity. Some, I rather suspect, want something or other, and think they will approach you through me. I am going to put a stop to all this. Could you make me a list of people we ought to know socially? I'll have an afternoon when they can come."

She saw by his expression that such a problem had never dawned on him. She had always been most scrupulous in not prying into his feelings about the girls' mother. What had she done, that pitiful predecessor, who had been hastened away, leaving a broken-hearted widower with two babies . . . and a life to live somehow? Perhaps she had been too occupied with babies, soon too ill, all too soon gone. He now did his best, like the good boy he always was.

"Yes. I see. I'll write down the names of the people we want to know. You can please yourself what you do about the others. We have to think about the Bank's customers."

That was it! She was part of an institution. She would be loyal, because it involved him.

"Thank you, dear, if you will. I'll send cards to give them a day. It needn't bother you, dear, they'll be gone before you come upstairs."

She kept silent while he made a note on his tablet with his special green pencil. It was rather touching, the care he took. When he had done:

"There's another thing, dear. Have you thought about what we must do for the girls?"

If the first question had surprised him a little, bringing into his field of vision something from outside it, so that he made a note to attend to the matter, that might not otherwise occur to him, the second question made him sit up, literally and metaphorically. He stared at her, then at the fire. His tone showed that he was startled to the verge of apprehension.

"My dear, what should we do? They have a good home. Lois did her best, and you will do more for them, I'm sure. They are devoted to you."

"Yes, dear, that's all very well. But Sydney must leave school shortly, and Evelyn after a year, at most. What's to become of them?"

His reply came haltingly, from the depth of an imagination dumbfounded.

"I really couldn't say. I suppose some young man will want to marry them. I really hadn't thought!"

Pellucidly true, he hadn't thought. He might have heard of "mould the woman to the fuller day" but would have dismissed it as ... er ... poetry.

"I think we owe it to them to think of it now. Supposing, for some reason, they don't want to marry the young men, or that no one asks them?"

His gaze shifted back from the fire to her face. There was real anxiety in it, as if he had been asked to contemplate a risk not commendable with the class of business the Bank did.

"I don't know what we can do. What do you suggest?"

"I think they should both go abroad, so that they have languages at their command."

For a full moment he stared at the fire.

"Will that attract the young men?"

"Possibly not. But they can teach. Anyhow the experience will fit them to meet the world."

"Good gracious!" He was genuinely astonished. Then he rose to the occasion with a new idea. "Couldn't they learn the pianoforte ... and ... er ... art, and do as well ... if I may say so ... as well, or nearly, as you have done?" He was evidently being complimentary. He had no inkling of "In the shadow will we work", of penury, of the limitations, the polite degradation of the sheltered, ornamental woman, only fit to be precariously married, like a piece of property changing hands. Still less had he any idea of what she had been through. Restraining any bitterness lurking from the life she had led as an art mistress, now so far behind her, she spoke in graver tones.

"Doughty, it's a hard life, only faced by those who must. Our girls need not go through what I and so many less fortunate have to. I'll make some enquiries through Hannah Scrivener, and my old pension, and let you know what the prospects are. But the first thing is to find out what the girls themselves wish. I'll ask them."

She waited just a moment to see if this assertion of her new duties struck against any prejudice he might still harbour, left over from an earlier conception of the place of woman in the world. She need not have wondered. His plain, honest mind flew directly to the facts, place, time, cost.

"What a woman of business you are! Certainly consult Miss Scrivener. 'Straordinary successful woman. I was looking at her account the other day. She must be saving money!"

Repressing a momentary impulse to retort: she deserves every penny she gets, and will need every penny too, with a possible long illness and early decline. She merely replied, "Very well," and let him stare at the fire again.

He might have said, as many of his sort would, "Pooh, girls of that age don't know what they want!" She knew well enough it was often true and she didn't want to be in the position of "putting ideas" into heads in which they did not exist. Nor of seeming to cast, by remotest inference, any slur on the mother, who had not survived to deal with her children's future. But he didn't. After a decent pause, she continued:

"One thing more, dear, then you'll have settled all the affairs of this interfering female you've married!"

That made him chuckle and might well have led to more of the demonstrations of affection to which he was rather prone. Complimentary and charming, but liable to cloy. She nipped them in the bud.

"Doughty, it's about the maids. Wellowes has profited by the pains Lois Marston so kindly took with her. She has become a passably good cook, and will improve. If she doesn't, we may have to make other arrangements. But so far she shows promise and she'll have to have more money."

This time he did show something approaching alarm.

"Why, my dear, she's been content enough so far. Has she asked for more?"

"No, but she's worth it, and there's nothing gained by paying her the least she'll take. Not to mention that, being a fairly bright girl, she will probably know or find out what other cooks get."

"She was glad enough to come here, as a child almost, to trundle the children in their pram. A shilling a week she got and was pleased."

"When was that?"

"When? Must be ten . . . fifteen years ago. When their mother——" He shut away the memory of failing health, deepening into tragedy. Facts again redeemed him. Dates! Passage of time. "Now I come to think of it, she must be getting on for thirty."

"Exactly. She'll have to have twenty pounds. Then Louisa, who is now doing what Wellowes did, and seems equal to it, must have fifteen."

"Oh, come, my dear. I think you exaggerate. They won't leave the Bank House. It's a recommendation."

"That's just it. Anyone will be pleased to have the maids from here. We can't stop them if they wish to better themselves. We should have to give them a good character."

"Wait until they ask."

"No, Doughty. I don't like accepting service I haven't paid for adequately. They may not ask for more, they may just say they want to go."

"Aren't there plenty more willing to come?"

"Plenty. Think of the ones we had to replace Mrs. Bumphrey. We'd better keep Wellowes and Louisa and the others. They are clean and sober, at least, and that's worth something!"

"Yes, of course it is——"

"Then we must pay something for it."

But she had sent his mind back to the previous fact.

"How I miss Mrs. Bumphrey."

"She had twenty!"

"Yes, but she'd been here a lifetime. I hardly remember the one before her. . . . Mrs. Cupiss, was it?" His mind groped for a moment back half a century to a set of people and a state of things long gone. He sighed. "Her batter puddings! Ah! We shall never see the like again!"

"You certainly never will. It's Wellowes or some one worse. And Louisa, Anna and Sarah."

"I suppose they'll be wanting something next?"

"I think I can keep them, on the present wage, if I give them a regular evening off, and perhaps one Sunday a month, and try and make their lives a little less like sheer drudgery."

"It's better than the sort of life they have at home, or they wouldn't come out to service."

"It ought to be. Think of all the blessings we enjoy. We ought to be more ready to share them."

He stared. He couldn't imagine sharing anything, except perhaps the air breathed by all Easthampton, with the maids in the kitchen. It was a hundred yards and over thirty stairs distant, another region, almost another world.

A little compunctious, and feeling she had tried him rather high, she made an appeal that she thought would succeed and she was not unwilling to test.

"Believe me, Doughty, I know what I am talking about. I used to enter a large number of houses. I know what the domestics feel. I know what I felt. I was treated little better."

It roused him.

"Good gracious, my dear, you don't say so."

"I do!"

"Monstrous. Well, you have me at a disadvantage. I never thought about . . ."

No. She saw that. Old Mrs. Bumphrey and some good-natured ignorant female had poured the slops down a noisome pipe, taken in milk in unscoured cans, bought food off barrows wheeled to the door. She thought: "I wonder what was the matter with the girls' mother. She may have kept some sort of control until she was brought to bed, and then . . . I wonder?"

Meanwhile his mind had travelled on.

"Fancy treating you as a——"

"Do as we would be done by, is a good rule. I'll see what I can do with the maids."

She left him, having at least not decreased his affection. He produced the list of people whom it might be well to notify of her "day". She had some cards printed and distributed. This left her with afternoons, at least, during which she could tackle the matter of her stepdaughters' future. At first she made no progress. Hints, allusions, seemed to be lost on them. This was not wonderful. They had lived sheltered lives. She was loath to demand point blank: what do you intend to do when you grow up? She felt sure they didn't know. At length she tried.

"How would you like a short time abroad?"

A pair of clear grey eyes surveyed her calmly. A rather bluer pair sparkled with anticipation.

"Like Monica Cavendish?"

"Where's she gone?"

"Abroad. On the Continent."

"What's she going to be?"

"Finished!" They repeated what they had been told uncritically.

"If you went, it would be to learn French and German."

"Oh! Monica's going to Paris." Very vague. Something in their complete blankness made her wonder. Not Paris perhaps. Some place a little more serious, and less expensive.

"Switzerland."

"Oh! Should we see the Alps?"

"Perhaps. But it would be more like school, only . . . grown-up. Not classes. Perhaps you could live in a family, and teach English."

Sydney, the elder, nodded gravely. Reliable like her father she absorbed the idea. Exchange of benefits.

"Evelyn might wait a little longer." She was too much of a child at present.

Dear, dear, what a long time ago it all was. How Providence (she still used that old-fashioned term) forced one to take decisions that, seemingly vital at the moment, appear years after of so little consequence. She had been so positive, on the brutal facts of her own experience, that the girls must be prepared to stand on their own feet, meet life, and offer valuable services as the price of freedom and self-respect. Armed with two languages, the only modern languages that mattered, French and German, they were sure of a future.

Hannah Scrivener had been a great help. She did not seem to harbour any grudge against the friend and sometime subordinate, who had left school-teaching for so much greater scope and security.

Both girls had a year at Morges, and learned fluent French and German and much else.

"How could one foresee that Sydney would get married and live abroad and never teach again. Or that Evelyn would go off to the League of Nations and spend her days doing an official job there, until it all came to pieces, and she went to America?"

But any feeling of futility she might have suffered was over-laid by the sequel.

"Well, I did my best, according to my lights at the moment. And here's Sydney's son, in this very house, sleeping soundly I hope. Who could ever have foreseen that? Why, Doughty might not even have approved if he had known!" Doughty was dead and gone, the Bank was so changed as to be hardly recognisable for the semi-domestic institution with a dwelling house, her home, upstairs. All gone? But had it? Hadn't something survived and spread from it. Security, fair dealing, affection, enlightenment, all of them contained in that great high safe old place, the hub of Victorian and Edwardian Easthampton until, in a new age, they had gone, those basic virtues, flooding out into the great clumsy, near-mediaeval village Easthampton had been.

That had been her final task. She was never sure if it hadn't been her most important one, the reorganisation of the domestic staff, it would be called nowadays. Lois Marston, in whom she had confided, was dubious but not altogether discouraging.

"Try and see, my dear. I quite agree that you'll have to pay more money if you want to keep the maids you like to have with you. I'd been wondering if I ought to say something to Doughty, but you understand what a position I was in."

"I think you did wonders, in a very difficult position."

"I was fond of the poor little girls. Who wouldn't be? Little Evelyn hardly stopped crying for weeks when her mother died. I could see things were getting out of hand, but daren't upset that old Mrs. Bumphrey. Well, that's all over, and I think Wellowes will serve you well. There's a young man, or a middle-aged one to be truthful. Gardener at one of the Bank partner's house. Widower. Not in a hurry. Neither is Wellowes, she knows when she's well off. I think they both look upon it as a sort of provision for old age. He'll get a cottage when the head man goes and Wellowes will have savings."

"But don't they——"

"Bless you, no. That sort have seen enough of early marriages and squalor in a brick-floored kitchen sprawling with children. They want to be genteel. My dear, you've no notion of the ideas people get nowadays."

"I see. Then I think I'm safe with Louisa."

"Yes, she's the serious sort. And no beauty. Goes to Bible meetings. Encourage her. Outlet for emotions."

"But they've never had any regular evenings off, sit gossiping among themselves, or flirting mildly with the tradesmen who are employed by the Bank."

"Ah, there you'll have to be careful. Give Wellowes her Sunday off when you can. She'll go home to Hoake and sit staring at her gardener and he'll stare at her. I've seen them when I let him come to tea in the kitchen. And you'll always know where Louisa goes. But the younger ones!"

"They ought to have an evening off, too!" She had bridled at the memory of her own evenings of incarceration.

"Depends what they do with it. You don't want to have one of them in trouble!"

Thus Lois Marston. Kindly but worldly, intelligent but rather cynical. It had been hard to admit that she was probably right, without surrendering the implication of "In the shadow will we work." It was easy for Lord Tennyson. He kept the men away from the Princess, and even the "plough maidens" who must have been as stocky and physically efficient as the Russian women police were today, didn't get involved with men until the word was given. If she left that young Anna and Sarah to their own devices, what might those devices be?

She soon found out.

That same Mrs. Cavendish, the lawyer's wife who had been her companion at the Choral Society, invited her to attend something called "The Ladies' Compassionate Meeting". She might have shied against an indefinable air of patronage about the name, or about Mrs. Cavendish's expression. But on referring to Doughty he had said:

"You'd better. Mr. Bird's sister is a leading light. I wouldn't like her to tell him you had declined."

This rendered her uneasy, but unwilling to embarrass him she had gone, and found herself in one of the larger houses of the suburbs, where the spinster members of the large and rich Bank partner's family resided. She noted that. They did not live there, they resided, with a porter in his lodge to admit visitors to the drive through the grounds, and footmen to fling open the door and usher one into a large, sumptuously furnished drawing-room.

She was kindly if austerely received, given tea, and had to listen to a long report on the activities of the Society among girls who had failed to get married soon enough to justify the inevitable results of associating with men. It was a very enlightened report, and among facts and figures, records of "cases placed in suitable employment" and "cases", nearly half, in which "your Committee must regretfully record that all trace has been lost and the worst must be apprehended", she heard "Your Society cannot but feel that the low rate of wages paid by firms in the City places in jeopardy the virtue

of girls who know of no other way of obtaining not merel
small pleasures and trivial comforts, but the very means t
live".

There had been a sensation, murmurs and mutters an
face-saving resolutions of thanks.

"Pious sentiments, all too late," she had said to hersel
but not to Miss Bird or even to Mrs. Cavendish. She ha
subscribed to the fund, shaken hands with the wife of th
Dean, and the wife of the principal Dissenting Minister, wh
regarded each other, in those days, with polite surprise
When she returned home, after her stepdaughters ha
retired, she had repeated much of the substance of what she
had heard to Doughty and asked him if wages were too low
in the town. To her surprise he looked rather shamefaced.

"My dear, it's always said that the girls at Vizer's take wha
he offers because they know they can make it up out of the
soldiers at the barracks!"

"He ought to be ashamed!" she had burst out indignantly.
"I'm surprised that the Bank keeps the accounts."

"Well, my dear, it's a matter of business. You can't expec
Vizer to pay more than the labour is worth. He's not in trade
for the good of his health. The kind of work the girls do,
sorting shoddy and making-up, is work that anyone can do,
and there are always many more wanting to do it than ever
get signed on. He can't pay fancy wages for the sake of it!"

"He's making money out of human misery."

"I don't deny it. I'm not defending him, I don't like him, as
you know. But he's only taking human nature as he finds it."

She had a sudden flash of vision. Of course. She thought of
the girls in the village of her birth, the sheer poor quality of
the humanity that existed to tend animals, commercially
more valuable. That was it. No use finding fault with well-
meaning ladies at the Compassionate. They were doing what
little could be done, with the sort of human material that
existed in all the courts and yards of the old City. There was
only one real basic remedy. Improve the quality. How right
Hannah was, "mould the woman to the fuller day"!

CHAPTER IV

"THERE IS A FLOWER THAT
BLOOMETH"

HE must have drowsed off as elderly people will, when they
re warm and comfortable and have not had quite their full
uota of sleep. She awoke to the agreeable sound of tea-
ups and opened her eyes to find young Jean setting down her
ttle platter, with her special pot and accessories.

"Thank you, dear!" Then the rumour of the house reached
er and she demanded anxiously, "Good gracious, what time
s it?" and reached for her watch.

"We're just getting the breakfast."

"All right. I'll be down in a few minutes."

"Why not let me bring you up a tray?"

"Because you spoil me, dear."

"That would be an achievement."

"No. The truth is, I don't like feeling helpless."

"Never mind your feelings. Indulge yourself for once.
ou've indulged all of us."

"No. I'll be down. What's been going on?"

"Excursions and alarums. Noises off. But they think they'll
trengthen the sea wall in time for the next tide."

"Good. I won't keep you waiting."

Jean disappeared with an alacrity which argued that she
ad left bacon frying and kettles boiling. Frances Dormer
ipped her tea. Cloudy rain-washed skies were brightening.

When, after the loyal battle with her elderly looks, in order
o be presentable to critical young descendants, she arrived in
he "refectory", it seemed crowded.

"Here's yours!" Nina Cresswell had kept her place at the
ead of the table. "I won't stop to introduce you. In fact I
on't know them all. But they'll be going out to the job
efore you'll miss them."

She accepted this introduction to the half-dozen men and
boys who were hastily finishing what was set before them
and disappearing with a word of thanks, and were replaced by
others. She made a little friendly bow to those who noticed
her entry and got sheepish, grateful or worried looks in
response. Victor and Steve waved to her with full mouths. It
was a scene of cheerful resolution, considering that several
of the "guests" had left their homes with two or three feet of
water creeping up the walls, or had spent the night ferrying,
swimming, coaxing or pushing unwieldy, frightened or
sodden animals to places of safety. Gradually the room
cleared, and Victor and Steve were able to move up and greet
her.

"I hope you got off to sleep, Gran'maman?"

"Quite well, dear, I felt rather useless!"

"Nonsense. You are the presiding genius of this place. We
all look up to you."

"It's very sweet of you, dear. I do admire you all, though I
can't share your travail."

"We like to show you what we can do. D'you remember
when I used to keep shop in your work-basket, and sell the
buttons out of the button-box?" They both laughed at the
childish memory. "I must go, Gran'maman. Are you ready,
Steve?"

"All present and correct."

The jolly boy presented his cheek to her kiss. He had
never grown up, that one.

"We must be going back. Look here, Gran'maman, you
walk as far as the sand-hills and see Uncle Archie's new wall.
He will be proud."

Half-inclined to retort: "Oh no, he won't. He'll think I'm
a nuisance," she restrained it, and substituted:

"Very well. Where are my goloshes?"

Emerging from the courtyard of Cockle Hall, one found
the coast road before one's feet, the sand-hills to the right, the
rising ground with its trees to the left. The upper part of the
village, well beyond danger of flooding, was called Church

Row reasonably enough, for the two-storeyed, flint-faced cottages spread for a distance of some hundred yards on each side of, and opposite to, the churchyard wall, beneath the old, many times altered and repaired tower. Amid them, the Lobster Pot Inn, Mr. Semmence's Stores, and the school, were the only public buildings.

"Some of Uncle Archie's men are on the church tower. They can see the whole way down to Seaton, and they've a field telephone. You won't see them from this side, but you will when we go down the Loke to the sandhills."

She glanced up to where the weather-vane, veering lightly in the brisk air, complained of lack of oil. Nina went off to see how the women and children in the schoolroom had settled down. Steve went with her in case there was still any heavy lifting to be done.

Just as, she leaning lightly on Victor's arm, they were about to turn into the Loke, she felt him withdraw with less than his usual consideration.

"*Sapristi,*" or some French expression escaped him, and he cried: "Why, Eleanor. . . . Miss Truman. . . . What are you doing here?"

A very presentable girl, neat and well turned out amid the workaday clothes and summary toilettes of Summerscale, gave him a startled look and dived into one of the cottages, ducking under a line of washing. Victor leapt after her. There was a sardonic call from a housewife who had to remove clothes-pegs from her mouth to utter it:

"Here, Liza, young gentleman wants you."

Victor halted and asked politely, "May I speak to Miss Truman?"

"No one of that name here!"

"But I saw her go in at your door."

"That was my Eliza. She come down from London to see how we are getting on. Triplet is the name."

"But this is absurd. I know the lady. She works for me. She's on my books as Miss Eleanor Truman!"

"Well, that's a good 'un. 'Liza, come here and explai
yourself. So you're her boss, are you?"

Good-natured, if slightly defiant, with the true Eas
Anglian "I'm as good as you" expression, the woman plante
her fists on her hips and surveyed him. Frances saw clearl
enough that, without the cloth cap, with a hair-do, a corset,
well-cut dark costume, she would be comely enough to be th
parent of the discreetly *soignée* daughter, who now re
appeared from behind the linen and met Victor's gaze wit
half-humorous bravado.

"What's all this, Miss Truman? Trading under an assume
name!"

"If you like. I can call myself what I please so long as
earn my money, can't I?"

"Indeed you can. I'm not blaming you. Come and mee
my grandmother. Gran'maman, this is my most intelliger
assistant."

"You needn't believe him, Mrs. Dormer. It is true I wor
in his shop, as Eleanor Truman."

"I don't blame you, my dear. Come and see what m
grandson has been doing to the sea wall."

"He's done a mighty good job, I believe. The village i
grateful."

The child fell in beside them, with that lack of false sham
and subservience which was one of the many engagin
qualities of this fourth generation. This one held herself wel
knew how to wear her clothes, which were of the simples
description and perfectly suitable for the grown-up an
earning daughter of the home from which she came, didn'
chatter or giggle. She had been a little startled at being dis
covered, but was neither brazen nor apologetic.

"Here's the works," from Victor.

In truth, the old Loke, used by no more than a handful o
longshore fishermen most of the year, and by the familie
which had discovered and frequented Summerscale in th
summer, could hardly recognise itself. In all its centuries o
pedestrian traffic, coastguard and smugglers, visitors an

llagers, it had never submitted to machinery, or led to
ything but the keen air, the constant sound, the immense
nptiness of the beach bordering the North Sea. Like many
other venerable institution, it had never been designed for
e burden it was now to bear. It had been narrow for the
dimentary, home-made trolley, a mere elongated wheel-
rrow, that had served to bring lobster-pots and creels of fish
om the boats to the carts that carried the sea harvest inland.
Frances stood amazed. The Loke was unrecognisable.
reat contraptions of which she did not even know the name
thered and chattered, emitting a blast of oily exhaust, or
natever it was, that easily overcame the salt and sodden air
the marram grass and gorse bushes that fringed the sand-
ls. Like intelligent elephants pushing things about in the
cus ring, complicated engines pushed steel slabs into
sition, another veered with the sightless intelligence of a
astodon, and suddenly poured an obscene vomit of liquid
ncrete where it was directed. A third, a great tripod, raised
th a menacing rattle a great metal bolt, which it suddenly
eased so that it struck the pile at which it was aimed a blow
weighty that the solid earth trembled.

"What a noise, what a mess, what a world!" were the
tinctive comments that rose to her lips. Teaching and
ternity, a certain social scope used for philanthropy, plus
old woman's physical shrinking from drilled and ordered
lence, made her survey the scene with helpless distaste, as
hung on her grandson's arm.

But she never uttered the words. As her old eyes re-
usted their vision, and tried to take in so multifarious an
ivity, while her nerves sought in vain to fend off the
fening clamour, she saw whose was the controlling voice,
dominating figure, in all that weird cacophony.

"Archie, come down, it's dangerous, what a mess you're
" The instinctive grandmotherly care for the little active
ing boy who had played round her feet forty years ago
ne welling up. Those momentary reactions were over-
ne by others, admiration, thankfulness, a kind of fierce

H

pride. How clever he was, clinging, insecurely it seemed
her, to a vibrating steel platform, swathed in a filthy servi
raincoat, bareheaded, the feeble straw-coloured sunshi
glinting on his thinning fair hair. As if the whole episode h
been staged for her benefit the significant thing happene
The Devil's symphony suddenly rose to new rauco
heights, a . . . beam, did they call it, with a great claw at t
end made two or three tipsy gesticulations and came to r
with a sickening clank, in a cloud of stinking blue vapo
Archie shouted something. She couldn't catch what, fort
nately perhaps, for he was clearly annoyed. Men wrestl
with wheels and handles. No result. Archie took wl
appeared to be a flying leap among them. He seiz
a long lever, which was gibbering helplessly, and ga
it a sudden down and forward thrust. He looked li
nothing so much as St. George spearing the Dragon. E
being a man of his age and an engineer, instead of destroyi
all that lethal bulk, with its immense potentialities,
serviceableness, its wrongly directed force, he tamed a
used it. In Archie's hands, the mighty engine, the mode
edition of a dragon, did not blow up, disintegrate, and becor
so much embarrassing dross. She had once been asked by
bright child in a class to which she had been reading t
legend of St. George, "Who cleared up the mess?" She h
been put to it to find a suitable reply, particularly as t
questioner was the daughter of a sanitary inspector, one
the new type in which she had such faith. At Archie's biddi
the great unwieldy box of tricks gave a shudder and a kind
cough, like a lazy sea lion or recalcitrant polar bear, prodc
into resuming its tricks. Wires tautened, valves (was tl
what they were?) slid, wheels revolved, and the great st
arm resumed its inarticulate obedience like some well-train
saurian. Then she knew what it was that had struck her w
an odd familiarity among so much strangeness. Archie's a
in command, was that of his grandfather, before the great r
that had broken his spirit and destroyed his physical capaci
She nearly said, "There's something in heredity after al

But what was the use of talking to her young companions about things that had happened thirty or forty years before they were born, in a different age?

She turned away from that scene, and with the help of Victor's arm and her stick, found her way back to the metalled road, and heard the conversation of the young things going on over her head. The girl said:

"Our house was safe enough. But there were the young children in Marsh Street. My Uncle Giles'. So I asked Miss Abbotts and she said she was sure you wouldn't mind, in the circumstances."

"No, of course I don't. Miss Abbotts wouldn't know that I had relations at Cockle Hall."

"No, she didn't seem to. So it's just coincidence."

"Now seriously, Miss Truman. . . . You are going on being Miss Truman?"

"Yes, please. People will laugh at my name!"

"Very well, though I don't know why they should. Now, what's happened at your Uncle Giles'?"

"There'll be a dreadful mess to clear up."

"Mud and debris?"

"And the sewage coming up!"

"What do you want most when the water goes down?"

"Brushes and brooms, swill cloths and fuel."

"Meanwhile, the children are being looked after?"

"Yes. The elder ones are in the school, the younger with their mother, at ours."

"Well, you must stay as long as you're wanted."

"Thank you."

It struck Frances as a queer conversation between employer and assistant, perhaps even queerer as between two very presentable young people. No condescension, no truckling, no noticeable consciousness that their ages were similar, their sex opposite. What a different world!

They stopped at the school to see how Nina's unforeseen tenants were getting on.

Frances, with her early memories of foreign populations,

herded in trains and market-places, of refugees from most countries in Europe, with whom she had had contact during two world wars, could hardly repress a smile that was not far from affection.

"The British!" she told herself. "No wonder they are incomprehensible but trusted, feared but courted!"

There were perhaps forty women of all ages, and all conditions from a beady-eyed, sallow-faced gipsy who lived, or rather existed, in her verminous and mysterious fashion in a caravan, in a field no one bothered to use, at the end of Hangman's Lane, to a decent, spectacled matron, a pillar of the Methodist tabernacle, who kept the shop in Marsh Street. Around them were grouped about the same number of small children. She could compare them with the populations flooded out from the neighbourhood of Paris, when the Seine was over the parapets, with the groups of Belgians, ferried from Antwerp in 1914, and the long stream of wild-eyed, terror-stricken refugees from all over Europe in the 'thirties. True, there was no political or religious terror hanging over them. No policeman or priest maintained authority, no spies lurked, and no officials fussed. There was no noise louder than the hum of normal individual conversation and the sound of elder children playing in the yard outside. There was a kind of dumb, unwilling resignation, no gratitude, and a strong determination not to get mixed up with those they did not consider their equals.

"We're a long way off revolution yet!" she reflected. "That kind of stolid humour never explodes."

"Well, Nina," she greeted the schoolmistress, "to what queer uses educational facilities are put!"

Nina took her up in the spirit of the greeting and laughed. "Isn't it luck to have it in the holidays? I suppose the place will be clear in time for us to get it scrubbed!" She turned to the young people. "Steve could do with a hand to move out those forms. Now, Gran'maman, everything's under control. We needn't stay to watch the W.V.S. with their mobile kitchen," and offered an arm.

She took it unwillingly. It was true if sad that she herself was useless. But she was intrigued by the way Victor, and this young woman whom she supposed she must call Eleanor Truman and not Eliza Triplet, had gone at once, to help Steve with the dismantling of the makeshift dormitory. It was not like employer and employed. It was not like two reasonably presentable young people, accidentally brought together. It was more like two companions going off to a football match.

"You know that girl, then. You nodded?"

"Eliza Triplet? Yes, I taught her. Nice kid. Ideas about bettering herself which I rather encouraged. She's a manne-quin, someone told me."

"She's employed in the shop Victor runs."

"No! What a small world. I heard some name, but it was not Galland."

"No, it's called Aristos, I think. She calls herself Eleanor Truman. Victor could hardly believe his ears."

"How quaint. I don't blame her. No wonder Victor was nonplussed. He seems to have forgiven her."

What did that mean? Was Nina hinting? If so, she hinted no further. They continued, talking of trivial things, leaving behind them the rumour of the village, the roar of the battle against the flood. She was not sorry to sink into her comfort-able chair in the empty refectory, and to hear the greeting of the flat-voiced, flat-footed Mrs. Kitchen, trailing off into a long story about village doings, mild scandal and gossip, muted by the closing door as she joined Nina in the kitchen. As with all old people, her own energies served her but fitfully. The exercise, fresh air, mild spectator's excitement, made her drowsy. She took up her knitting, relinquished it for her book, closed her eyes.

She was conscious of the flood, a sort of catastrophic back-ground to her thoughts, what they called an Act of God, a Crisis of the Elements. Possibly partly on account of the queer encounter of the young people, partly from some lingering spark of vitality in herself, that memory blew into

a flame, the element that threatened Summerscale and the
neighbouring coast, translated itself into that other flood,
that spread over more than half the people in the world,
fertilising and threatening, the source of birth and life, the
cause of innumerable deaths, the means of communication,
and at the same time the separating barrier. She herself had
once felt it wash round her ankles, as high as her waist, if
one wished to continue the image, and had escaped total
immersion.

Here she was. Incredibly, that same she, looking and feeling
so different, had once contemplated that escape.

> Scenes that are brightest,
> May charm awhile,
> Hands that are lightest
> And eyes that smile!

As so often happens to musical people, it was the phrases of
the old opera that recalled the images to her.

She saw herself, sitting in the high-perched bedroom
window of the old house over the Bank, looking out across
the acres of the enclosure beneath the mound and walls of the
castle, black with the crowd that gyrated, yelling and laughing, in half-tipsy horseplay, before the merry-go-rounds,
coconut shies and raree shows of the Easter Fair. "Scenes
that are brightest". That was the link! The brassy mechanical
organ in the nearest tent was jerking out the tune in a
series of eructations, and puffs of steam.

> Yet, o'er them above us,
> Tho' nature beam.
> With no one to love us,
> How sad they seem!

Coarse and brazen, and not more coarse and brazen than the
gesture of the spangled and frilly-skirted girls who twirled
the enticement of their never quite exposed limbs in the face
of the onlookers; not more coarse and brazen than the

allusions and insinuations with which the clown and the hero
beckoned and handed-up the gaping sightseers to the pay-box,
where for a shilling they were admitted to the performance of
the "Gaiety of Paris" advertised in the life-size posters that
covered the entrance. There it was, the turgid, boiling flood
that brought men and women together, tore them apart,
created life and often destroyed it, an animal fever, a rut,
a divine institution that had to be embanked, canalised,
controlled, dominated.

She had sat there contemplating the scene with her eyes,
her ears alert to the uneasy breathing of the sick child in the
cot at the foot of the bed. She had by no means taken the full
measure of what had happened to her, by that date, the second
Easter after her marriage with Doughty Dormer. For that
was how it seemed to her now. Everything around her
remained static. She had seen the Easter Fair before. It looked
no different. The change was in her. The bedroom, their
bedroom, her "nuptial couch" as poets ridiculously called it,
was the same. She had turned Doughty out, to sleep in the
dressing-room next door, and had installed her infant in its
cot, at the foot of the bed they had shared.

Sounds in the long passage that led from the stairs. No
mistaking that confident tread. Doughty was most considerate. She choked back the reflection that he was pleased as
Punch. Fond enough of his daughters, he had wanted a son.
She, Frances, had provided one. And nothing could undo the
fact.

She could hear him now, taking infuriating pains not to be
his loud assertive self, opening the door with precaution,
poking in his head, beaming at her, and immediately trans-
ferring his glance to the cot.

"All right?" Doughty Dormer was one of those men so
transparently honest by conviction and training and profession that it just never occurred to him to conceal anything
he did or thought. It had become plain, the moment she had
been indisposed, that he was delighted. His brave attempts at
solicitude had been maddening. He was now trying to

remember her, before he turned to the prize that had crowned his middle age, the son so eagerly expected.

She had nodded with as much patience as she could muster, and with another smile to her, he had closed the door and gone on with his busy useful exemplary life. Having a son didn't interrupt him. It had transformed her.

Puzzle as she might, she could not define what had happened. She had been taught, like all civilised people, to keep old animal nature under control. It was not only Christian morals. It was common-sense. The fate of human people, particularly of girls who didn't keep it under control, was plain enough. Then she had been further strengthened by Hannah Scrivener's ideas about the liberation of women. She still believed every word of it. So she had become an Art Mistress, instead of a drudging housewife, or a hunted, deceived, helpless and hopeless non-wife, without a house, husband or home, as plenty of women did. She had made her way, in spite of the great flood of creative instinct that had tried continually to sweep her off her feet into its power. She had succeeded. She had succeeded only too well. She had been good enough to sing a small part in *Maritana* in place of a professional, she had captivated Doughty Dormer.

"What was wrong with that? Isn't he everything one could ask? All the better for middle age and widowhood, rather than the silly inexperience of so many younger men!" she demanded of unanswering fate.

All quite true. Yet there she was, sitting watching a sick child, in the middle of a fine afternoon. She had lost control of her life. The great flood had engulfed her and swept her along and it was just good fortune, Doughty's fine position in the City, and his amiable if not deep character, that enabled her to swim, as it were, instead of being just tossed about, in danger of drowning, as plenty of women were.

"Scenes that are brightest!" brayed and bleated the steam organ out there. The people were pouring out, with shame-faced guffaws and nudges, from yet another performance of the "Gaieties of Paris". The girls who took the principal parts in that egregious piece of as near pornography as they could get, would now, once more, make as if to gratify the Peeping Tom salacity of the males in the crowd, egged on by most of the women who thought they could profit by it. She almost wished them the luck, that the male characters now parading in front of the entrance were no doubt suggesting to them, in every barefaced hint.

There went the legs! Those girls would be lucky if they finished up in half the comfort and security she had managed to secure for herself.

But that did nothing to assuage her feelings. She had little use for irony. Few people had when they themselves were the object. It had seemed to her, in that far away time, that she had been surrounded with irony. It had not been absent even from the visits of Hannah Scrivener. During the spring and early summer of the year of her marriage she had been full of the affairs of her stepdaughters, the care of the great house she was trying to rearrange, the domestic staff she had reorganised, the club for the pathetic weekly wage-earning girls from the factories, whom she tried to teach to sing simple cantatas, and make simple clothes.

In the middle of it all she had been obliged to say to Doughty hurriedly one morning, as he came running upstairs summoned by the maid:

"I shan't be down to breakfast. I'm . . . not quite myself. . . ." How devastatingly true!

She could see his plain, fresh-coloured face between its whiskers, the expression of concern, melting to something like hope. He hid it hastily at her look.

"Very well, m'dear!" Downstairs he went, and evidently sent for the doctor, who shortly arrived, and soon made up his mind. He was very nearly arch about it. She had then learned the lesson that every human being found so hard to believe until it happened to them! She knew at least as much as most women of the "facts of life". No one reared in a village could very well remain oblivious of them. She had defended her physical integrity well, during her professional years. She had accepted Doughty Dormer, because it was an opportunity too good to cast aside, for a fuller, better life. What had she expected? Even so few months after the event, she couldn't remember. But she had let the current sweep her off her feet, and there she was.

Hannah Scrivener came to see her when she excused herself from some engagement in which they were mutually interested. She told Hannah of her . . . plight? No, she refused to look upon what had happened to her as such. But she feared the avowal had been rather sulky. Why? Hannah hadn't done it. No one had. It had happened . . . to her!

"My dear, I congratulate you." Hannah had come up to her and kissed her on the forehead. She had burst into tears. It was . . . magnanimous of Hannah, who perhaps couldn't, and certainly wouldn't, in those early days, feel this to be a matter for congratulation. It was more like an illness. And instead of the privacy that muffled illness, everyone had to be told. Indeed, in a short time there would be no point in not telling. It would be obvious. And instead of commiseration she got congratulation. Everyone was so pleased; not only Doughty, but the girls, a little awestruck and solemn, but bright-eyed at the idea that they might have a little brother. She had one moment of sardonic amusement when she found that he assumed the sex of the coming infant.

"Well, my dear," Mrs. Marston had greeted her, "we must see after you. I know a very good nurse." Practical and kindly, with just a hint of, "What did you expect?" natural in a rather older, more experienced sister-in-law. Time had moved relentlessly on, she had had to abandon the Choral, and the Girls' Club as the autumn advanced.

"In the shadow will we work," came also to have an ironic *double entendre*. Was this "moulding the woman to the fuller day"? So to the final stage when, with a kind of exaltation she had abandoned herself to her fate, and been rewarded by . . . the helpless little creature in the crook of her arm.

That phase, too, had not lasted. She began to resume her former command of her life, as, one by one, the small dis-bilities of infancy had been overcome and she had resumed the existence of a woman who was not merely a woman, but a responsible member of society. She could still sing and play and teach others. Above all, she could direct and plan the beginnings, at least, of the life of another human being. She was scrupulous not to neglect the two girls. But the "baby" who became the "boy" was her very own.

"And if I told anyone under this roof what it was like, they would hardly understand what the words meant." Nina might be interested in the changes in social habit, Archie would be contemptuous, if it were not for affection, the younger ones would find it comic. But it was rather advanced for those days.

She had been first, so far as she knew, to start the fashion in early morning tea. Now, half a century later, she felt mildly compunctious at the thought of the maid who, starting work at six, or Doughty would have gone to the end of the corridor in the servants' wing, and roused them all with a stentorian bellow, had to carry it up the fifty-odd stairs from the kitchen and along to the relatively new wing over the garden, to her bedroom. She consecrated that hour to accounts of the previous day, and plans for that to come. Her next innovation had been to abolish morning prayers. It seemed to her unchristian to stop the maids in their work, bring them trapesing up from the kitchen, or down from the upper stair-head, beyond which they might be making beds and emptying slops, in order to have a passage of scripture, and a prayer, read over them, when they must be famished. They could come to her Girls' Class and hear scripture not only read but expounded if they wished, and much else. After breakfast, she had nurse remove young Stephen of those days, to the high wide nursery on the second floor.

"At least I saw what sort of breakfast he made and the nurse got hers in relative peace and quiet."

Doughty might be totally concerned in the business of the

Bank, and at least half a century behind the times in his notion of the needs of the children, but among his many virtues were his punctuality and his readiness to leave everything concerning his offspring to her. Having read the paper, with a cheerful and final, "I'll go down now, m'dear; up at one," he would disappear through that door under the front stair that led into the office, which reminded her so much of the entry to the Cave of Aladdin. For it was one of the rules that only major disaster could break, that, once that door closed behind him, he had entered "the office", and must not be disturbed. Many a priest had a less devout feeling for the House of God than Doughty Dormer had for the century-old, adjusted and altered, but spiritually unchanged, ground floor in which the meek old Quakers had installed their "banking office" a century before.

She herself then descended to the kitchen and expected to find cook waiting to receive her, with slate and pencil to take her orders. She gathered that, in that earlier time of her predecessor about which she was so careful not to enquire, cook had come upstairs to see "Mistress". Well, she had altered that. Wellowes had responded to her promotion and was as loyal to the interests of the family as anyone could wish, and as intelligent in her work as her capacity allowed.

"Now, Wellowes, what have you got for dinner today?" was the formula, putting the responsibility on the senior occupant of the kitchen, encouraging initiative and scope. Wellowes would make suggestions all carefully within the framework of a very slightly varying routine, for Wellowes was not endowed with imagination, and perhaps it was better so. The kitchen week began on Saturday with the sirloin that only gave place to rare presents of game. The Bank partners would sometimes send venison or grouse or feathered game, as the season might allow, or their easy-going approval of their resident chief clerk suggest. Once, during some exceptionally mild weather she had found herself (and Wellowes) faced with a great chunk of high-smelling deer's flesh and had said:

"I wish Mr. Bird would let us know when he is feeling kindly towards us."

"My dear, how can he? We're on his list, and very fortunate to be so."

She had to tell Wellowes to burn a good deal of the rapidly deteriorating remains and resign herself to the whims of those who, under Providence, and nearly as remote from the daily lives of their social adherents, dispensed such promiscuous bounty.

But for three-quarters of the year, week in, week out, there would be sirloin and Yorkshire pudding on Saturday, cold sirloin and salad, the latter serving the double purpose of making a cold dinner and thus setting free all but one maid, on Sunday, and hash, mince or collops on Monday or Tuesday, depending on the lighting of the great old built-in copper. If that feature of the big washing ceremonial was in use, then there would be steak and kidney pudding, slowly boiled until the lachrymose and dilapidated Mrs. Long, the cabman's wife, was ready amid her tale of daughters who had gone astray, and sons who had enlisted, to use the water. A joint of mutton would provide for Wednesday and Thursday, and Wellowes was incapable of omitting mashed turnip and caper sauce with boiled, and red currant jelly and leeks with roast. Friday meant fish, and so the week ended. But, habitual or no, she solemnly walked through the kitchen, with its mural decoration of dish covers and the no-longer-used kitchen service of pewter, the back kitchen, with its shelves of saucepans, fish kettle, dutch oven and Heaven knew what high-up and out-of-reach, never-used iron-mongery of spits and toasters, basters, frying-pans, warming-pans and objects of which she, and perhaps Wellowes, never learned the use. It all dated from the eighteenth century.

"I suppose one could sell that junk for a substantial sum nowadays, the warming-pans and much of the pewter any-how, and some other items for curiosities. Or even by sheer weight for scrap!" she mused.

.   .   .   .   .   .

Beyond were two larders, one with a marble slab like the entrance to a mausoleum, one with a great ice-box lined with lead. "And the whole barrack range was scrubbed once a week and turned out once a year, all the years we were there. I wish I had a graph of the foot pounds the maids moved, and were glad to have the job." No one would believe her nowadays.

Then there were the no longer used buildings, which might originally have been brewery or still-room, and a shed in which the Boy cleaned boots. And the earth closet, on the very last patch of what remained of the garden.

"We could have stood a siege!" she told herself. "No flood could have had terrors for us. We could have lasted out any visitation of nature."

After the kitchen floor, she had usually passed up to see that the bedrooms had been duly put in order, and so to the nursery to luxuriate for a few minutes in the company of little Stephen, and incidentally to impress on his nursemaid that constant vigilance would always be exercised over that remote corner. If the weather were fine she saw that he was taken out for an airing, for, as he progressed from a little bubbling and blah-ing infant to a small trotting boy full of questions, and thus to a sailor-suited youngster, an increasing apprehension grew on her, "Was he getting enough fresh air in that house built up in the middle of the town?"

So she drove the not so willing girl forth, with careful instructions: "Today, the Close!" or "Today, the Castle gardens," or "Riverside, but by Prospect Place, not Bishopgate". For coupled with the fresh-air question, was the very nature of even the best sort of girl of the long series who filled the post. They all came from the country, and to them fresh air meant nothing except escape from the noisome interior of a crowded cottage. They just could not conceive why anyone should want to leave those high, light rooms, well-heated in chilly weather, amply shaded in hot, ventilated (not that they noticed that!) in stuffy times, and well enclosed in damp or fog.

"No notion of hygiene. I wonder what all the Sallys and Marias and Jessies would have thought I meant if I'd mentioned the word? High jinks, possibly."

There had been yet another purpose in that day-to-day variation of that restricted trot. "Remember, Master Stephen not to play with just any little children he happens to see." She had discovered on the occasions when she herself had opportunity to take him, his egregious friendliness, and blamed herself. But what was she to do? Brought up surrounded with love and affection, care and forethought, he assumed that all human beings he caught sight of enjoyed similar advantages. She had to restrain him, as best she might, from returning the beery salutations of the awful old man, whose naked flesh protruded through boots and clothes, who swept the rich greasy mud and horse-droppings from the street crossing; from the cheerful and calculated gifts of the drowsy market women, who would offer him fruit or lollipops, and catching her agonised look, would wipe the offering clean on their unspeakable skirts or shawls. He wanted to bowl the hoops or drag the little wooden horses, or fondle the pets, live or fabricated, of funny-nosed, smeary-cheeked contemporaries in the Public Gardens. He responded, all too prettily, to doubtless well-meant but insanitary endearments from proprietors of the smaller shops, proffered with, "Oh, isn't he a little love!" at which she ground her teeth so as not to answer, "He's not going to be a little victim!" and curtailed her purchases in order to get him outside and go over him, much to his annoyance, with a clean pocket handkerchief.

There were other dangers which she sought to forestall and hoped she succeeded. She felt, more often than saw, that all "maids", save responsible senior ones like Wellowes, or a few ill-favoured or evangelistically minded ones were always accessible to men. She mentally added, "At least, creatures wearing trousers!" There were the smart, well-set-up soldiers of the garrison, the blatant would-be mashers, with waxed moustaches and canes, there were senile,

debased, semi-invalids, in all public places. One of th
Cavendish relatives found that their infant was regularl
taken to a not-too-particular public house, left outside to i
own devices, and brought within doors if it rained, an
finally trundled by a garrulous, malt-breathing maid, lurchin
home through the traffic, who when followed and caugh
replied: "Well, all children (hiccup) like company. The
don't howl if someone takes notice of 'em!" All too tru
alack.

This, among other things, led inevitably to the questio
"Why are they like that? Why is it that Doughty and I, th
Marstons and the Cavendishes and all our sort would neve
think of entering a public house, for company or for an
other reason. We have too much . . . ?" The word that fitte
was "self-respect", but she soon saw that the real answer wa
"privilege". It began with the beds that the servants slept in
little low narrow pallets on wheels, filling one side of th
little cell-like attics. More than once she thought she ha
detected the presence of what were referred to in conversa
tion with other housewives, when they discussed the domesti
problem as "er . . . insects". A faint odour, brown stain, o
a tendency to scratch reddish spots on those rough menia
skins that had enough spots and stains at any time, and sh
had the suspect place cleared (thank God, there were enoug
spaces, on those wide, street-like landings, to turn out a whol
room) scrubbed, fumigated, disinfected. She harried th
younger and newer girls over the changing and washing o
their underclothing. "But the fact that they were as they wer
because they were what they were, remained. Except Wel
lowes, they could only offer brute strength and endurance
so common that it commanded only the lowest wages."

No use to talk to Doughty. It had been much that he ha
consented to her drastic reforms of the eighteenth-century
conditions she had found in the kitchen and servants' wing
He sighed heavily when he brought her, every quarter, th
enlarged sum of money for wages, the weekly housekeeping
bills. She went as far as she felt reasonable:

"Wouldn't you rather place so much a month in a separate account and let me draw cheques as I need?"

He was plainly staggered by the suggestion, which to him was rather as if she said, "If you will buy me some fur boots, I will make a journey to the North Pole!" But, as always, his respect and affection triumphed, and he tried to absorb the idea with an almost audible and visible mental gulp.

"I don't think I need trouble you, m'dear. But I'll bring up the money on the first of the month in future." Evidently some little trouble and forethought was readily accepted, rather than the spectacle of a lady, his wife, armed with a cheque book that was as foreign to the nature of the "fair sex" as a musket and bayonet. Ah! he little knew or guessed what women would be up to, fifty years after his death, and women of his own flesh and blood!

But she would not join in the lamentations of the professional class matrons who came to her "Afternoon", or to whose she went. To them, there was no solution to the problem, the Lower Classes were lower, they never asked why? She thought she knew, and asked Hannah.

"Of course, my dear," Hannah replied patiently, "Higher Education for women. The school age ought to be raised, and Further Education added for the free evenings. It would provide the maids with a very wholesome alternative to parading up and down Bishopgate, in the hope of attracting the attention of a soldier. Look at Jemima's case!" Jemima was the maid who had made impertinent and salacious suggestions with the congratulations on her, Frances', engagement. Jemima, from being hilarious and humorous, had become morose and moody. The usual story. The man was long-service enlistment and there was no chance of her being "married on the strength" of the regiment. Hannah had done what she could for grudging thanks. Jemima had gone to a much worse situation, and would not keep it probably. They had sighed, Hannah over the perversity of human nature, which she was bent on correcting. She, Frances, could not help a tiny gleam of sympathy. Having a child was

I

sufficiently solemn and exacting a business, as she had found,
if one had a husband like Doughty Dormer and the whole
resources of the Bank House to help and sustain one. What it
could be like where it occurred most often, in the yards and
courts of the City, the cramped, sodden, dilapidated cottages
of the country. And she had a range of experience Hannah
lacked.

"Men are like that. Even Doughty. Even parsons and
professors. Read the marriage service and see what the church
thinks about Holy Matrimony."

Presumably Hannah had never read it!

There was the class she had helped to start for the girls in
the factories. Could she induce the maids to join that? They
"worked", "in the shadow" most of the time, it was true.
Could they be said to be moulding "the woman to the fuller
day"?

She had a certain hesitation in proposing it, that might
have arisen from the realisation of how strongly she would
have resented the most well-meant attempts to improve her
from all but a very few people, like Hannah, to whom she felt
devotion.

However, when the day came round for her Class, she
invited it to meet in the big drawing-room looking out over
the street, which would hold forty people comfortably, and
leave ample room for her great Bechstein Grand. She asked
Doughty.

"So long as they arrive and leave in an orderly manner,"
he had replied. "Seven o'clock. The young men will be gone
by then."

How realistic of him! Of course, it wouldn't do to have the
young clerks, who left by the house door after the office was
closed, involved with a straggling group of girls, who, however they might spruce themselves up for the occasion, came
from poor homes and might be susceptible to masculine
charm. She gave orders to have chairs brought down from
the bedrooms and landings.

"When one thinks of it now, what a house it was. N

difficulty in finding forty chairs, in order that the members might sit and practice 'Heather Bells' and numbers from Sterndale Bennett's *May Queen.*"

She found her two younger maids puffing and blowing a little over the exertion. They had made, she thought, ten journeys upstairs and ten down, with two chairs each.

"Now, how would you like to bring two from the kitchen, then you can join in."

Blank stares! They looked at each other.

"Wouldn't you like to learn to sing?"

Hesitant shakes of the head, and silent, they withdrew. Somewhat disappointed, she asked Wellowes, when she was down giving orders in the morning.

"Why didn't they want to join the singing?"

Wellowes produced the grin of the privileged upper servant humouring the foibles of the mistress.

"Singing in front of all these girls in your class. No, M'm, they wouldn't like that!"

So, smarting under defeat, she was obliged to fall back on seeing that they did their work, kept themselves clean, and took their evenings out, according to their own devices, and hope for the best.

She might have persisted, had it not been that she was able to forego the nursemaid. It was time that Master Stephen went to school. She turned to that task with relief and zest. It would be odd if she, with her experience, and Hannah with her bigger and bigger and more and more prosperous school, couldn't find the very best early steps for a young intelligence. She dutifully explained to Doughty what she had decided. As he was preoccupied with the business of the Bank, and his outside interests, she felt it was his right to know about his son's gradual growth, though she doubted if it would ever have occurred to him to do more than say:

"Hrm! School! Yes, I suppose the boy must go to school. Come to think of it, I did. Learned my letters from an old dame in Fellmonger's Yard. Pah! I can smell the place now. It's all gone, of course. Yes, he must go to school!"

He might even have added, "Ask Lois Marston!"

So she took the initiative: "Doughty, I think Stephen must go to school now. Hannah Scrivener will have him in her Infants' Form. I don't suppose she'll charge much at his age. She may not charge at all except for books and implements. . . ." He had been very good about money and she wanted to make him feel that she was aware of the importance of economy. But his reactions were quite other.

"Implements!"

"Yes, children of that age nowadays don't learn their letters by rote. They do things to train eye and hand and ear, and are then taught the names of the objects they handle, and then the letters that make up the names."

He looked at her as if she were a long way off.

"Very well, m'dear. All progress, no doubt!"

Then he added surprisingly, "But we mustn't be beholden to Miss Scrivener."

"Oh, Doughty, she's fond of the child."

"Hrm! It's very good of her." And he seemed to have dismissed the matter.

Not so she. With a feeling not far removed from self-indulgence, she promised herself that, for the first term or so, she herself would take him the few minutes' trot round to the other side of the Castle, where stood the great mansion in which Hannah strove to contain her hundred and more and ever-increasing pupils. It would spare an awkward dislocation in the maids' duties involved by one of them dressing up to do it. And who knew what they might not encounter in the way of temptation to loiter, during even so short a journey.

"It will be a nice break from this upstairs, indoor life, and I shall see something of the school again . . ." she hurriedly suppressed such thoughts as being not quite kind, perhaps faintly disloyal to Doughty, and substituted: "It's the only sure way of seeing that he gets there safely. And it will make things easier for Wellowes if I'm those few minutes later before I go down to her."

So the new regime in young Stephen's life began.

      •   •   •   •   •   •

She sighed, roused herself to pick up the knitting, listened comfortably to the morning sounds in the house, and again drifted away.

"Can I ever have been that impossible figure in a bonnet and mantle, black button boots, holding by the hand a little chattering boy in a sailor suit, and making him dodge the heaps of ordure on the pavements, not to mention the filth of ages between the cobbles. How dangerous it was, with errand boys, such errand boys, barring one's way with ten-foot shutters that had to be shot into a cellar down a cavity that opened before one's feet; the runaway horses; the high speed dog-carts being driven to the station; the general cheerful hit or miss of those years. I wonder what the road casualties were? No one ever counted. If anyone were knocked down he was carted to the police station, if not to the mortuary direct, on a wheeled bier pushed by bearded police, amid an interested clamouring crowd!"

Ah! Another memory pierced through the thick protective covering that subsequent events had forced her to grow over all those old memories. It was like the Flood, mastered and kept at bay from tide to tide, year to year, for decades, and then, on the impulse of some exceptional wind and moon or whatever it was, bursting through and brimming over.

It must have been during the summer term for she had the image impressed on her mind of a fine day, with streets drier and cleaner than they often were. She had been telling little Stephen to admire the old stonework on the Toll House, for she believed that education went a long way beyond the classroom, and that no child could have too well furnished a mind, when she became aware that she was being stared at and passed hurriedly on, tweaking the child away from a window full of toys. Were those hastening steps following her? She crossed over, and made as if to take the short cut by the passage that led through the churchyard to St. George's by the Bridewell. But she was overtaken, a shining top-hat

flashed in an arc of salute, and a voice she instinctively dis-
liked accosted her:

"Good morning, Mrs. Dormer, you look even more
blooming than usual."

She saw what a mistake she had made. It would be harder
to shake him off in this unfrequented place of old gravestones
surrounded by new warehouses, than in the busier street.
She drew herself up and faced the pursuer.

"There's no need to speak to me like that, Mr. Vizer."

"Oh, come, my friend Dormer would be gravely offended
if I passed his wife without a word of politeness!"

(Was he slightly drunk? She had sometimes wondered at
rehearsals at the Choral. But at this hour in the morning?
No. Just impertinence.)

"My husband would be gravely offended if I told him I was
pestered while taking the child to school in the morning."

"But you wouldn't tell him that, surely!"

"I certainly shall, if you don't let me pass."

"By all means. But he won't like it. He doesn't like to hear
anyone speak disrespectfully of the Bank's customers."

He did stand aside and she hurried on and he ranged beside
her. Was it true? Would Doughty feel that?

"I happen to be going this way. I will see you through this
somewhat undesirable quarter."

The persistence! She took a deep breath.

"Mr. Vizer, have I made it plain to you that I do not desire
your company?"

"My dear Mrs. Dormer, you look magnificent when you
assume that expression."

"For the last time, Good morning!"

On the three steps that led out of the alley into the busy
Palace Street, where the school was, he raised his hat and
turned away. She was tingling all over; the feeling was not
unpleasant. Did she really attract that sort of man still, with
a child's hand in hers? How ridiculous! She would ask
Doughty to give the individual a sharp reproof. No, she
wouldn't. It was true. Doughty wouldn't want to be at cross

purposes with an influential citizen, wouldn't credit the sense of distaste she felt, would pass it off as a shopkeeper's habit of fulsome politeness. She supposed it was—Doughty was beginning to show his age. Well, she had got rid of the intruder. She arrived at the school, flushed and speechless, but everyone there was too busy to notice.

She received something like a shock when her husband came stumping up the stairs from the office at dinner-time. He began calling for her as soon as he reached the top.

"My dear. Hrm! I've something for you!"

As they moved into the dining-room he handed her, with a little bow, a small ornamental basket in which were set off to advantage by an arrangement of leaves, half a dozen expensive hothouse peaches.

"What . . . ?"

"Vizer came into the 'shop'" (his familiar way of designating the Bank counter) "and handed them in. I thought it very obliging of him!"

What to do or say, she couldn't think. Some part of her prompted, "Take the things and throw them in his face and tell him I'm not the sort of woman with whom he associates!" But the words didn't come.

Doughty added, "There's a card."

There was. She took it up and read, "In appreciation of your singing last Friday!" and some initials. Well, of all . . .

"It's very nice of Mr. Vizer," she got out weakly. "I met him this morning on the way to school with Stephen . . . he didn't say . . ."

What had he said? Blandishments that would sound stupid if she repeated them. She couldn't remember much except her feeling of outrage. How could she convey to Doughty that the innocent peaches were dirty, she felt, like the fruit the market women offered Stephen. But Doughty was so single-minded, he would never understand her feelings.

"You'll be a great success in the *Dream of Jubal*." This cantata was being rehearsed by the Choral and she had not unwillingly taken a part.

But if it were going to expose her to this sort of thing! She managed to fend off the danger . . . no, that was nonsense, there was no danger . . . the encumbrance, by sending a maid with young Stephen; on a wet day, taking a cab on the plea that she was afraid of the child sitting in wet things; then there was the week-end. Then she arranged to have tea with Hannah, and unbosomed herself to her friend. She found it harder than she expected. It sounded so . . . odious . . . no, so silly. Hannah soon found a remedy.

"The Cavendish girl comes with her nurse. An elderly person. Most reliable. Get Mrs. Cavendish to let them call for Stephen."

So it was arranged. She sighed. She missed the morning trot. She didn't like handing over her boy to that female griffin of the Cavendishes. But he was very biddable, and went without difficulty, holding hands with the Cavendish girl and their formidable escort. She took care to arrive at the Choral and leave it, either with Doughty or someone of her acquaintances. She avoided Vizer's shop, avoided his eye when they had to meet. Perhaps he would learn his lesson.

But no! The new arrangement had not run a fortnight before the nurse, returning with Stephen and her charge in the later morning, produced a paper bag of lollipops.

"A gentleman stopped us this morning, that Mr. Vizer from the Emporium I think, and said, was it Mr. Dormer's little boy, and would he like butterscotch? I didn't know what you would wish, Ma'am."

"Thank you, I'll take charge of them."

She stilled Stephen's clamours and thanked the domestic, moderating the gratitude she owed, which it was not perhaps wise to emphasize. But she would have no secrecy about it, and said, as soon as her husband appeared:

"I don't know why Mr. Vizer feels so indebted to us. He offers Stephen sweets in the street!"

"My dear, retailers are all alike. He probably thinks it stands him in good stead with me."

Hopeless! But the whole thing was a nuisance, and she did

not intend to allow it to take up any place in her life. She threw herself into all the activities that she considered to be worth while, the Browning Society in which Hannah could not help being a dominating figure, the Choral, to which she generally had Doughty's company, the class for the girls from all the factories, the Ladies' Compassionate, and the small social engagements she rather despised but did not entirely neglect, the two latter rather to please Doughty. She felt she owed it to him to present, beside him, the figure of the correct and dutiful wife; he was so easy to manage, kept to his dressing-room at nights, amused and occupied himself so well that he left her, to so large an extent, to her own devices.

Among the few calls she made, there was, from time to time, Lois Marston in the Close, for whom she retained that kind of liking one accords those who could patronise or criticise, and who forbear. The house in the Cathedral Close was a pleasant one, and she did not much regret this particular instance of what she described apologetically to Hannah as, "The time I have to waste, the married woman's social burden."

The accoutrements of those days! She had been wearing her best afternoon frock, frilly petticoats no one ever saw, corsets that creaked slightly, black button boots, the toque of the period, with a short veil, and carried a sunshade.

She glanced down the vista of over sixty years, marvelling at that distinct if remote figure that she had once cut, walking in leisurely fashion down from the Bank House, through the Crusaders' Gateway, avoiding the patches of ordure in the road, and seeking the pleasant shade of all the great trees in those gardens in which the utter peace of seven centuries seemed to have formed an almost solid residue of stillness and silence, hardly ruffled by bird or bee. She preferred that way, although the Marstons' was in fact nearer by the Bishop's Walk outside the Close wall, for it lay beyond the little "kissing-gate", or iron wicket that effectually prevented the

Close being used as a convenient short-cut from its Seaton Road end.

She approached this barrier, light-hearted and without a care, admiring the snapdragons growing out of crevices in the old walls, and humming over to herself the four-line refrain of the Cathedral chimes, when a figure emerged from the shadow of the overhanging ivy.

"Ah, Mrs. Dormer, how charming you look. Now where might you be going?" It was Vizer.

The voice, the greasy assurance of the manner, roused in her feelings the strength of which she had forgotten during her easy sheltered life as Doughty Dormer's wife. She divined in a flash that this was no accident. He had guessed she would be going to Lois Marston's, knew which was that hostess's "day", or might even have seen her set out and posted round by Bishop's Walk to meet her. She stood an instant petrified, trying to find words and voice to utter them. It gave him a chance to say:

"You know what they call this? You must pay toll!" He flicked the ancient iron grille that complained of lack of oil, but somehow, the shrill, uncouth sound gave a final whisk to the feelings seething in her. Without a thought, acting from pure instinct, she jerked up the parasol she had just furled, and brought it down with all the force of her arm, on that fleshy, wide-lipped, open-mouthed impudent, lascivious face that he was surely offering her. The blow was so instantaneous, that he staggered; the arms that were . . . could it be, reaching out for her . . . failed to save him, and he slumped in a heap by the wall. She twisted through the kissing-gate and scuttled across, as fast as her skirts permitted, to the Marstons' gate. Mercifully, no one was in sight. She couldn't have controlled herself if there had been. She must have rung the bell as unconsciously as she had mounted the steps, for she came abruptly to herself, at the look and words of the maid who opened the door.

"Oh, Ma'am!" the horrified decorous whisper of those days, from such a one. "Your parasol!"

Mastering her gasps with effort, she managed a half-apologetic simper, that sounded in her buzzing ears like someone else speaking.

"Isn't it unfortunate, I caught it in the . . . er . . . kissing-gate. Put it out of sight until I leave."

She profited by the moment while the girl disposed of the broken torn object behind a large flower-pot containing a fortunately bushy and prolific azalea, to glance in the gilt-framed circular mirror over the great dower chest against the wall, hurriedly going over toque and veil, and composing her agitation as best she might. Announced, she took a deep breath, gripped herself and marched up to her hostess, exchanging the necessary sister-in-law's greeting, and turning to acknowledge the salutations of the guests she knew, and to be presented to those she did not.

"Very warm, is it not?" she was met with.

She conceded that, hoping it excused her flaming cheeks and flashing eyes that the veil barely shielded.

"I walked. It's no distance from the Bank House, it did not seem worth while to have a cab. And the Close is so lovely."

She wondered at her own voice, uttering this apology and hoped it sounded convincing. Here was the tea-tray. "Thank God," she suppressed. As she received her cup, and chose one of Lois' little rolled-up pieces of bread-and-butter, she felt the maid's downcast eye flicker, and was conscious of old Mrs. Higginbotham, on her left, regarding her covertly through a lorgnette. She knew why. A gleam of white was registered by the corner of her eye. Her right sleeve must be split underneath. She managed to keep it close to her side, and used her privileged relation's right to linger out the others, bound by the conventions to twenty minutes.

"Look, Lois," she said, with returning calm when they were alone. "I stupidly caught my sleeve on that absurd little gate coming out of the Close."

"Oh, my dear, what a nuisance. I'll get Thurza to tack it up, until you get home."

So repaired, she felt she had regained her habitual poise,

even a faint air of triumph seemed to surround her as she returned home, making sure to keep to Bishop's Walk, where there were too many passers-by, just in case.

So the violent moment passed, died down, became part of the life she had lived. She had adjusted herself by the meeting of the Choral in the week following. As she and her husband walked down to the Institute Room in the Monastery in the spring twilight, Doughty had said:

"That chap Vizer's got a rare black eye. Says he ran into the kissing-gate in the Close, when some stranger slammed it on him, not knowing how it works!"

She glanced at her husband just to make sure that there was no purpose in the imparting of this information. She need not have troubled. Whatever shortcomings she felt in her husband, subtlety and manœuvre were not among them. He just repeated what came into his head, for her amusement, and because he was incapable of hiding anything, except, of course, the business of the Bank.

Feeling comforted and fortified, she replied, "Poor Mr. Vizer!" and allowed herself a little secret smile.

"Pooh!" Doughty blurted out. "No one believes him. The fellow keeps all sorts of company. He probably deserved it. Goodness knows what he mayn't have been up to. Don't pay, the way he goes on!"

"No, I should think not," she agreed with a kind of glee. Was she growing malicious? Whose fault? She managed to avoid any direct contact with her tormentor. He was, in fact, rather subdued at the Choral, when they arrived, with a large green shade over one eye, which did not entirely conceal the discoloration. She had to keep her eyes on her vocal score, and her lips firmly closed until her entry. But within her breast echoed, "Don't pay, the way he goes on." She marvelled. How right!

Somewhere in the house people were moving about. The sun was shining and the beams struck the wall rather near her chair. Whatever time could it be? From her chair she had to

ean forward a good deal, or to get up, to see the face of the
lock. Before she could do so, the door opened, letting in
a whiff of dinner preparation and the rumour of people in the
kitchen. The face that was poked in was that of young Jean,
who regarded her quizzically.

"Can I come and set the table, Gran'maman?"

"Yes, dear, surely!" Generally they brought her a cup of
coffee in the middle of the morning. Had she had it? Better
not make any remark. She might have been dozing.

"Let's see. Not Emil today, but Eliza!"

"Oh, is she coming to dinner?"

"Yes, Victor asked her."

Busy hand swinging the long cloth over the refectory table
and smoothing it out. Victor had asked this young woman
employee of his he had discovered. What was the meaning of
that? Not quite sure if she understood how the young people
of today managed their affairs, she said uncertainly:

"It's very kind of your Uncle Archie to keep open house
like this!"

"I expect he likes to have his helpers under his eye. Eliza's
people are all right. They are well above flood level in the
street. That was all that worried her!" Here came a shower of
spoons and forks from the long shallow drawer in the dresser.
What a way to set a table! What would Wellowes or any of
the old domestic staff at the Bank House have said? But these
young people had spent so much of their time in hostels and
camps and all sorts of semi-public places that they seemed to
think that all that mattered was to shovel enough provender
into enough mouths. Had she caught a faint acerbity in the
voice? Was there something going on, among all the young
things? She said tentatively:

"She seemed a nice young woman. I didn't know that
Victor wanted to invite her in."

"I expect he did it to please Steve."

There was a whisk and a subdued clatter, and away went
young Jean with that air of never a wasted word and never an
unnecessary action that was so efficient and not unattractive.

By the time she had tidied herself, they all came flocking in
the girls all helping with the table, the men getting rid o
waders, muddy clothes, and all the apparatus of flood fighting
in the back kitchen. She was tickled to see the social amenitie
of the new age.

"Good morning, Gran'maman," from Jennifer.

"If it is a good morning, which I doubt!"

"Really, Barney, do you remember *When We Were Ver*
Young, as well as all that?"

"I don't know about remembering, but it seems the sor
of thing to say in these topsyturvy summers."

"Well, Archie, what's the one o'clock news?"

"It's going down. Of course it is. The S.M.O. says so, a
if we couldn't see! The thing now is to stop these unlucky
people from flocking back into their sodden and stinking
houses before they're dry and disinfected by the S.F.A
However, the bridge at Seaton Road is clear, so we shall ge
in extra fuel, and the M.O.H.——"

"The what, dear?" She found these strings of initials some
of the hardest of the incomprehensible jargon they all picked
up in their training, or their service, or their clubs and associa
tions, and all the rest of it that coloured their lives today.

"Medical Officer of Health!"

"Don't you believe him, Gran'maman, it's Mothers' Often
Helpful!"

There arose a clamour of competing versions, as she knew
they had for all these wonderful code words, out of which
Archie's bass boom and habit of direction emerged.

". . . we'll let 'em go back as soon as he sees fit. He doesn'
want an epidemic on his hands, you may be sure!"

And a lot more of the modern technical talk that was so
different to the talk . . . no . . . conversation that had been
played like some decorous social game, in the drawing-rooms
of the 'nineties, over afternoon tea, handed round by girls
. . . maids . . . by profession, wearing what was essentially
a uniform.

She couldn't join in, didn't want to, was grateful to get on

ith her dinner, and sit back and watch them at it. No one
ould want better grandchildren. She made a mental com-
arison with her own outlook, aged twenty. Left over from
he drowsy ruminations of that morning was a taste on her
mental palate. What was it? Ah, Vizer! All that subterranean
ex and shiftiness. Here, among these young people, how
ifferent.

"They'd discuss sanitation, I don't even put obstetrics past
hem, at table too, if I weren't here and they didn't feel some-
hing due to my grey hairs, bless 'em!"

She was right. Nothing in the conversation offended her
nineteenth-century ears. On the contrary, it was all des-
erately common-sense and business-like, presided over by
rchie, and made up of accounts of the various activities in
which they had been absorbed. Jennifer began.

"Funny, you'd think the van-dwellers from Hangman's
Lane would be the toughest. But they're not!"

"Tough enough!" from young Steve. "Superstitious, that's
heir trouble. Remember, Dad, when you tried to park the
equipment on Tunforth Rough?"

"Don't I? Never heard such a hullaballoo!"

"But they're not superstitious about concrete-mixers and
ulldozers," from Victor.

"No. It's the evil spirits of the place. They think harm will
come to the horses."

"I have a deep suspicion that they work up all that belief in
evil spirits, to keep people away from the waste lands, where
they want to settle."

"But they never stay on the Rough for more than a week
or two."

"Ah, that's not evil spirits, that's Goodbody!"

"Who's Goodbody?" from Victor.

"Mr. Goodbody, please. Our policeman." Eliza corrected
him.

"He's not a spirit, evil or otherwise," young Barney
added. "I shouldn't like him to haunt me, if he were. They
go ten to the ton, the Easthamptonshire police."

"What's he to the gipsies? They're nomads, or near."

"That's just it. He will turn up, no one quite knows when, looking for things."

"Things! What things?"

"Lost, stolen or strayed. Various animals and oddmen find a mysterious attraction round the caravans."

"Isn't that just plain thieving?"

"Oh, no, I don't think so." Archie was getting very judicial in his pronouncements. "Different morality. If you'd been born and bred where and how they are, you'd feel differently about strays and anything you found lying about."

"But haven't they a real feeling for the trees and the wild? Some of our people have, in the hills." Young Jean spoke so quietly, but people paid attention.

"Something perhaps," Archie was also very tolerant. Was that the effect of having had trouble? It was a contrast to the rather downright attitude of his son. "Living so near to nature they may have a feeling for it we miss."

"I dare say," added young Steve, "but you'll never make me believe that was the only reason they wanted you not to dump your stuff in the Rough. They don't like being seen about their affairs. They're not sentimental about trees and bushes as such."

"Our people are. My mother would never have May blossom in the house."

"We shall see." Victor had the scepticism she often attributed to his gallic-mixture heredity, if there was such a thing. "A new generation will have to use tractors, and go to school. I give all that sort of life another thirty years at most."

"Besides, they are few and don't increase," Barney added. "That's why they're so striking perhaps. They haven't the latent good humour of the local stock."

"You may call it that. I must say I saw hardly a smile as I looked round the schoolroom this morning."

"You couldn't expect it," warmly from Jennifer. "Think of being roused in the middle of the night to leave your home and belongings and not knowing what sort of a mess you may be going back to!"

"The children think it fun, once they get over any little fright they had," Nina put in.

"Or is it the free gum-boots?" from Jennifer.

"That may be."

"Can't understand it. Uncomfortable things and always moist inside." Barney took more interest in his appearance than most young men.

"I believe it's the easy slip-on that does it," young Steve assured him. "It's less trouble, isn't it, Nina?"

"Or do they think they look grand so?"

"Just novelty perhaps. It's not very long since they were children in the village wearing the cast-offs of grown-ups."

"In the Highlands you will see children going to school with boots slung over the shoulder, so as not to waste them," Jean admitted, half smiling against herself.

So the talk flickered on, until the men went off to see what further effort the emergency would demand, and the women gathered up the dinner-things. They installed her in her chair beside the unlit fire.

"No," she told herself as she closed her eyes. "It is a better world, even with these Atom Bombs and things I can hardly pronounce, let alone understand. No inhibitions. Little sentiment, lots of common-sense. Old Hannah Scrivener was right. We have moulded the woman to the fuller day, even if it is a washing day with a machine that goes by electricity. In the shadow will we work'. Well, we did. I was lucky. Poor Hannah, they little know what they owe her, the girls for her share in making possible what they are, the boys for not being encumbered by the sort of woman so many of us used to be!"

CHAPTER V

"YES, LET ME LIKE A SOLDIER FALL"

SHE had never got over the sensitiveness that had been
enforced on her during her husband's last illness, her over-
anxious care for her son, and perhaps she had never been
a deep sleeper. In any case she woke readily enough with the
sense of someone in the room. It was that little Jean.

"Had a nice nap, Gran'maman?"

"Yes, dear, thank you. What is it?"

Jean wanted something, plainly enough.

"Uncle Archie would like you to come in the truck and
give out the cleaning materials and things that have been sent
for the flooded-out folk."

"My dear," the reluctance of old age to move out of its
chair besieged her, "surely you can do all that without old
me!"

"Uncle Archie says not. If he does it the people will say it's
not enough, or not what they want, and that he gets between
them and the authority. If the Palgraves do it, they'll say why
should the gentry have enough and to spare when they are
short?"

"My dear, what nonsense. Barney and Jennifer work as
hard as any of the labourers on the place."

"Yes, but Jordan will make a lot of it——"

"Jordan? Is that the old man who looks after the roads for
the District Council, or is paid to, and doesn't, your Uncle
says——?"

"Yes. You see he's a Communist."

"Is he? I wonder why."

"Uncle Archie says it's because he's got a pension and is
allowed to work just the same, but he thinks he could make
more if he had a van and went round with the diddykoy...!"

"The what?"

146

"That's what they call the travelling salesmen—gipsy pedlars we call them."

"What a foolish old man!"

"Yes, but there he is. Uncle Archie says that if you go round and say a word to them, they'll think it's you being kind to them, and that's what they want!"

"Why old me?"

"Well, you're the Squireen, or Squiress, and you take the place of old Mrs. Thaxted, who used to live here."

"That old——! I hope I don't look like what I remember of her!"

"No, dear, but will you come?"

Trust Jean for sticking to the point.

("I wouldn't be surprised if that were not why Archie sent her. He knows how fond I am of the child and how persuasive she is!") But aloud she only said:

"Very well, but I must go and put on something more suitable to Uncle Archie's truck!"

"I've brought your big lined boots, so that you won't be cold or damp."

There, sure enough, on the other side of the empty hearth, stood her boots.

("Oh, so you'd made up your mind beforehand I was going, had you?") but she substituted:

"That was thoughtful of you. Help me!"

She gave Jean a sharp glance to see if the inferred sarcasm went home. But on that neat little face was an almost prim unconsciousness, as if butter wouldn't melt in her mouth, as she kneeled and slipped on the footgear over rheumaticky old feet, and gave her arm so nicely. Something, it might be merely the rebellion of long-lasting vigour against the helplessness of old age, made her say suddenly:

"You know, young woman, you ought not to be taking courses, and spending your holidays looking after an old thing like me. You ought to get a young man."

"Gran'maman, how thoughtful of you. I had the very same idea myself."

Frances grunted.

"Ah! And may I enquire his name?"

"Dear, I was expecting you to tell me that."

"There was a time when girls used to get their ears boxed for speaking like that to their elders."

"Yes, dear, but it's a long while ago. And all the people like you made it unfashionable, so now you just give me a kiss instead."

Who could resist the proffered cheek . . . ah! cheek in two senses of the word. She took the nice firm young arm, kissed the child, allowed a rainproof coat to be put round her, and they emerged into the humid steamy afternoon.

"Faugh!" she muttered instinctively. "Duckweed it used to be. Now it's drains."

"You can't wonder, Gran'maman. The whole of Marsh Street has been washed out, and what ought to have gone into the sewer, is drying along the hedges, Uncle Archie says."

There he was. Could that tough commanding figure with thinning hair on the bare head be the son of her son? Strange but true! He broke off his conversation with some men who looked like County Council officials and waved to the young Palgraves who seemed to have taken Victor and the Triple girl and a load of parcels in their big old car.

"Hullo, Gran'maman," was Archie's greeting. "Come and be a fairy godmother to all these lucky people."

"I hope I look it, Archie. I don't feel it. But I like to help. It's about all I can do." This sudden burst of candour made Archie laugh.

"Just listen to the poor old thing. Come on!"

He adroitly pushed a wooden box labelled "Keep away from Kerosene" against the rather high running-board of what she knew as his "truck", one of those vehicles with a kind of cabin in front containing a broad seat for driver and several others, while behind was a capacious float, filled at the moment with piles of household goods and implements among which were seated young Steve, Emil Tisch and two or three youths who looked just sufficiently different to be identified as other members of the German scout party.

She was greeted with a volley of incoherent applause as Archie swung her up on to the seat and young Jean followed. Archie made the contraption give out appropriate noises and it moved forward amid cries and warnings and the applause of assembled village urchins, swaying and vibrating along the street, past the church, and turning down towards the lower part of the village known as Marsh Street.

"We seem to be creating quite a sensation," she could not help exclaiming, feeling her old heart beat with unwonted vigour, and trying not to let them see that her eyes were dancing with excitement.

"Triumphal procession, Gran'maman!"

"Nonsense. Where do we start, Archie?"

They ascended between the gardens that sloped down from the back of the houses in Church Street, and she could not help marvelling at the almost universal signs of radio aerials. What a world! The labourers had gadgets! Archie swung to the left, and they came by a sharp corner into Marsh Street, the heavy wheels hissing in the glutinous, stinking half-dry mud.

The street ran east and west, with the houses mostly on the lower side, where their gardens and back premises were a few inches only above the pastureland of the estuary. She knew the place slightly, for a little further on was the entry to the "staithe" or landing-place where Archie kept his boats. More than one jolly water picnic had she joined, in propitious seasons. Now, from the backs, and in some cases from the very interiors of the cottages, a great sheet of glittering water spread away, divided by forlorn gates and posts, sticking up to show where, normally, the entry lay to the various "goings" or grazing grounds, while in other spots, hairy-looking areas meant that some slight rise had already brought the grass and rushes above the surface of the receding inundations. In the misty sunshine it did not look too bad, save for the wide margin of floating debris, posts and boards, which lapped and bubbled as the breeze made miniature waves splash against the gradually re-emerging barrier of the firm ground. She hoped some of the unrecognisable shapes were not drowned animals.

"Poor dears!" she could not help exclaiming, at the sight of the forlorn little groups, treading cautiously and in some cases wading down what had been little front gardens, some of which had been kept with no little pride. Others were poking gingerly into the houses themselves, fetching out bedraggled furniture and belongings and stacking them in any dry spot, or on improvised stands, wheelbarrows, coops or rails, that would keep them out of the mud. Archie drove slowly to the seaward end of that thoroughfare of misery so as not to splash the evil-smelling silt over those who were begrimed enough already. Opposite the last houses he drew up and backed, and the "rescue party", as they had been calling each other, leapt down and set to work, helping fetch and carry, distributing brooms, brushes, cloths, hearing lamentations and giving advice.

"Where do I come in?" she enquired meekly.

"Here. They're sending the children. You give them a bag of toffees and a kind word!" Jean lowered herself and produced a wide lid, from which she handed down to grubby little fists belonging to round-eyed and solemn, or cheeky and giggling youngsters, small packets of goodies that were eagerly clutched. Leaning out from her elevation in that twentieth-century vehicle, she did her best to fill the part for which she was cast so unexpectedly.

"What's your name? Is that your little sister? Would you like a sweetie? Ask Mother to come and speak to me when she's not busy."

That was all she could think of, while Archie and the men, joined by the people she took for County Council officials, made the more serious examination, for settlement, unsafe walls and roofs. As the news of the truck's slow progress spread, some of the women did come to it, and delivered their several verdicts on the event which had overtaken them.

"Not so bad. We shall get it dry sometime."

"They ought to have given us warning. What do we pay the rates for?"

"It's a fine old mess. I don't care if we don't go back there. I've told him it's time we moved."

"You should see my sofa. That'll never dry!"

"Thank you very much. It is a climax, isn't it?" (Climax! term learned from the picture house?)

"As if there weren't enough trouble without all this! D'you think you could get us into one of those new Council houses?"

"I was born here, and here I'll stay!" This one, she learned later, had remained in the upstairs bedroom during the crucial forty-eight hours, and had resisted all attempts to rescue her.

"It's all in the day's work, I suppose. Home sweet home with the chill off!"

So it ran on, she gained an overall impression of strong underlying individualism. Not that they refused or omitted to help a neighbour, but mostly, they regarded the whole incident, not from any common standpoint, nor with the least curiosity as to its cause or cure. For them, it was a personal grievance, against which "they" (any conceivable authority from the Government of the Realm to the landlord) ought to have protected them, but, they felt with the ready cynicism of those who are unlikely ever to rise above the standards of a minimum wage, never would.

Amid the long shifting line of unfortunates, some half-dozen people stood out. Archie dominated the whole scene. But grouped about him and taking his directions as if they had been orders, instead of the ideas of Mr. Dormer from Cockle Hall, were Goodbody the policeman, Emil Tisch and his young Germans. The former caught her eye and motioned, with a broad grin, to the active and efficient Emil who had marshalled his youths in line, and told them off to various duties, some at least of which were done by the undisciplined, glumly good-tempered victims before he could

organise his helpers. Then there was the incumbent of the
parish, almost ostentatiously non-clerical in clothes, passing
from group to group, most of which received him with
patient toleration.

"What a shame," she told herself, "he's doing his best. He
can't help being a parson. It's his vocation!" But she knew
what it was that accounted for the attitude towards him.
Along with his canonicals he had put on a way of looking and
speaking. How could he do otherwise, a priest of an establishment? Only it reduced his commerce with the parishioners
to: "Quite, quite. . . . We must see what can be done. . . .
Mercifully, it's going down."

On the outskirts of the busier groups hovered an old man
whom she eventually recognized as the roadman, whose
advanced opinions might be a matter of conviction or might,
she shrewdly surmised, be a matter of *amour propre*. She heard
him commiserate with one of the women who was most
voluble:

"That's right, Mrs. Sadley. That's the lot of the worker."

There he miscalculated, if what went on in his head could
be defined as calculation, for the other drew herself up.

"Speak for yourself. I dunno if you call what you do,
work. I reckon you're lucky to get the job with the Council.
You'd have to sweat more if you were doing anything worth
the money."

There it was, the farouche contempt of the "industrial
classes" for anyone who was employed by a public body.
Foolish and irrational, but what a standard of conduct it set
for those who administered England.

They came to the staithe, where the ex-fisherman who
looked after Archie's two boats grinned his sardonic grin, of
those who have to forestall and beat the shifting moods of
the sea.

"You got 'em out just in time, Barnacle!" Archie commented.

"Ah!" was the sole response, but there was a gleam of
satisfaction in the far-sighted grey-blue eyes that had gazed

so long and so often at the immense stretches of broken water of the North Sea. Both looked, with satisfaction, at the cabined cutter and the all-purposes ship's boat that lay bobbing in the small waves of the dyke, securely moored some yards from danger of grounding, collision with debris, or swamping.

Beyond this again, Hangman's Lane, that led down on to the marsh, ended yet in a couple of feet of water, from which the caravans had been drawn up far enough to leave their wheels but half-submerged. Here swarthy lank-haired people, the men affecting canary-coloured neckcloths, the women ringlets and earrings, were congregated round a pile of baskets, the contents of which they seemed unwilling to disclose. Frances made the same approach to them as to the villagers, but was met by a queer silent defiance, and a drawing close of the children about them. When offered the same help that the others had received, they moved forward and took whatever was there.

She was greeted by a kindly but fatigued-looking woman in W.V.S. uniform, who was the vicar's wife.

"Difficult people," she commented. "Won't have our excellent district nurse. Prefer to manage for themselves."

"One can but offer!" she agreed, for she sympathised with the well-meant kindliness. In her heart, however, she had a gleam of understanding. The diddykoys were suspicious of authority. The inference might be slight, the feeling unworthy, yet the wife of the incumbent of the parish just couldn't help being that, the wife of the person whose lot in life it was to tell others what to do, and when they were wrong.

Beyond Hangman's Lane the ground began to rise, and the few houses remaining before Marsh Street twisted north and uphill to join the main road had suffered no more than an inch or so of water over the back kitchen floor, and an already drying soggy mess in the back garden.

"Help me down!" she commanded Jean. She would see for herself.

The entry of the nearest cottage had not been submerged

and the ration of coal had been dumped beside the doorway. She ventured into the "front" room into which it gave and at first could see nothing but the photographs on the cheaply papered walls, the clock and group of china vases and one or two astonishingly good pieces on the purple velvet cover of the mantelpiece. Two good old chairs, two cheap new ones occupied the room, with a table safely tilted up, out of harm's way. But she could feel that she was not alone, though she started a little when a voice assailed her ears, and she saw the hindquarters, back and head turned towards her, of a woman kneeling before the little iron grate, trying to induce the fire to burn.

"Ah?" the East Anglian interrogation, equivalent of the North Country, "Na", and conveying, "What is it?"

"Can we help you?"

"You can stand out of my light."

Frances moved from the doorway to where a board on two boxes supported the regulation half-dozen pots of geraniums, a fuchsia and other plants she did not stop to verify, all flourishing as they will only do in cottage windows that are never opened. She was immediately recognised.

"What?" (the salutation had lingered in East Anglia since Anglo-Saxon days). "That's Mrs. Dormer!"

"Yes. Have you all you want?"

"That'll be a funny day when I have that!" It was good-humoured enough, the robust instinct to miss nothing, and never, never to admit satiety.

"I'm sure it will. I see you've got your coal."

The woman stood up, easing herself, hands on hips, the upper part of her face surrounded by wispy hair, darkened with an habitual scowl, the fleshy lower part relaxed with an instinctive grin.

"Yes. I've got that. Harness brought it!" (No mention of the Authority which had ordered, or the administration that had organised the distribution of fuel. Harness was the local dealer who supplied coal among other things.) "I told him to put a sack down and lay it on that. But he say he hasn't any sacks to spare. So I shall have to scrape it off the path and half the gravel with it."

"Men don't understand these things," she put in gently. "Are your children all right?"

"Yes. They're out playin'. I don't want 'em in here until I've put things to rights."

"You're dry upstairs, anyhow?"

"Dry as it ever is!"

"Rain through the roof? Shall I try to get someone to put the tiles right?"

"That'd save trouble if you told someone to pull the place down, as soon as we're out of it. That's past repair."

It looked to Frances none too bad and immeasurably better than others not far away, and in a different class to the sort of dwelling such a woman had had when she herself had been a District Visitor.

"You're on the list for a house?"

"Bin on the list a twelve month. If this hurries 'em up, it will have been worth it!"

Frances pushed open the door leading into the back parts, meeting the odour of damp bricks, but not the nauseating stench of flooded sewer or overflowed cesspit.

"Earth closet down the garden?"

"That was a stroke of luck. Garrould had just cleared it out!" Frances had lived long enough in the village to know that the name thus introduced indicated the husband.

"You'll get a ticket for groceries."

"I'll see I do. Thank you very much, ma'am."

There it was! No good explaining how the tickets were distributed among those whose food supplies had been washed out or spoiled. It was taken to have been a personal effort on her part, and she ought to disclaim the gratitude, but did not. It was pleasant, all the more because it did such a woman good to feel the personal touch. Jean appeared in the doorway, and bidding the woman good day, she allowed herself to be led back to the truck. Young Steve appeared and volunteered to run her home to Cockle Hall. She had a suspicion that Jean gave him a look or nod to do so, but felt she had better acquiesce, though she never admitted the frailty due to her age if she could help it. Duly installed in the chimney corner, she obeyed Jean's injunction to rest while she put the kettle on and helped Nina with the tea.

The image that was most prominent on the underside of her eyelids as she closed them with a faint fatigue, caused by unusual exertion and drowsiness resulting from so long a dose of fresh air, was that of Archie directing operations. She knew where he got that confident certainty, that loud-voiced decision. She could hear his grandfather on the night of the great fire that had ended his career in Doughty's Bank taking charge of a situation as alarming as the floods of these sixty years later. She could hear him speaking with authority to the Inspector of Police:

"You understand. The Bank must not burn!"

There it was, the great social change of half a century, from the day when some institution, Doughty's Bank or another, propped up the daily life of a whole district, to the present day when all the effort seemed to be directed to the well-being of the least conspicuous members of the community. As so often happened, certain salient characteristics missed a generation and reappeared in the next. Her son and Doughty Dormer's, who had witnessed the catastrophe that had reduced his father to an impotent invalid and brought his life to so unexpected a close, had not been half so true to type as this grandson, in whose house she lived, and who was always a commanding figure, never more so than when physical danger threatened. Perhaps one prepotent generation used up all the vitality, which had to lie dormant and renew itself, to reappear in the next.

"There's something in heredity, after all. You can't train leaders, they are born, and all the more likely to be, in a line that has produced others." Yet why? She and Doughty, so far as he could spare attention from the business of the Bank, had done their best by the boy. Had they missed anything?

Nothing in her whole life had been so absorbing as the care

she had taken over Stephen, her boy. The grandson, Archie, she now admired so much, had not had half the attention lavished on him. Was that why he was so much more effective than his father had been, in spite of anything she could do? Had she been wrong, had she taken too much care?

She saw him now, as he emerged from infancy, in the little kindergarten form at Hannah Scrivener's school. Since that decisive encounter with Vizer, when she had given her pursuer that black eye that had caused her such wicked satisfaction, and so much unusual secrecy, she had resumed her morning walks to take young Stephen to school. On one fine morning later in the summer term, as she handed him over to the mistress on duty at the side door, where the hundred day pupils, nearly all girls of course, but with a sprinkling of little boys like hers, the young woman stopped her.

"Miss Scrivener wants to see you, Mrs. Dormer."

She found Hannah in her room, reclining . . . the first words that came to her mind were "laid out" with all their sepulchral significance . . . on a *chaise longue*, a writing-board on her knee.

"My dear Hannah! I heard you wanted to see me. Are you fit to——?"

"My dear Frances, I am as well as God wills," came the answer from those discoloured lips in the pallid face. "Sit down!"

There was no mistaking the will power, the absolute compulsion residing in that moribund frame.

"About our breaking up. We're having Professor Holland down to address the parents. You've read his book, of course?" (She had only skimmed it, but what was the good of saying to Hannah: "I have a husband, a son, a large cumbersome house needing constant attention, and all of them bring with them certain social duties. I haven't time to read all you do, though I should like to!" Hannah might reply, and she sometimes feared she would: "Frances, you deserted us. You left the ranks of professional women to become a wife and mother. It is all the more your duty to keep your mind alert, and not let it become like the mind of the average unthinking woman, who just obeys her creature instincts!" But Hannah didn't say it, if perhaps she looked as if it were unnecessary. The thought passed in a flash.) "We must have some little formality. Edith Raingold will present the list of successful pupils in the Institute Examination, as Head Girl. How would you like your little Stephen to offer the buttonhole . . . ? We feel we can hardly offer a gentleman a bouquet. . . . What do you say?"

"Oh, Hannah!" she was more deeply moved than she had thought probable. It was as though Hannah were offering her a renewal of friendship and confidence that had somehow lapsed slightly since her marriage. "Dear Hannah!" she had stepped forward and kissed that fevered forehead. "It will be delightful of course. How kind of you!"

Hannah had nodded, as if she too felt more than she was willing to express. They chatted a moment on trivial matters, but Hannah was plainly struggling against ill-health to keep a close grip on the formidable and growing business of the school, and she herself had to return in time to set the servants about their work, and the interview ended with expressions of affection.

"Ah! Deary me! A long time ago. Is it believable that I dressed Stephen up in a white sailor suit with singlet and lanyard and scarf, and little gold braid anchors and crowns and Heaven knows what foolishness on the sleeve!" Yet such had been the case. The scene started up with the vividness that distance lent to it. The "main schoolroom" Hannah loved to call it, into which the ballroom of the noble mansion she occupied had been turned. Four great windows were open on the acre or so of City garden, with its magnificent apple trees, none like them nowadays, its gorgeous beds of flowers, wide walks, and at the back the remains of what had been one of those mock-classical shrines, in plaster, all overgrown with a great spreading fig tree, and a magnolia with stems the girth of a leg. In flowed the sweet air, flower scents and hum of insects, with, just audible in the background, the rumour of the horse traffic, street cries and vibration of the busy street beyond those high walls.

"There must have been over a hundred children and I suppose nearly a hundred parents packed into the place. Nothing but Hannah's will-power could have brought it about. All those girls with hair pulled back and tied with ribbons, clad in their 'best' frocks, whispering and eyeing their parents, and other girls' parents; mothers in all the frills and furbelows they could carry; not many fathers, most of them like Doughty, couldn't spare an afternoon off from business. Those who could, precious, uncomfortable, collars cutting into their necks, fidgeting with hats which were about as convenient as pails in all that crush!"

Into the middle of it all, exactly as the great gilt clock that set the time for the school went ping, ping, ping, Hannah marched. There was no other word for it! Doomed and sickening, she had levered herself out of her *chaise longue*, dressing herself with a kind of nun-like simplicity, but a sister superior's dignity, her one gew-gaw a fine thin gold chain with a crystal lorgnette at the end. Behind her (such a contrast) waddled Professor Holland, the "new" man whose books and speeches had created such a sensation in the awakening world of education, whose dawn had been illumined by a gaudy sunrise of high hopes and excellent intentions: a fat man in a perpetual perspiration, with a neck that overhung his low collar, ringlets that overhung his mighty brow, large gold-rimmed spectacles gleaming, and a great frock-coat that flapped about his knock-knees and turned-in toes like the cloak of some figure of romance. The girls all stood, the parents just shuffled. There was no great feeling in the middle classes of that day about the prestige of a professor, or whatever he was. Few of the parents knew, or greatly cared, but if Miss Scrivener, who had been so successful with their girls, said so, he must be all right.

Hannah mounted the platform, the Professor blundered after, and at a motion of her hand, the girls subsided. That was the cue. She herself, wedged into a corner with little

Stephen, gave him a loving push. He joined the handsome and
capable Edith Raingold, all in white with a great cascade of
golden hair flowing down her back, so brushed and brushed
that every single glistening thread seemed separate, and side
by side, the two, the big girl and the small boy, advanced.
Edith, with a neat curtsey, handed up her illuminated list, little
Stephen reached up the nosegay he had been carefully
shielding with his free hand. The Professor suddenly caught
sight of them, rose awkwardly, nearly blundered off the
platform, took the list with a beaming smile, bent down to
get the nosegay, dropped his glasses to the full extent of the
chain by which they hung, stammered something and flopped
back on his chair. Edith turned with grace and aplomb, took
Stephen by the now free little fist and led him back to her
corner. There was a burst of clapping, turning to laughter
as he covered the last few steps at a run and buried his face in
her lap.

"That's how he was, and that's how he grew up. Dutiful,
lovable, honest and careful, but . . . overshadowed by the
great old house in which he was born, the lofty traditions of
a Quaker Bank, too much Past, too many elderly relatives,
too high a standard to leave him any initiative. It's a good
thing that his son is so different. If not, I don't know where
we might be today."

Somehow that period when she was the mother of a little
boy who appeared, on occasions, in a white sailor suit, had
always been precious to her. She had been in complete control
of him then. Before that he had been merely an infant. After
it, all too soon, he became a separate person, a boy, a young
man, a creature of different sex and age and only partly hers.
For a few years only had he been part of her.

"Perhaps it was the greatest danger he had to run!" she
now thought with the clear sight of old age. No, she would
not admit it. There was the ever present danger that beset all
men as they grew up, of becoming self-centred, and there
had been in his case the danger, special to his generation of
what she, and all her contemporaries, would always think of

as "The War". Nothing that had happened since had cut off the Past as that event of 1914 to 1918.

The end of his white-sailor-suit life had come swiftly. Perhaps she knew subconsciously that it must, but as usual it was Hannah Scrivener who said what her conscience thought.

"Frances, your boy must go to a boys' school. He's getting too big for my kindergarten!"

Of course she was right. The obvious school was the ancient foundation that took its title from King Edward VI. She interviewed its Head Master, a kindly old clergyman. Queer to reflect that nearly all the masters in a school of that description at that date were in orders. He received her with faint surprise, and she felt bound to put forward her husband's preoccupation with the Bank, and her own experience as a professional teacher, to account for her visit, instead of the approach through the parson of the parish.

"We shall be pleased to have the son of Mr. Dormer of the Bank. The ... ah ... curriculum ... will he be looking forward to the Services, or the Universities?" (She noted that Stephen was Mr. Dormer's son, she was merely Mr. Dormer's wife.)

The question left her dumbfounded for a moment. It was years since she had encountered that sort of mind. It was the same tone, the same outlook that had made her fly from her native village and become a professional woman. This time, however, she had not merely her own feelings and instincts to consider. When she had mentioned the matter to Doughty, after being at some pains to detach him from the easy-going stereotyped round in which his mind worked, she had said:

"Of course, one can't tell what he will become!"

That had touched some basic conviction in his breast.

"Why, he'll enter the Bank, as I did. What else should he do?"

It was so final, so limited, that for once she was overawed. To the Head Master therefore, she replied:

"Our son is destined for a career in the Bank!"

The Head Master had given a little bow, as of resignation.

"So that's how it all happens! Is that what Providence, the very name of which we used to repeat with such awe, really amounts to? There was Doughty Dormer, the third generation of managing clerks in a bank in Easthampton. And because I accepted the offer to teach in Hannah Scrivener's school, and she liked her assistants, as she did *not* call them, to ... well ... advertise the school by taking part in the public activities of the town, I join the Choral Society. So Doughty Dormer falls in love with me. He did. It was rather an elderly desire for comfort than the pasion of youth, but it was honest and kindly. Then I had Stephen, much to my surprise. Stephen goes to the School of King Edward VI and one of his school friends is a French boy called Galland. We invite him to the house because it is good for Stephen's French ... what a forlorn hope ... and he marries my stepdaughter, Stephen's half-sister. And Stephen marries his distant cousin Blomfield. Here they all are, Stephen's son and grandson, Victor Galland's son, young Jean Blomfield. That's Providence, is it? It must be surprised at itself!"

No good telling them so, all those young ones. They might listen to her, out of affection, but to them the whole story was part of the dim past, barely believable, almost comically outmoded. She, only she, of all that household, could remember the daily sounds, sights, the very feeling of the Nineteenth Century, the long, and it now seemed, accidental Peace that lasted three generations.

"They call it a century of progress! What I remember was the awful inertia. There was Hannah killing herself to make the daughters of the middle, shop-keeping class into a new kind of woman. In the Shadow will we Work! Hannah worked in the Shadow of the Grave. Only by that sacrifice did she Mould the Woman.

"There was I, mistress of a great old mansion, kept going by the sheer hard labour of the daughters of labourers who didn't want to be improved. They wanted to get married and produce more labourers and maidservants. There was Doughty directing the whole structure from his desk in the Bank, on behalf of his masters. There was I aiding and abetting him."

Well, it was all gone, a page of history that only a few scholars would trouble to turn from time to time. And here was she, living with the results. And very nice to her they were! But for the life of her, she couldn't say exactly when and where the change had begun. What part of her was still nineteenth century and what twentieth? What made the difference? The date? Was it the 31st December, 1900? Or was it the death of the "old" Queen, or "Good Old Queen" as she was often called? No, a lot of it went on unchanged, right up to The War, as she would always call it. But to her the dividing line, that made her today the Granny, the Gran'maman, the old thing of another time, of another life, was the Diamond Jubilee!

"That was the real culmination. There was nothing gradual and indistinct about that. It happened. And the very night after came the great fire, and the end of Doughty, and the life we had all led. It was never the same again."

Yet she ought to have known, even then. The time was ripe, had been ripening a long while. She had told Wellowes to have the "summer" curtains changed for the occasion, for the Bank House must set a good example to the street.

Wellowes, clucking slightly, had remarked: "That's no good, mum, they get black again in a week. It's the smuts!"

Good, honest, if not very intelligent, old Wellowes. It was the smuts. And what were they? The evidence of the mounting, roaring prosperity of Easthampton, of the whole country, the great Empire so loosely strung round the earth. It was smoked out by the smoke of its own boastful ill-regulated vigour. Smuts!

"No one ever knew what caused the great fire in Middens Lane that night. No one ever knew what caused a fire or other catastrophe. They just happened. Providence, or the lack of it perhaps!" That was what the nineteenth century had been like. Prosperity for those who were prosperous, like the Queen, and the Bank, factories and shipping companies, all mounting up into a great beer-swilling, cheering, firework-blazing Diamond Jubilee. Then a great fire, and the whole scheme of things collapsed. Or, at least, the scheme of things by which Doughty Dormer always sat where his father and grandfather had always sat, and where he expected his son to sit. It all went, overnight. Perhaps it was too good to last, almost too good to be true.

"How often had I not heard Doughty say, 'poor so-and-so, he's done badly', or 'his business has gone down', or 'he's dead, and left his widow badly off'. People did. But Doughty Dormer didn't. Until that night. Anxiety, or a blow on the head, or was he, like the nineteenth century, just ripe to go?"

Anyhow, he had gone, and she had been glad to take a job. And as if there had been something symbolic about his declension, the whole scene of Victorian England of which, in Easthampton at least, he was so prominent a figure, began to dissolve. The Queen died. The Electric Trams came. Easthampton with Electric Trams! The Bank amalgamated with other banks and became one of the "Big Five", did they call it now? And somehow the First Great War had been the master stroke, the quickening, the final seal set upon it all.

That, however, had been years ahead, when she had, in her reduced circumstances, set about the task of making her own way, and starting off her son in life. There he was, a mere schoolboy, not ready to step into his father's shoes, although the Directors had promised to find a place for him when he was. Step into his father's shoes he couldn't. No one wore the sort of shoes Doughty Dormer had worn. The boy seemed to suffer little from their changed circumstances. Neither did she. Perhaps the old domestic life in the middle of the City had had its day. Her stepdaughters seemed to think so. Born and brought up as they had been in the Bank House, she was a little surprised to hear Evelyn say, when told of forthcoming changes: "I should think so. You couldn't possibly have gone on, in that insanitary old barracks, even if Father had lived . . . though I suppose he would have wanted to."

Was that what Hannah Scrivener had been about, working in the Shadow, to Mould the Woman? She herself couldn't feel quite like that about the great old house, the upper floors of which had been her home, and which were now to be incorporated in the offices, until the whole place, people said, would be pulled down and rebuilt.

She had paid a final visit after the domestic staff had been paid off, all except Wellowes, who elected to come with her to the small house she had taken in the suburbs after the great sale had emptied that score of rooms where three generations had accumulated so much. From room to room she had passed, the row of little attic cells in which the maids had been content to sleep; the passages and corridors with their imitation "marbled" walls, some so long that Stephen and his school friends had been able to play cricket in them; the extraordinary contraptions such as Doughty's shower bath, with its leaden cistern; the room entirely devoted to deed boxes and account books; the evil-smelling closets that had contained the sanitary arrangements of other days; the stone stairs down to the cellar, the yard and its domestic offices. It was not merely her home to which she was bidding farewell. It was a state of civilisation which was becoming an anachronism. The certainty, the assurance, born out of the religious convictions of the Quakers who had founded the Bank a century and a half earlier, that was the element of which she had to take leave. Already, she noticed once she was outside it, people spoke about it in a different way. When she first came to Easthampton, to teach at Hannah Scrivener's school, people who alluded to the Bank, if they did not quite bow or cross themselves, adopted a tone of voice that would not have been disrespectful if they had used it about the Cathedral or the Castle of the old City. Indeed those buildings, symbolic of heavenly authority and earthly power, were far less present to the minds of Easthampton of the nineteenh century than the Bank. It was the real temple in which they worshipped, the real stronghold from which government proceeded.

"And then, in what seemed like a few months, the Bank became a public institution, like the post office or the railway. Queer? What was it that had happened?"

And for the first time in all those years, she thought she saw. It was because no one lived in the house, above stairs, any more. There had always been a Dormer there. Now there was nobody. Her main preoccupation had been with the boy Stephen of those days. Her stepdaughters had taken posts which were satisfactory enough, luxurious she thought them by the standards of her own hard struggle of twenty years earlier. When she had done her day's work, teaching, and her greatly reduced housekeeping, she would sit sewing or reading, but covertly watching him, at his homework, or, if he were out with young companions, wondering about him, and herself, and life. As though the nineteenth century could not die without a flurry, that man Vizer, whose very existence had been a noisome spot in her otherwise tranquil and easy life, had suddenly set all the tongues in the town wagging, filled the columns of the local Press, and caused a small crowd of would-be sightseers to congregate outside his office.

"What a fuss!" she now thought. "How sanctimonious people were, with tongue in cheek, all the time. As if all the men hadn't known what sort of a character Vizer was, as if all the women hadn't tittled and tattled to each other about his goings-on?" She could hear it now, plain across the distance of time. Even solid matrons like Lois Marston could not keep the whispered confidences out of "her afternoons."

"My dear, they say he put her into that house in Shady Grove, as his tenant——"

"A foreign-looking woman . . . well, she was foreign, of course."

"They tell me the police took action, but she had Winkler, the lawyer, to help her, and now there'll be a case!"

There was, in fact, a law suit at the Assizes. She had never had, thank goodness, to take much stock of such matters, but was a little disturbed by the "unsavoury details", and the effect they might have on Stephen's adolescent mind. Had his father lived, no doubt he would have told the boy something . . . ? Or would he? Didn't all children find out for themselves? Stephen was very reticent, if quite correct on

such matters. "Weren't we all? In those days no one alluded
to the things that occurred, at habits that must prevail, at
facts that all knew existed. It was a great game of hide-and-
seek, or hunt the thimble . . . no, hunt the scandal! Should she
ignore it, explain it, make light or grave of it? She was saved
the decision by Stephen himself. One day, during Assize
Week, he was late for the midday meal.

"Sorry. Just couldn't get through the crowd!"

"What crowd, dear?"

"Round the Tollhouse. It's this case of Vizer's."

Did he know how near she had been to being involved
with that precious individual? Of course not. No sign. She
could only reply, helping him to stew:

"What a nuisance! Perhaps it won't go on long."

"All this week, Basher says. They've got barristers down
from London."

"I shouldn't pay too much attention to Basher." (Was that
the name of a boy, or of one of the masters?)

"Well, he knows law, so he advises both sides."

"What sides . . . of what, dear?"

"We've formed two sides. Vizer's and Lapetrière's."

She always tried not to forbid him any knowledge, or to
prevent any activity to which he seemed inclined. But this
had shaken her. These children mixed up in this public
scandal between Vizer and the woman he had brought down
from London and installed in a house he had acquired in
Shady Grove on the Seaton Road, the use she made of which
had caused the police to intervene. She could only say:

"It all sounds very sordid and unpleasant. I didn't know
you took so much interest!"

"There may be an appeal . . . it may run into another
term."

There she had left the matter, unwilling to make more of it
than the sort of foolishness boys got up to at school. But the
seriousness of the infants about a law case, and a dirty one at
that? The town was holding a kind of surreptitious carnival,
the local paper printing special additions that were sold out

before they were dry, no other topic possible in any public place or vehicle, the excitement in the streets. Just disgusting! And just like Vizer! She could hardly forbear a small satisfaction in having held him at arm's length. And dealt him a blow with all the strength of her arm. If she hadn't, goodness knew whether she might not have been dragged in to some sort of smirching publicity.

But that was not the last she was to see of Vizer. One morning during that week Hannah sent for her. In the parlour was a gentleman she knew slightly by sight, as a lawyer, a partner in the important local firm of Forster. Hannah introduced her.

"Mrs. Dormer. Ah, I knew your late husband."

"Mr. Forster requires a translation made of some . . . er . . . papers."

"We require someone with a sound knowledge of the French language. Are we right in believing that you spent some time in France, before entering the teaching profession, and speak the language fluently?"

"I believe so."

"Then I will leave these papers" (he produced an envelope tied with pink tape), "and may I call for them, not later than..."

Too late to draw back. Was she going to be involved in this wretched case? The lawyer was brisk and authoritative, and before she could frame some countervailing disclaimer, he had settled the matter and taken his leave. Only then she found her tongue.

"Couldn't your Mademoiselle Estrée have done this translation?"

Hannah replied: "Apparently the other side got hold of her to make her version of the same papers. I didn't know what this was leading to, Frances, how could I?"

How could she? What a good job she herself had always kept Vizer's pursuit a profound secret. Suppose he blurted out something about it now if he were as desperate as some gossips said? She took the papers with a heavy heart, but, she hoped, a face that betrayed nothing more than a natural

nnoyance at an irritating *contretemps*, which Hannah fully
hared, with far less reason.

Worse was to follow. Young Mr. Forster called for her
ranslation. He scanned her neatly written script. She had
ome a long way since, as a young woman, she had first
ecome aware of the attitude of men . . . some men at least
. . towards her sex. She had not been shocked, certainly not
urprised, at the matter she had to turn into English which
utomatically became frigid as she wrote it. That any woman
hould bargain about her person was so deplorable that she
might have thrown up the task, had it not been for a counter-
ailing feeling that Vizer had met his match and was getting
vhat he deserved.

Young Mr. Forster, who had the manners and appearance of
gentleman, and whose firm inherited and maintained a reputa-
ion only second to that of the Bank, seemed aware of her feelings.

"We lawyers have some unpleasant tasks, Mrs. Dormer."

"Yes, indeed."

"We have to do our duty, even when it involves washing
lirty linen in public."

"It seems so!" The very words. Dirty linen. That was just
he impression the closely-written pages gave her.

"I think you had better be at hand, in case any question
urises as to the translation."

She answered with a kind of frozen stoicism, "Very well."

That was how she found herself elbowing her way through
he crowds that besieged the Tollhouse, a few mornings later.
With a kind of sullen anger she repeated again and again:

"Pardon me . . . would you allow me to pass?" until she
got to arm's length of a policeman to whom she showed the
etter of admission she had been given.

She had never in her life been inside a court of law, and the
majesty of the Legal System she found ill-represented in the
ll-ventilated grubby interior into which she was squeezed,
among a number of people who seemed to be fulfilling some
modest function in the wings, as it were, of the drama for
which the stage was, apparently, set in this peculiar place.

"Something of a concert hall, with a kind of mock holiness in the atmosphere, as though, at a touch, the solemnity might break out into ribald laughter. I remember that. I remember gazing at the figure of Justice, and thinking what a good job it was that she was blindfolded. The sword and scales looked as if she were about to argue with the butcher about the weekly joint. Well, that brings one round to Shylock, doesn't it?"

But the tragic earnestness of the *Merchant of Venice* was not to be found in the Tollhouse of Easthampton on the occasion which started up before her mind. The Court became full to inconvenience, sometime before the proceedings were due to begin. A number of people, among whom she recognised Forster, and who might be solicitors were laughing and joking, discussing social and sporting events with barristers in a queer sort of semi-uniform. After all, a wig and gown were really only formal and archaic editions of night-cap and dressing-gown. Was that why these good-looking, clean-shaven young men had an air of a dress rehearsal for amateur theatricals?

"There was a moment, though, when something respect-worthy emerged, when the judge entered. Everyone rose, as in church, and there he was, in his vestments. No, I suppose his robes would be the word. Charles II and very gorgeous. A lot of fuss by various officials, reciting incantations and handing about rolls of parchment and paper. One of them called out Vizer and Lapetrière, and made me jump!"

Somehow, while she had been admiring the judge, Vizer had come in and seated himself near her, but fortunately looking the other way. She received the impression that he had gone downhill a good deal, sagged, burnt-out, since their last encounter. Anyhow, he was evidently in no mood to be annoying. As far away as possible, on the other side of the barristers and lawyers grouped in the middle pews, if that was what they called them, another figure now appeared. Veiled, withdrawn, with the stillness of a cat, and yet emanating an atmosphere of watchful malignity, the woman Vizer had brought down to Easthampton for his pleasure, could not be

herwise than conspicuous. Soberly, neatly dressed, there
is about her something that had been noticeable before—
course, when they had been rehearsing *Maritana*, and
ere had been the row with Vizer over just such a woman?
slickness, a professional air, as if to say:

"*Qu'estcequ'il y a pour votre service, Messieurs—Dames!*
ere are the goods, the price is not shown on the ticket, it is
duel of wits!"

Of course every eye in the Court was on her, either directly
by implication. Vizer got a glance or two of ill-concealed
musement, she thought. He had always been too sharp,
ough men had praised him; she had heard them. But he
dn't, she had then felt, a friend in the place.

"It does not pay, to take advantage of everyone!" she
ought to herself, and was abashed at the thought, feeling
mething not far removed from compunction. He hadn't
ken advantage of her. And, somehow, he had failed to take
lvantage of this Lapetrière woman. Odd that there should
e that link between two people with such immeasurably
parated views of the whole purpose and scheme of life!
hey had both beaten Vizer. Otherwise they might have
een inhabitants of different planets.

Madame Lapetrière raised a gloved hand and adjusted her
eil. Was she trying to catch the eye of the judge? If so, it was
discreetly done that its failure was unseen. But a gleam of
. . complicity? . . . flew to one of the lawyers. "How many
w that?" she wondered.

But her thoughts were forcibly absorbed by the proceed-
gs. And they soon amounted to one solid exclusive im-
ression, "Disgusting!" That was all she made of it. The
hole place, its atmosphere, dialectic, personnel. Over it all
esided the judge. Down below under his averted eye but
rominent nose . . . did he form his opinions by sense of smell
he wondered, for the whole business seemed to her to stink
udibly? . . . the game, the nauseating game, as bloodthirsty
nd sadistic as any bullfight, but with the triviality of some-
hing dirty scrawled on a wall, went on. It seemed to consist

in reading out statements with a perpetual *sous-entendre* th
caused the spectators to lick their lips, she could hear the
and then standing the . . . victims . . . in a sort of pew, call
the witness-box, and baiting them. "I had read about bea
baiting and cock-fighting, and all sorts of revolting eighteent
century pandering to the gory lusts of overfed, tipsy an
debased men. I had just no idea that it still went on!"

It did though. All that morning. Apart from the discon
forts of the place, the outrage to decency that the enti
establishment was, there were awful moments when sl
feared she might be called upon to give evidence. She felt th
piece of blue paper and the shilling that had been pressed upo
her like a stigma, an infection, a leprosy. But she need n
have worried. She and her humble rôle of translator wou
never furnish the sort of fun this thieves' kitchen appreciate
Indeed, she heard with a sense of outrage, one of the slic
young men who had been such boon companions until th
Court opened, and were now engaged in a deadly cut-and
thrust of argument, interruption, and objection delivere
with irritated and contemptuous smiles, allude presumabl
to the script she had supplied:

"My Lud, if it will get my friend out of the difficulty i
which he has involved himself, I have no objection to agreein
that the version in English of the letters he has just put in, i
substantially correct."

"Substantially! Thank you for nothing!" she muttere
with a fury she seldom experienced. The Jackanapes! No, sh
regained control. The air of the place was getting her dow
It even made her drowsy, once that sharp stab of anxiety les
she be hoisted up as a target in this pestilential shootin
gallery had died away. She sat, uneasy as in a nightmare
while the facts, so simple and inevitable that anyone coul
have guessed them, and spared all this noxious ingenuity
were teased out like the torments of Hell in some medieva
morality. Vizer had induced the woman to come to East
hampton by promises he didn't mean to keep. He and sh
quarrelled, as anyone could have told they were boun

quarrel, in such a relationship. Even devoted married
ople found life together difficult enough. It had been one
the triumphs of her marriage with Doughty Dormer that
ey had had sufficient interests in their lives other than mere
xual attraction, to enable them to treat each other with
vility. Vizer had tried to get the person out of the house in
hich he had put her and which she had made to serve her
wn ends, including spite against him. She had relied on his
nwillingness to set the law in motion, but had goaded him
ntil he had done so. And here they were.

In the middle of the tale of recrimination and subterfuge,
voice as from another planet had fallen on the vitiated air.
he judge was speaking:

"I shall rise now!"

"All stand!" shouted the ushers.

She had been swept by the giggling jostling rout into
corridor, and suddenly halted. Ahead, where the gothic
oorway framed a blessed space of pure outside air, were
noutings and scamperings, the clatter of hooves and rumour
f a crowd. She was thrust forward and found herself on the
avement, where the judge had just entered the state coach
ent for him, in a wide space cleared by mounted police.
here was something almost heartening about the stolid good
umour of the moustached constables on their great golden-
rown animals that brushed back the yelling sightseers like
o much dirty water. She slipped away into Middens Alley
nd through into less encumbered streets.

Stephen was home and it was dinner-time. She did not go
nto explanations, but saw to his needs while he, fork in hand,
lodded through the columns of the special edition of the
ewspaper. She had to make an effort not to try to forbid or
nterrupt that perusal. It was far removed from anything she
ad ever imagined as his education in social and personal
elationships, the "facts of life", and delinquency. He must
earn what people were like, and how different was the current
iew to the high-minded, dutiful and tranquil atmosphere of
is home. If she dare comfort herself, it was on the score of

his serious calm. The things that he read, scarifying enoug
for a well-bred youngster, moved him neither to chuckle n
horror. That was something. He put the paper down witho
a word and prepared for his afternoon's cricket.

When he had gone she heaved a sigh and went and bathe
her face and hands, as if washing the contact off. Your
Mr. Forster had passed her a note, dispensing with her furth
attendance. A gentlemanly consideration. Once again t
flood, the raging torrent that swept all humanity along, draw
ing some, flinging others high and dry, and yet fertilisin
stimulating, motivating all existence, had ebbed away fro
her and left her. Until it was the turn of another generation
course.

The door opened, and young Jean came in carrying a gre
tray filled with tea-things.

"Dear me, have I been asleep!"

"Oh, no, Gran'maman, just closing your eyes. You ha
a tiring afternoon."

"Rubbish, child, I sat in a vehicle, and was trundled dow
the street, and spoke to half a dozen people and two scor
children. I oughtn't to be tired!"

"It was a splendid effort. They'll never forget it, as long a
they remember the Floods. You're a kind of Mrs. Noah
letting them out on to dry land!" They both laughed.

"Meanwhile, where are all the others?"

"They'll come, when they want their tea. Some may hav
gone off with Barney and his sister."

"Where's Steve?"

"Helping his father, I expect."

No, she must be wrong. She had begun to wonder if Stev
were the destined young man. The relationship was not too
near to matter. But there was no trace of a blush, or lowere
eyelids. That wasn't it.

"Are we to see more of that young woman of Victor's?"

"He may bring her along. She's a useful girl, she know
the Marsh Street people."

"That's what I thought. Queer translation from the village being a mannequin!"

"Nina's doing. She says she saw that there was the aptitude en Liza went to the class in Easthampton!"

"So I gather."

The words were hardly out of her mouth before the crowd   ne surging in, chattering and joking, as young people   own together by some mutual interest will. They made   reat fuss of her, but once she was installed at the head of the   ole, there wasn't much she could join in. Sports, jobs,   ospects that the Floods had for the moment pushed into   e background were taking their proper place once more.   olleges and courses would resume, the football season   ould start, the exciting Calendar of the Autumn Session   ould soon be upon them. By the time they had demolished   e great plates of bread-and-butter and canvassed all the   ates for the ensuing weeks, she herself felt she would like   stroll before the evening drew on, and slid away from the   ble as inconspicuously as possible, to get her walking shoes.   omeone, she could not think how they managed it, heard   e telephone bell above the din. Jean went. Call for Victor.   his left young Eliza Triplet unattached as it were, and she   neeled at once to her aid.

"Thank you, my dear, it's terrible to be so helpless, but   can't bend."

"I expect you've done your share of bending these many   ears!"

"Perhaps. It doesn't reconcile one though."

"Can I give you an arm?"

"Oh, no, I mustn't take you away from the others." But it   vas half-hearted. She couldn't get far with any certainty   vithout a companion. And she did not conceal from herself,   hough she hoped she did from this nice friendly young   voman, a certain curiosity. Would this one reveal anything   of the exciting and interesting life of the third generation she   aad seen on earth? Or would there be shyness and reticence?

They turned away from the village and mounted the little

path that led up to the sand-hills. Archie's great engines w
silent, it seemed the first time for days, the wind had dropp
and as they reached the broad summit, just where it curv
back and became cliffs below the higher ground, instead
dyke running down into the marsh, the whole expanse
evening sea, so deceptively calm and harmless, opened
swathes of grey-green and lilac as the light caught it.

The slight ascent had used up her breath and she was g
to sit on a tuft and gaze, and beside her the girl who had l
the village for such an unusual vocation sat, smiling slight
but silent. Was she waiting for something or someone?

"Well, my dear, how do you like your lot in the great City?

"It's a good enough job. All I'm fit for!"

"Come, no more enthusiasm than that?"

"I've no complaints." It was rather hurried as if she h
been caught in a breach of manners.

"Mr. Galland is very considerate, the pay is good, com
pared with anything I could get here, and he thinks of man
things the bigger places overlook."

"That's right. A good boy, Victor, not that you'd brin
tales to me, if he weren't, I'm sure!"

"No, indeed."

"Hours not too long? I suppose you have to live som
distance away?"

"We have a flat between four of us. When we get to it."

"How strange that sounds, and what an improvement o
my day, sixty years ago. It was lodgings then!"

"Miss Cresswell said you used to work in London."

"I did indeed, for years, until I came down to Easthampto
and married."

"Ah! You got out!" A shade of envy?

"I was like you. Couldn't stand the village in which I wa
born, and went to better myself."

"Wasn't it rather awful?"

"I didn't think so, at the time, but when an old frien
invited me to Easthampton I wasn't sorry to make the move
To a better job, of course."

"I should think so!"

"You don't care for life in London?"

"I don't mind London, but it isn't much of a life. And no future at all."

"Curious. I thought most girls liked it."

"Most girls may!"

"Aren't you one?"

"That's just the trouble, Mrs. Dormer. Too many of us, too many people, too much of everything."

"Not enough room? I thought you did a . . . solo act . . . do they call it?"

"We do indeed. We're on show. We're not people, we're what they hang clothes on!"

"A new light. You all look very happy in the advertisements in the papers."

"Professional, I assure you. It sells the goods."

"Well, well. Live and learn. I used to think teaching was an overrated game, repetitive and thankless, and that you, and of course the stage, did at least get applause!"

"Anyone can have mine. And they'd better be quick, while it lasts."

"I can see that there isn't a long career to it. But you expect to get into management, don't you?"

"If one accepts backers. You realise what that means?"

"I do, or did. Believe me, music mistresses of my day were not immune. They were selling an attractive accomplishment to the parents of young ladies, to render them more marriageable."

Eliza—Eleanor laughed.

"It was simpler when a girl had so many cows to her name. And would be much more use, with dairy stuff the price it is!"

"Oh, come, there are alleviations. The peasant's daughter with her dowry didn't get a good seat for the Coronation. Even the music mistress used to have the summer holidays. You don't really think it's a worse world than your mother's?"

"Mum didn't get much holiday, or such trimmings with

M

four of us, and Dad away for months. But these perks come
to an end. We re-open on Tuesday."

"Then it's very nice of you to spare some of your short
respite for me. Now, I've had quite as much of this evening
air as my old bones can put up with, unless I'm going to be
rigid in the morning. Help me down, dear."

It was a nice firm arm, crooked solicitously for her. Yet she
thought there was a kind of hesitation. "A long while ago I
knew that expectancy," she thought. "I wonder if she's right?"

With a long and last look round, for she could never escape
entirely the sense that her opportunities for sea-gazing on
a fine evening were now numbered, she turned and let Miss
Triplet-Truman help her down the steep bank. It was only
a few yards from the perch at the top of the gap, back to the
road that led to Cockle Hall, but it was enough to provide an
answer. There, against the stunted and wind-torn elder
bushes that alone could maintain, in that salt and sandy soil,
their grip against wind and weather, was young Steve,
strolling, hands in pockets, his head "pointing" like a dog's.
There could be no mistake about the intention of that easy
pace and hopeful demeanour. She put on her Gran'maman
voice to which her great-grandson had never failed to respond
since she had spoiled him in infancy.

"Stevie, dear, here's poor Eleanor got to go back to work,
and so worried about leaving her family in this danger spot.
Do take her along and show her your father's new sea wall,
so she doesn't have to worry. It's too much of a scramble for
me. I'm going in."

She tried with all her might not to squeeze that shapely
forearm as she relinquished it, nor to seem to give the
slightest push. But she did turn her back resolutely and stump
away homewards, leaving behind her a silence that almost
tingled in her ears, lest it be broken by some dutiful: "Oh,
we'll see you home!" or what not. But silence it remained,
and she found entertainment in her surprise, in being so
delightfully wrong.

"Not Victor. Steve! You're an old fool, Frances Dormer!"

CHAPTER VI

"SCENES THAT ARE BRIGHTEST"

SHORT as had been her excursion to take the air, it made her third outing that day, and was quite as much as she felt fit for. She was not sorry when Nina brought her a mug of cocoa, saying:

"I've taken your bottle up. You've been overdoing it, you know."

"Quite right, dear. I deserve a sleepless night and aches and pains tomorrow. But it's worth it!"

She surprised herself by the vehemence with which she spoke, and it made Nina laugh.

"You've said it yourself. I hope it is."

"My dear, I just can't bear to be left out of things. I find these young people desperately interesting. I've just left Steve taking Eliza Triplet, if that's what she likes to be called here, along to look at his father's works. Did you know?"

"I won't say I hadn't any suspicions. It's very natural, isn't it?"

"Very. And rather pretty. After all, and in spite of everything we're told nowadays, boys will be girls' boys, and girls will be boys' girls, won't they!"

"It seems so."

Nina was standing leaning against the table, gazing out at the dying evening.

Frances thought to herself: "Now if only Archie were a little less . . . if he could forget his unfortunate experience, he might make her very happy. But he's so tough . . . or likes to look it. I wonder. I wouldn't be surprised if he weren't sore enough sometimes. . . ."

As if in answer to her thoughts, the door from the kitchen passage opened with that noiseless decisiveness so characteristic of Archie, who closed it behind him, just as quietly. He was in slippers but there had been no sound of his discarding great boots, a matter over which most men made such a clatter.

"I must be thinking about supper," and Nina slipped past him. If there were anything between them, they managed to cloak it well.

"Well, dear, I hope you're reasonably pleased with the state of affairs."

"Yes, we're past the peak tides and the weather looks better."

"I'm so glad. And these unfortunate people will be able to dry out their houses?"

"Oh, yes, those that have got the sense to set about it reasonably. They've every chance."

"I hope they're not too disgruntled."

"No business to be after the splendid job you did with them this afternoon."

He was beaming suddenly, with that ready good-humour all the Dormers possessed just below their authoritative gruff exteriors. She hastened to disclaim:

"I'm sure I'm very glad if I cheered them up. It was the least one could do."

"Well, you did it. Not forgotten in a hurry, that sort of direct personal approach. The thing is to get to the children. They'll remember you!"

"It's very nice. And our little circle did their best. I feel quite sorry it's all over. That's ridiculous. No one wanted them to be put in such a predicament. But now I suppose our party will break up!"

"That's what they say." It didn't appeal to him of course, armoured with trouble and responsibility as he was, and not yet old enough to be aware of that feeling of very aged people, that there is not much left. In spite of herself, she said:

"I don't suppose I shall see you all together again, like this."

That reached him, for if professionally insensitive as an engineer with a public appointment will be, he was an affectionate and dutiful fellow.

"There, there, old lady, don't take on so. We've overdone you a bit today. You go and get a good night's rest. You'll feel better in the morning."

He was right, of course. When he bent over and kissed her, she patted his firm leathery cheek.

"Help me up, dear." She took his hand, but she refused his arm. She nearly said: "Go and put it round Nina. I've had heaps of loving in my life, she hasn't had quite enough. And yours was spoiled. She could make it up to you."

But of course one didn't say that. She was a little amused to see that he accepted the independence with which she left him, bearing heavily on her stick. Perhaps Nina would come back before the others came in, and perhaps her will would make itself felt and draw the two together. She would have liked to watch it, but knew better, and stumped her way upstairs. That was the last word, the only riposte old people had. Go to bed. Particularly so comfortable a one, warmed and lighted and turned down. On the little bed table, besides the lamp, was an abundance of reading matter, the one or two contemporary magazines she could understand, a volume of travels that she liked, for she got the occasional thrill which is all that the most exhausting and hazardous journey could have procured her without the exhaustion and hazard. There was a volume of poems that she liked to dip into, and a book of devotions that she seldom opened, but which it was pleasant to have within reach.

"They say we old people should 'make our soul', as the French call it. I don't believe it. We should enjoy the small comforts which may be paltry and trivial, but which mean that those about us, care for us, or they wouldn't provide them!"

She opened the book of travels, but her thoughts wandered, but gradually took the turn given them by the latest human impact, her grandson Archie, whose good night salutation was fresh on her cheek, and whose blunt words still meant so much to her.

Even now, well as she knew the facts, she was filled with

wonder at the stuff life proved itself to be, the sort of person her son, directly the fruit of her own body, her grandson and his son had become, and the others, only a little less.

"Who was it who said life was like one of those tapestries, of which the weaver only sees the back? He works by knowledge of the pattern and his fidelity to what he believes makes it come out right . . . or not. Faith and Works they used to call it. Allowing for the margin of human error and frailty, that was how it came out. Heaven and earth might pass away, but a certain pattern, and a degree of fidelity in its execution, remained. I ought to know," she sighed. "I've seen Heaven and Earth pass away. Who would ever have thought I should finish up in Cockle Hall, depending on Archie and being asked to hand out to flood victims the bounty of their neighbours, their county and their fellow countrymen? Who indeed?"

What was that legend about the child, led into the dark forest, with the purpose of losing him, but who kept a handful of little bright stones that he dropped from time to time, so as to find his way back?

All wrong. There was no going back. There was only going forward, out of the dark forest, into the light of day again. The notion that the goal lay behind one, down the path one had come, was a medieval superstition. There was no going back. There was only going forward. Or was it going round? Here she was, utterly dependent, helpless as she hadn't been since childhood. That was why old age was called second childhood presumably! It was middle life, activity, the power to do and to be that was now so misty. Could she ever have been that energetic woman, left a widow with a small pension and some power to earn, to finish her boy's education and launch him out into the world?

In her mind's eye, as she lay there, so well looked after, listening to the sound of the sea, held back by the wall Archie had built, dimly aware of the household sounds, hushed she feared so as not to disturb her, as those vigorous young people came in for supper, she could see the distant past better than that which was much nearer in time.

But it was there and not to be re-crossed, back to the old City where she had dwelt in the massive old Bank House, and Hannah her friend had kept school only a few hundred yards away, in a City in which everything happened within the walls.

Well, she had left it, and found a little cottage in the southern suburb, just where the small garden plots began and modest houses, with a window each side of the door, three windows upstairs, and if you were lucky, a green painted shed and some kitchen outbuildings. Trams had come to East-hampton, and she who was a country girl by birth, and a City matron by marriage, found herself going down on a tram every day to take classes for Hannah. That had been a lesser, little recorded revolution. To live outside the City, in a street in which there were no shops, only a series of gardens, and gates with numbers, that was something new.

"A dormitory. A place to which one went to eat and sleep, but in which no one worked. The City was too full, too prosperous. It burst out to that!"

It was the same with everything in those rich Edwardian days, for they continued to be Edwardian, even after George V succeeded. The old legend was not so far out. Just as the woodman took the children into the forest to lose them because there were so many of them, so all the institutions of Easthampton, one after the other, began to seek new sites outside the old congested streets, where, as Wellowes had told her, the smoke and grime were now too dense for any-one to live. After the Bank House the same influence began to bear down upon Hannah Scrivener and her all too success-ful school, in spite of the ample old garden and its trees. The day came when, on presenting herself as usual in the study, where the staff congregated after the opening hymn and prayer, before dispersing to their various forms, she found a group of agitated women round Flora Scrivener, who was in tears.

"She can't speak to me. She can't speak to me!"

Hannah had had a stroke. Of course she had. That was bound to happen sooner or later to a woman who was never much more than an invalid and who had driven herself along, and driven a great and growing organisation along, by sheer will-power. "In the Shadow will we work!" Hannah had worked in the shadow. She had moulded, if not the abstract "Woman" in Tennyson's "Princess", at least a private school of a few pupils until it had become so numerous that the inspectors had asked her rather searchingly what she proposed to do.

Hannah had replied, "I shall build!" and had sent for the best architect in the City.

"You see," Hannah had unrolled the plans her architect produced on the table of that very study where they stood on the fatal morning in a huddled panic, "I am planning for five hundred girls, of whom a hundred will be boarders."

"But, my dear," she had remonstrated mildly, "will you have room?"

"Oh, not here," Hannah had replied patiently. "Even if we pulled it all down. No. I have a site in my eye, on the Seaton Road. Ten acres."

That was how Hannah had talked, and looking back on it afterwards, she had wondered if there wasn't something a little feverish and incoherent at the time, in the way she spoke and looked, and the trembling of the hands that unfolded the plans. She had never, of course, questioned Hannah's better knowledge, and never dreamed of asking if, perchance, Hannah had thought of the financial responsibility involved. She had only remarked mildly:

"It is an undertaking, isn't it?"

"Undertaking! It will be the biggest and best school of its kind between here and the North London Collegiate!" Hannah had replied proudly. Perhaps too proudly. Perhaps the excitement over, the vision of, the enthusiasm for, this super-school had been the last ounce of overstrain. Anyhow, there it was. Rigid and dumb, Hannah was in the charge of two nurses, and the doctor called every day.

By that date, of course, she herself was the most senior of the staff, a person of age and experience compared with the bright young women Hannah had recruited, some from among her own former pupils. She had taken the initiative, comforted Flora, reassured the others, seen the doctor, taken charge of the domestic working.

"It was venturesome, but it worked," she mused, not without a certain pride.

After a day or two she had been allowed to see Hannah. She had never forgotten the experience, the polite, rather deferential doctor, the awed nurse.

"None like them nowadays, I'll be bound," she told herself. "The proprieties that had to be observed. The tacit assumption that a person of professional status such as Hannah, must have all the attention of which she stood in need."

But it all made a mere framework about the central feature of that sick-room scene. Hannah's eyes. The only living thing in that moribund body. But so alive; not beseeching, but commanding! How she managed no one could ever have told, but by sheer intensity of her glance she had conveyed that she wanted something. In spite of the doctor's disapproving gesture, she, Frances, had grasped that fact. Perhaps women, especially those who loved, as she loved, nay, adored Hannah, understood where medical skill could only hesitate.

Something on the desk.

"I held up one after the other of the business papers. Not this one, not that, the eyes said. At last, the cheque book. Hannah had written a counterfoil when she was 'taken'. I explained to the doctor, he agreed that she might see her lawyer. I don't think she could hear then, but she seemed to grasp our looks."

So the school had been kept going from day to day, as, painfully, agonisingly, inch by inch, the invalid fought her way back into partial use of her faculties. "Her signature was so bad that the lawyer drew up some kind of document, enabling me to sign with Flora, and we carried on. By the

time she could sit up and say a few halting words that clever
and sympathetic young Mr. Forster had found a person
willing to buy the goodwill and take over the school. It was
the only thing to do. The doctor said she would never walk
again, it was a miracle she was alive, sheer will-power!"

It hadn't been so easy though. No one dared tell Hannah
that they were going to sell the school, her school, under the
Power of Attorney to which she had put the quavering mark
that was all the signature she could manage.

"Hannah dear," speaking very slowly, distinctly and
gently, she herself had undertaken to break the news. Who
else? Flora was no use, too cowed by a life-time of being
a younger sister. "Hannah dear, we're getting you a partner,
to help until you're fit again."

No one dared suggest that she wasn't going to recover and
resume her hectic activities, her grandiose schemes. Gradually
the words became clear, one could almost see the process in
those dilated deep brown pupils. Little by little the sense
registered in that stricken but still active brain. Slowly the
maimed faculties functioned and the words came, one by one
as if the vital force was such a trickle that it could only drop
one word at a time.

"I . . . must . . . explain . . . to her."

Somehow she had not forgotten. In spite of the blow that
had nearly ended her life, that indomitable will had kept hold.
She was still thinking, planning, imagining, however dimly
the great, new, perfect super-school for girls on the ten-acre
plot on the Seaton Road.

Luckily the feebleness and delay with which her partial
recovery was accomplished, dragged on until the normal
time of breaking up. It was arranged that the "new Head"
as they did not call her to Hannah, was to be present.

"We thought we managed so cleverly. I was to take
Hannah a glowing account of the proceedings, the new
proprietress, Miss Purslip, was to appear and be introduced
to the parents, and it was to be allowed to become plain that
this was really the new Head Mistress. Then there was to be

after the usual choral items and recitations, and prizes, a touching reference to Hannah's indisposition, I think we called it. Then, when it was all over, I was to go upstairs and tell Hannah all the nice things the Mayor and the Dean and the visiting speaker had said about her. Miss Purslip had the brilliant idea of providing a marquee on the tennis lawn, for the number of parents and pupils just wouldn't any longer go into the Great Schoolroom.

"But not a bit of it. When Miss Purslip called, Hannah managed to drag herself into a sitting posture, to the terror of the nurse, and talked, haltingly and slowly, but connectedly enough, about the new building and what was to be said to the parents."

Ah, dear! A long time ago. She had outlived Hannah by a good deal. She turned over in her warm bed, and pushed the hot-water bottle further down.

Miss Purslip had heard her out with admirable patience and reassured her:

"That's all right, Miss Scrivener. I'll make it plain to them, and then we'll tell you all about it afterwards."

Hannah had stared for more than two long counted minutes, and then said:

"But I shall be there!"

"Oh, yes, of course!" Miss Purslip had replied with admirable aplomb, and gone on to talk about the new scholarships the Institute was providing.

Once they were outside the sick-room what earnest consultations were held! The doctor joined them, the nurse was called in evidence, Mr. Forster was sent for. It was his shrewd counsel that prevailed.

"You're more likely to give Miss Scrivener a final and fatal stroke by trying to forestall her, than by letting her have her way. Besides, it will give a sanction to the action we are contemplating if she is present. You'll be there, Doctor, in any case . . . and the nurse. Then we must take the risk. I feel sure it is the lesser one." And so it had proved.

Never, never to the end of her life would she forget that

last prize-giving at "Miss Scrivener's School for Girls".
"Somehow it impressed me even more than leaving the Bank
House. Not that I wasn't fond as any happy woman could be
of husband and children and home, and perhaps a little
proud of the position it gave one in the City, and the possibilities it opened up. But after all, I had known Hannah and
her school first, and had returned to Hannah and her school
after Doughty died. I had spent more time there than I ever
did in the home of which I was the mistress, and Doughty,
bless him, never 'moulded' me 'to the fuller day' as Hannah
did!"

It had been high summer, and the great old mansion's thick
walls kept it cool. The garden too was especially spacious
when full foliage and abundant creepers almost hid the fact
that it was a City garden, surrounded by other houses and
not five minutes' walk away from the market-place of a big
provincial town. The marquee, by contrast, was stifling. But
she had arrived early and helped poor little Flora, utterly
cowed by a life-time spent in the shadow of masterful
Hannah, to receive the parents and guests, to introduce Miss
Purslip to all the proper people, make sure that the staff
marshalled the girls correctly and brought them in, form by
form, and had the recipients of prizes and the choir separately
seated in the Great Schoolroom, whence they could come into
the marquee as required, through the great French windows
that gave upon the garden. Then there was constant watch-
fulness to see that the moment the Dean and the Mayor made
their appearance, the whole assembly rose.

Not a bit of use pretending she hadn't enjoyed it, she was
conscious that she was the senior, had known Hannah best,
had seen, by that date, a whole generation of girls pass
through the school and out into the world, and send their
children, for hardly one of those who had ever come under
Hannah's influence could believe that there had ever been
anyone like her anywhere; she had revelled in it.

"It was rather a moment when the Mayor and the Dean
met on the threshold, and stood bowing precedence to each

ther, and then both taking precedence together so that they
collided and both withdrew a yard, bowing once more and
looking so foolish. And it was another precious moment
when poor little Flora went to greet them, blushing and
bowing and managed to mix up their titles so that she saluted
them. 'Mister Mean, I mean Mister Dayor!' and giggled.
Fortunately someone started clapping and no one heard, and
motioned them to their proper chairs."

There must have been four hundred people in that marquee. All brought together by Hannah's quarter of a century
of "Mould the Woman to the Fuller Day". It became almost
a travesty to repeat, "In the Shadow will we work," but there
it was, in letters six inches big, on the backcloth of the
marquee, so that Hannah's motto that she chose all those
years ago dominated the whole scene.

"What a pity Lord Tennyson couldn't see it. He would
have been pleased!" she now thought with a chuckle.

And then, when the whole concourse was seated, there
came a breathless pause, and in silence so complete that
footsteps approaching were audible, a little procession had
entered the Great Schoolroom, moved across it, along the
lane between ranks of girls, hastily rising once more, out
through the great window, and up by an inclined ramp to the
platform. It was led by the doctor and young Mr. Forster
marching abreast. Behind them came the nurse, pushing an
invalid chair in which Hannah was propped up. They
reached the space that had been left on the platform, and
from all over that assembly of dignitaries and staff, parents
and pupils, went up a unanimous sound, half exclamation of
wonder, half commiseration, as if the words "Poor Dear",
never articulated, had burst from every heart.

Then the music mistress who had succeeded herself, raised
her baton and the choir burst into "God Save the King".

"The rest of the ceremony leaves no impression!" she
reflected. "I don't even remember who made the speeches.
Was it the Dean and the Mayor? If so, I expect we got 'Be
good, sweet maid, and let who will be clever' from the one,

and from the other something about 'Immense strides o
modern education, I can remember when there were n
careers for women such as are contemplated today!' Ther
was, of course, the Report which I wrote out and poor littl
Flora read. Did we have an H.M. Inspector at that date
What did the choir sing? The detail all recedes into the back
ground, and leaves me the picture of Hannah, sitting there, s
motionless, staring in front of her. No one referred to he
presence. No one dared. It was as if she were a spirit fron
another world revisiting the earthly scene. Perhaps she wa
I have often wondered. The only sign of life was when, afte
the National Anthem, little Grace . . . what was the child
name? . . . came tiptoeing up, in her Sunday best, and offere
Hannah a bouquet of lilies. There was a gleam in Hannah
eyes, a tremor just visibly moved the jaw as if she would hav
spoken, then little Grace who-was-it, so nonplussed, laid tl
bouquet in her lap and retreated, slightly scared, and we a
burst out clapping, and the music mistress hurriedly calle
up the choir for a part song.

"Well, we got through. Heaven knows now how we di
with Hannah sitting there immovable and dumb, but we di
and at the very end her little procession trundled out and w
dispersed in a sudden wave of clatter, parents seekin
children, and children parents, all beginning with 'My! di
you see Miss Scrivener!' For the disappearance of that la
figure in the invalid chair, whose glance none of us da
encounter, let loose the so-violently suppressed feelings o
that hour and a half. I remember leading away the Mayor an
the Dean and the guest speaker to a special cup of tea in tl
study. Surely H.M. Inspector was there, and Flora of cours
but whoever else I can't imagine. It was an unspeakabl
relief. We were almost jocular about it, I recall."

"A very remarkable feat of psychological control!" Tha
was the Dean.

And from the Mayor: "What a woman! What happen
now, I wonder?"

There was no need to wonder. Hannah never spoke agai

Did that last effort use up what faint spark of vitality was left? Did she, by some equally mysterious feat of intuition, succeed in gleaning from something in Miss Purslip's speech, some atmosphere, possibly some last gleam of deductive reason, grasp what the school as she had known it and the sort of person she was were coming to an end, and that in future state aid and state control, trained and certified teachers and pupils chosen by examination would replace an institution which was Hannah? For that is what I remember. Breakfast Hannah had ordered. Prayers. Hannah officiated. Classes Hannah had organised. Dinner. Hannah had ordered. Recreation, Hannah had imagined. Evening meal, preparation or some occasion, play or reading, lecture. Bedtime. Some two score people slept in beds Hannah had provided. Well, it had been so well and adequately done that it had burst out of its limits in all directions, as a well-fed child bursts out of its clothes.

Perhaps it was Hannah's child! All the devoted maternity, the loving care, the forethought, the aspiration that I concentrated on Stephen and my stepdaughters was thwarted and diverted in Hannah, and embraced the school. "In the shadow will we work". That was it. Obscure and indirect, all the babies Hannah never had became not merely the pupils, but the whole organisation under her roof. She had worked in the shadow, and moulded that. People might say she killed herself over it and became the victim of her idea. It is truer of Hannah than of most of us. She must have been a potent influence in Easthampton for two generations, by the time the youngest of those who were present at that last prize-giving sent their children to a very diffrent sort of school.

For die she did.

The doctor forbade anyone to see her, when all the guests were gone, the grandees thanked and taken leave of, the parents and children clattering down the street, the staff having a high tea at which they gorged out of sheer relief. It was all over, the great marquee empty of everything except

the scent of pot plants, the school-room summarily tidied b
maids in haste to be off on their board-wages until th
mansion could be closed. When I had seen little Flora up t
her room with a cup of tea and a wet compress on her fore
head, I went off to Laurel Cottage to look after Stephen.

"You should have been there," I told him. "You are
former pupil. Your 'Aunt' Hannah actually sat there lik
a statue through it all."

"Good for her!" He seemed to register something, bu
not much, and went off to his Territorials.

Then, in the morning, a mistress came on the work
men's tram to summon me.

"Miss Flora says, will you come at once."

"Is Miss Scrivener worse?" I demanded.

"I'm afraid she is," she answered, "the doctor has been
Poor Miss Flora is in a dreadful state."

Well she might be. I was too late. Hannah was gone. Sh
was cold and rigid when I came to her bedside but her eye
wouldn't close. Odd! It made one wonder how long she ha
been dead and if she really were. There was no other sign o
life and the doctor signed the certificate. Flora was prostrate
I took charge, saw young Mr. Forster about the money an
old Grief about the funeral; saw the remaining members o
the staff off, got the maids away and the charwomen in
locked up after them and took Flora with me to Laur
Cottage and put her to bed.

Even then I don't know that I quite realised that, just a
the Bank had been rebuilt and no one would ever be agai
what Doughty had been there, in the old house, on the firs
floor, so no one would ever be again what Hannah had been
and the mansion would be replaced by a block of offices
There was so much life in both places, and the sort of perso
that Doughty was in the Bank, and Hannah was in her schoo
made such institutions so personal. And now, hardly anyon
remembers what they were like.

There were faint sounds outside, it might be of the othe

coming up to bed. She twisted over to look at her bedside clock. Ten-thirty. Like all very old people, she just could not sleep or wake, lie or sit, stand or walk for more than a relatively short time. Softly and with precaution, she levered herself up, reached for her dressing-gown, pushed back the clothes and then drew them over her bottle, while she took a dozen turns, up and down the room. She halted at the window embrasure which Archie had had widened and fitted with a steel casement. She drew the curtain and looked out, it was moonlight, few clouds about. The sea, where it became visible as the coast shelved away southward, was bathed in soft light and moved with a soothing rhythm as if rocking the world to sleep. Who could credit that, only so few hours earlier, it had been an imminent danger, and that people had fled from it, while it broke down their defences, submerged their homes, destroyed the effort and care of years? "After life's fitful fever, he sleeps well!" she quoted to herself. There was little enough sign of alarm now. The submerged portion of the marsh was not visible from her viewpoint. On the higher ground, inland, one or two lights were visible, steady and unwinking. What a reassuring thing a lighted window was at night. Far to the west, a glow on the clouds, faint because of the moon, showed where the City lay. The sight gave her just the right respite and deflection. She let fall the curtain she had drawn aside, opened her bed, and pushed the hot-water bottle down. "Creature comforts!" she reflected; "a cup of cold water, a hot-water bottle; a cup of hot tea, a kind thought. Who would despise such trivialities? Until, of course, the day came when all triviality was past."

That was what had happened to Hannah, half a century before. Nowadays, people took for granted the new spaciousness Hannah had been one of the foremost to add to life by her teaching and her attitude to the position of her sex in civilised society. But not then. She had never contemplated what sort of funeral would crown Hannah's long devotion.

N

Who did? The modern world was far more familiar with death.

The arrangements Mr. Grief (yes, that indeed had been the name of the undertaker, believe it or not) had made at her instructions had been simple enough. There were only herself and Flora who was quite unfit to stand by her dominant elder sister's grave, and whom she had firmly kept in bed. Miss Purslip expressed a wish to come. Mr. Forster and the doctor would occupy a second carriage. The nurses could come in the third. There was no one else. The Scrivener parents were long gone, the family relatives few and distant, and the elder ones had always disapproved of Hannah's new ideas and revolutionary methods.

"My dear," she could almost hear the shocked tones, "she dresses the girls in . . . ah . . . pantaloons and shifts, for . . . er . . . gymnastricks!" (Blue serge knickers and tunics for gym.) "They act Shakespeare . . . and learn . . . science." (Shakespeare was not nice. Science even less so. It was about insides!)

If there were a protest, "Well, you know, most schools do science."

"Yes, dear. Botany perhaps. But biology?" the horrified whisper trailed off.

Or the other approach, the prosperous merchant: "Needn't bother with all these learned subjects, Miss Scrivener, my girls won't have to earn their living. I want them to be ladies."

The prosperous bearded farmer standing respectfully near the door in the study, so as not to leave the print of his great boots on the carpet, and holding out the bill he had received: "Look here, Miss Scrivener. I could ha' bought a bullock with what you've charged me for my girl!" Hannah had replied: "How many bullocks is your daughter worth?" The man had moved his head uneasily, just like a young short-horn, thrusting against the stout iron rails of the pen on the Cattle Market. "Well . . . a course . . . I du!"

Hannah had that power of coercion. Undoing the double-breasted box-cloth coat, the fellow had rummaged deep in a great pocket, brought up a fistful of golden sovereigns and put them down one by one.

"Have you got the change, ma'am?"

"Oh, yes!" Hannah was never heavy or grudging once she had made her point. "Frances, ask cook for the silver, while I write the receipt."

Long ago, of course, but at the date of Hannah's death it hadn't been so long ago, and she had been surprised when, on the morning after the brief notice appeared in the obituary column, she found, when she went down to the mansion, that Flora was sitting up in bed, turning over bewilderedly a trayful of letters.

"Look here, what cook has brought me!" Flora was completely unstrung.

Sitting down beside her, she had methodically opened the letters. Condolence, expressions of sympathy, reminiscences, offers of help even, from former pupils; old members of staff, friends, such as Hannah had had time to keep in touch with; H.M. Inspector, visiting masters and mistresses. She sorted them out, into official, semi-official, those that related to the school and left Flora the few relatives. It had taken her all the evening, and when it was done she heaved a thankful sigh and bade Flora good night. That was that!

She little knew. The small funeral cortège clattered over the cobbles in front of the mansion, that Hannah would never bestride again, left the imposing housefront with its drawn blinds, for Flora's room looked out over the garden, and there Flora sat, not weeping, but handkerchief in hand lest it might be needed.

She and Miss Purslip, an intelligent and sympathetic person, conversed lightly, as the heavy black horses walked their ponderous way. Nothing warned them that they were engaged in anything but a rather painful but necessary and essentially private rite, until, some hundred yards short of the cemetery, the cavalcade came to a dead stop. Even then, they made no remark until Grief put his head in the window.

"The police are clearing the way, miss!"

Police! They stared out of the window. The carriage followed the hearse, between a dense bank of people, the men removing headgear and the women bowing their heads like a field of corn as the wind passes over it. At the little chapel where the parson awaited them, every seat was filled, and beyond it the cemetery staff were hastily roping off the path that led to the grave.

She had always felt a little on the defensive at funeral services, believing that a good deal of the emotion shown was the spectator's fear for his own fate, rather than thought of the deceased delivered from pain and weakness, or the sorrow of those near and dear. But there was no mistaking this unrehearsed tribute of respect. Hannah had never attempted to solicit approval, would have scorned to do so. And this very quality had impressed. The mainly unimaginative middle classes of Easthampton had drawn the conclusion that anyone who cared so little what was said of her revolutionary ideas, must have a strong belief in them, or some occult assurance of their value.

So the brief sentences were said and the prayers offered, and they moved on, behind Hannah's coffin to the place appointed for it, between dense packs of, she hoped, sympathisers, she feared, sightseers. The brief graveside ritual concluded, and they sought the carriages, and returned to the workaday streets of the City in state to which they were little accustomed. Miss Purslip was evidently moved. So was she herself. This was public recognition. Hannah had been proved right.

That had been the end of Hannah Scrivener and her school. The premises sold well, Flora would be able to retire, Miss Purslip would take most of the pupils, and the goodwill to a great new place outside the City walls. Stop! It wasn't the end of Hannah Scrivener. Though her gravestone in the cemetery might be of the humblest and no public monument perpetuated a name which in any case would mean nothing to the new public that thronged the old City and was bursting out in every direction, in new factories and hastily built dormitory suburbs, Hannah had a living memorial that no erection of a few cubic feet of soot-covered granite could rival. Hannah's memorial was the new education, the new outlook, the women's colleges, the bursaries and scholarships that took girls, almost as many as boys, abroad or at home to educational establishments that had, so short a while ago, been the privilege of the few. People had deprecated Hannah's insistence that women should be useful, capable, independent and not merely ornamental. Hannah had won. How many girls today failed to enter a profession or at least, take a job?

"My girls won't have to earn their living!" Wouldn't they?

"What do girls want with science? Science is not nice!" No, it isn't, but women will master it. Hannah had set out to mould the woman to the fuller day, and now the fuller day had dawned. All the same, she recollected that she paid a last sentimental visit to the mansion, claiming the keys from Mr. Forster's office on the plea that the now vacant and echoing place might still contain something that had been overlooked.

"Somehow I wanted to see the very walls and ceilings among which so much had happened, to Hannah, to me, to a whole generation of English girls. Of course the place was stuffy with being shut up and unused for weeks. That didn't matter to the firm that had bought it to pull down. It mattered to me. They had shut in something that had caused perhaps the biggest revolution in English life since the Reformation and the destruction of the monasteries!"

A sudden thought struck her.

"Of course, that's what it was . . . the destruction of a monastery. Hannah had dedicated herself, and imposed a sort of vow on every pupil in the school. Instead of seclusion they were vowed to expansion, that's all!"

So she had let herself in and strolled, savouring the silence and emptiness where, for twenty-five years, there had been, for at least two-thirds of the year, the footsteps and voices, scuffling and singing of five score new young Englishwomen, to the Great Schoolroom where they had assembled, to the remote classrooms where preparation for public examinations had taken place. She had poked into the dark kitchen and sculleries, gone out by the back door and trodden the length of the main gravel walk, between neglected and overgrown beds, but still the very walk on which the drill-sergeant had drilled the first young women of Easthampton ever to receive such instruction at such hands. "How smart he was, all gold braid and scarlet, pipe clay and shining boots and buttons, with a wonderful fair moustache and a blue eye which tried to look at the young women as if they weren't."

Re-entering, she had climbed the main stair to look in at music-rooms, bedrooms, the bath behind its gravy-coloured partition, and that other place with its extraordinary erection like a grand piano, up three steps. Why three steps? How cheap mahogany and labour must have been.

Last of all she came to Hannah's room, the brain cell of the whole vast establishment. Hannah's bed and desk were gone. Flora had taken the one, Miss Purslip, gratified, had accepted the other. The room looked bigger, in its emptiness, but she remembered that there had been room, and only just room, for Hannah to turn round.

"Then something made me go to the big cupboard in the corner and open it. What a sight it was!" On the floor, beneath the lower shelves, stood row on row of medicine-bottles, the various doses by which the doctor had contrived to keep Hannah alive. Above, in neatly docketed envelopes, twenty-five years of Annual Reports, growing bigger and bigger as the years passed, delivered at the prize-givings. She plucked down the first, a meagre and tentative affair, had it not been animated by Hannah's determination to turn her personal weaknesses into new facilities for more fortunate women.

She put it back and took another. "And there was my own name. That is what the parents and others heard about me . . . and look, here was another, the year of my marriage with Doughty when I left the school. Hannah congratulating her friend and assistant on the 'Happy Event'!" Had Hannah ever grudged her the happiness she could never share? Well, she had concealed it very well.

There was nothing more to be done. The housebreakers' men would warm their billycans of tea over the reports Hannah had so laboriously compiled, and would make a few pence by carting all those medicine-bottles to the nearest dispensing chemist. She never entered the place again. Very few people nowadays knew where the old mansion had stood, and fewer still recalled the name of Hannah Scrivener. Yet the education given by public bodies and private establishments was what it was, owing, in part at least, to what Hannah had been.

Easthampton itself was changing. She might keep up her small teaching connexion, but she foresaw that the day would come when Stephen would want a house of his own and a wife, and she would have to find somewhere to go. But, like many another elderly person of the Georgian era, she little suspected what mighty forces were to be unleashed to make an even greater change in her life. "Whatever did we do to the Germans?" she couldn't help asking, whenever she thought of that great gap or rift in all European life, on the far side of which, clearly discernible, but hopelessly remote, lay Victorian and Edwardian England, the old certainty of a few people, that they must and should control the habit of the time, teach their standards and set up their way of life as if it were the only one. But she knew well enough what she and all her generation had done to the Germans, and perhaps the rest of the world.

"Too much easy success, too much money, too many ships, too many places where English was spoken, English habits implanted. And no one could make out why? When I went abroad with Hannah and Flora and the others, we were welcomed. Our money was always good. And we had no political ambitions. How well I remember the visit of the customs officials in the middle of the night. Was it at Pontarlier? I forget the names. They passed us through with a grin. But with French or Germans, and still more the Russians, what an inquisition there was! And the awful row in Geneva and Lucerne about the cheap Italian labour filtering in, living on a plate of macaroni, when the local Swiss needed beef and bread and beer. We were not admired or liked, but besides our money, there was our irrelevance. We were thinking about India and Canada and South Africa, and we did not interfere with Continental politics." That set her off on a different track. South Africa was the one part of the ill-named "British Empire" that did excite the excitable feelings of Continental people. She remembered her fiacre being held up, and finally diverted, in Paris. The driver explained, "*Ils vont conspuer la reine Victoria!*" Although her French was fluent, it took an appreciable minute for the sense of the words to sink in, "*Mais pourquoi?*" The face of the *cocher* under his waterproof top-hat was contorted by an almost comic struggle between his national feelings and his hopes for *pourboire*. "*Il y a qui disent, Vive les Bo-ères!*" *Vive les?* Then she saw. The Boer Republics! That was it, was it? A lot she cared. While she had an instinctive dislike of Rhodes and no sympathy at all with those who held shares in gold mines, she had difficulty in feeling compunctious. Doughty, true to the old-fashioned integrity of the Bank, had said:

"Undesirable lot. All foreigners."

"But I thought Cecil Rhodes was English?"

"Irish. Worse than most foreigners."

She had given it up. Chamberlain was a nonconformist who had once been a socialist, who had worn a red tie and refused to drink the Queen's health. That was rather like "*Conspuer la reine Victoria*". Oh, it was too complicated and she couldn't explain it all to a fierce-looking driver of a fiacre in the middle of Paris. She wanted to get to the Gare de Lyons. So she said: "*Eh bien, Vive les Bo-ères si ça vous fait plaisir. Maintenant, allons vite, à la gare!*" Over that sallow face passed in lightning succession a kaleidoscope of feelings: fury and a kind of admiration, apprehension about the tip, and conviction that all English-speaking people were unreasonably, unrighteously rich. He made a gesture with his whole body and his whip, slewed round and drove like mad. But he took the few coins she added to the fare with a reverence that would have been appropriate to a kind of person she certainly was not.

All that was ages ago, but it came back to her memory much later in 1914. She had not taken much stock of the murder of the Archduke at Sarajevo, except to breathe once more the not infrequent prayer of thankfulness that our politics were not like Continental politics. "Never mind, poor dears, they have their cooking and their scenery and their climate!" she always added to correct herself, for she hated complacency. There was something, too, about the German Emperor, which offended her sense of decorum. But *Punch* made too much fun of him, and to be made fun of by *Punch* was a serious matter.

All of a sudden, the whole scene changed, the habit of a life-time was broken by a violent jerk, as a placid, slow-flowing river suddenly plunges over a weir.

Stephen said, "We shall be called up."

She had never opposed his joining the Territorials. She secretly felt it to be a little like playing soldiers continued into adult life, but men were like that.

"But the Germans . . . no, it's the Austrians . . . won't come here!"

"At the Drill Hall they say we may have to go overseas to help the French!"

The French! She was fond of France, of French people, delighted in their life, their art and forgave them readily enough the religion that some of them professed, and the habits that others of them followed. The idea that a great military nation like the French couldn't fight their own battles without our aid was new to her. Then she had remembered something else.

"But your Territorials are Home Service?"

"Unless we volunteer, and we may be asked."

"I see!" She left it to those two dreary little words. In a few seconds something had happened she never thought could happen to her again. Her heart was beating agonisingly, and she had all she could do not to say: "Stop. Stop. This mustn't go on!" so strong had become her instinct to direct and control her life.

From that time onwards, something else took control. Not all at once. She had found herself involved in a process. Stephen was called up. He put off his sober suit that had sufficed for his situation in the Bank. He appeared in rough, dim-coloured khaki, not just for Monday evening, as he had for years, but for a brief, hectic few hours.

She had steeled herself not to show unworthy emotion. It took all her will-power. They sat together, in her little modest dining-room at Laurel Cottage, filled to overflowing with pieces of furniture much too big, from the demolished Bank House, but which she had never been able to bring herself to part with, for it would have seemed disloyal to Doughty's memory. The tall old bookcase, full of books, histories and biographies she never read, jostled the big sideboard whose cellarette, full of decanters that were never filled, stuck out so that there was only just room for a chair to be pushed under the table. She had kept a few of the pictures. The whole had been intimate enough, a proper background for the widow of a bank manager, and for a young clerk following in his father's footsteps. Now, an odd thing had happened. She had retained these objects of wood and glass and upholstery, so as to preserve a decent, useful, modest way of life. That way of life was going to be entirely altered, although the inanimate witnesses of it, guarantees of family virtue handed down, honesty, industry, simple pleasures adequately earned, and all based on a scheme of things, one couldn't call it anything so profound as a religion, were going to remain. The polished surfaces, the solid texture seemed to deny it. But there sat Stephen, turned into a soldier.

It was he who gave the next twist to the wheel of Destiny, or whatever it was that had taken charge of their humble, satisfying lives.

"Look here. If I don't come back——"

She failed to control a gasp, and he continued with a patient grin:

". . . some chaps have got to be killed to clear up this mess. I may be lucky. If I don't come back, I wish Jean Blomfield to have this ring."

He produced a plain sensible gold ring from a pocket, showed it, and put it on the mantelpiece. Jean Blomfield! The cousin in Scotland. They had exchanged visits, she had been pleased and relieved that their two families got on so well. She had never dreamed that there could be any serious feelings between the . . . children, she still called them, though Stephen had been earning these ten years, and Jean was teaching, she believed. In a flash she saw that with her own part-time teaching, her interest in social work, the Girls' Club, the Choral, she had not known what was going on in her own home. Neglectful? Not she! She did not believe she had failed in her duty as a parent. She had meant Stephen to have a life of his own, to be a separate individual, not tied to her apron strings. She had obviously succeeded, and she must not now complain of the result. She put all the accumulated affection for her son, and belief in the general goodness of the Universe, into her smile.

"Well, you will come back, Stephen. And then?"

"Then I expect we shall want to get married!"

"Dear, nothing could please me more."

She said it lightly and brightly, he kissed her, she felt the rough smelly khaki next to her, heard him say:

"Well, I must be off!" and was grateful for his strong command over his emotions.

She stood at the door of the little house they had shared ever since they had left the great old place over the Bank. Her eyes misted a little, for she saw that he was already a different person. He was going away, not merely from her, but from himself, from what his father and grandfather had been, obscure but honest clerks of a superior, confidential kind, the very backbone of the nation that lived on credit.

At the gate he turned to wave and she had waved in response, as he leapt on to the tram. He had to report at the Drill Hall, and the troops would be travelling all night, he thought: she must not worry if he could not write for some days. Nor would she run down to the station and try to catch a glimpse of him as the battalion marched to entrain. All that was for weaker and smaller-minded women. She would show her faith in him, and in . . . whatever it was that presided over such events as marked the closing months of the year 1914 of the Christian Era. Was it the God of Battles? That was Kiplingese and already unfashionable.

She need not have worried. That peak of heroism and sacrifice dwindled to months of anti-climax. What was the high-falutin chorus in *Maritana?*

> Come, let me like a soldier fall,
> Upon some fatal field.
> My heart, expanding for the ball.
> Beats high and scorns to yield!

No, that wasn't exactly the verse, but it very well represented the sound of military bands, the trample of feet, the cheers and gesticulations.

Instead, Stephen wrote, with a kind of stoic dolefulness, that they were in a "coast town" (so like the son of his father, not to say where, because it was against orders, as if anyone didn't know they were just outside Seaton). There would be weeks or months of drilling and the battalion might never go abroad at all, he glumly reported. She shared his impatience, if not its object. She had volunteered for assistance at the War Hospital that had suddenly arisen and found herself with Mrs. Cavendish and others of her set, meeting trains which conveyed miserable, dirty, ill-provided hordes of refugees.

"Some have too many babies, others ought to and haven't!" as Mrs. Cavendish, always abreast of the movement, put it.

A new vista of human history opened up, that she had never suspected. She replied somewhat tartly: "The best people get killed or captured at their posts. The ones that run away are the dregs!" It was unkind, but not altogether untrue. Some of the crowd that had seemed so piteous at first, soon found jobs. Others preferred, plainly, to be housed and fed and not found jobs. Mothers of families quartered themselves on any kind-hearted householder who had room, or made it, and were reluctant to leave, and difficult to move, short of sheer brutality. Those young women who had no families, rightly or wrongly, in a matter of days spruced themselves up, by any and every means, and seemed to look round for any available man, not always unsuccessfully, to give them one.

"I need not have been so affronted. They sorted themselves out, just as Stephen did. He took a commission and I was proud, I admit. The first Dormer ever to do such a thing, but looking the part."

He had, in fact, looked bronzed and well when he came home on leave and once more events caught up on her, and she seemed to have moved more than a year or two from the time, receding rapidly into the remote past, when she planned and controlled her actions, knew what was right, did it, and saw it done.

"Ask Jean down to stay!" he said.

"Oh, that will be delightful." She thoroughly approved. If only all the young officers she saw about the streets had such good taste and faith in the future. The next shock came in the next sentence:

"What does one do about a marriage licence?"

Perhaps it was meant as a kindly way of informing her. He must know that it was not the habit of a previous generation. Her own, careful, responsible, decorous courtship and marriage rose up before her. Licence! Such formalities had been looked after, of course, but that was not the main thing. Did he, could he, realise how grave . . . ?

"Dear, I suppose her parents have consented?"

"Parents always consent, in present circs, you old Mum!" he said, giving her a squeeze.

He went off to see about the licence and she sat down to write to Jean. And to Jean's mother, surely? She was delighted of course. Of course she was. If anyone had told her even six months before that she would lose control of her son, so soon, so suddenly, she would have been surprised and perhaps antagonised. But the war had made everything move at such a rate. She pulled herself up. She liked Jean Blomfield and was ready to surrender Stephen to her, and thankful enough that it was to no other.

"Faster, Faster!" Where did that quotation come from? *Alice Through the Looking-Glass*, apparently. Odd that the classic of childish and childlike foolishness should prove to be so vividly descriptive of the history of the second decade of the Twentieth Century. But it was. "Faster, Faster!" Was she like the Red Queen? She was not altogether pleased, nor was it sensible to strain the simile too far. It was the merest fancy that lent to real events the rhythm of the fantastic imaginings of Lewis Carroll. It became known that a great offensive was planned for the autumn, and all the troops who had been drilling and receiving tardily their equipment during that summer would go overseas and sweep the Germans back to their proper side of the Rhine. People of her sort, to whom the Continent had been open and free for thirty years, never envisaged anything else. The Germans must go back where they belonged. It still seemed strange, in 1915, not to be able to go to France or Switzerland if one wanted. One had not wanted to go to Germany quite so much. But apart from the Kaiser, and the unfortunate penchant of all great European countries for huge conscript armies, customs barriers and a foolish thing called the "Balance of Power", there must still be plenty of plain sensible people in German-speaking countries as anywhere else. Beyond that, English public opinion, among the people she met, did not go, and was not going to be led by the newspapers, which never accurately represented what middle-class England, the Dormers in fact, thought. "Faster! Faster!" meant that, in order to clear up the mess, Stephen and his generation would have to go and do what the French and the Russians had unaccountably failed to do. It was to be hoped that it would all be "over by Christmas", already Christmas 1915, instead of Christmas 1914 as all English people had believed and said. There might have to be some . . . er . . . adjustment about Alsace-Lorraine, and perhaps Poland. But Eastern Europe was rather irrelevant, wholly incomprehensible, perpetual enigma without solution, including the Turkish Empire and Egypt. The rest of the world, America, Asia, Africa, didn't come into view at all, except that the "Overseas Dominions" as people were now calling what used to be the "colonies", sent some very useful troops to this sideshow in the Dardanelles.

Only . . . and this is what stuck in her throat, and in the throats of all the mothers of her circle . . . Stephen and the young soldiers of the Territorial and Kitchener's Armies were all saying, "We must get married now . . . in case!" No one ever finished the sentence. It stuck in the throat like some bronchial affection, common in the bitter East Anglian spring, impeding speech. In this case, free speech. No one wanted to say what followed "in case. . . !" just as no one wanted to irritate the lump in the throat that the March winds of Easthampton so often produced.

"A war-time wedding!" she said brightly to the few people to whom it mattered. There was no difficulty about it. They also were finding that their sons and daughters were getting married in war-time "in case . . . !"

"It's rather like having a picnic instead of lunch!" Ella Cavendish proffered. She always said things like that, mildly outrageous, but not really untrue. "Not a proper marriage" used to be a term of deep reproach, used of those who went to registry offices, or who preferred the rites of the less usual denominations. But this was a case of haste, quite commendable haste, necessitated by imminent embarkation of all the bridegrooms. The old sly hint, "She had to get married in a hurry," began to have a new meaning. The young brides were proud to be married in a hurry, "allowed them to share the risk . . . in case". It was becoming harder and harder to leave the prospective battlefield out of it. Meanwhile, unpatriotic as it might seem in mid-war, she still had her private feelings. "No one could want a better daughter-in-law than Jean. Nice to look at, without being expensively got up; well informed, good social manner without chatter; fond of Stephen without being sloppy or possessive; a qualified teacher if . . . 'in case' became the case, that one never specified." Yet it was "heads I win, tails you lose". If Stephen survived he would be Jean's husband. If he became the case of ". . . in case" he wouldn't be there. Anyway, she would lose him.

She turned on her side with effort as old people do, and looked at her clock. Past midnight! Outside, the country and sea coast sounds, soothing and satisfying now there was no danger to the lower part of the village. Wind and sea, foliage and grass, a bird making a flutter for some reason, a dog barking, very likely for no reason at all. Inside, no sound; they were all safe in their beds, and sound asleep. Only she, so old that her bodily habit no longer ran smooth, couldn't sleep for more than an hour or two continuously. And also she had these long, long memories, her particular possession.

"Why? What have I done or not done that I have outlived so many, and been so relatively lucky, and am left here, in a new age, just watching it?"

There was no answer. Something moved somewhere that was not human will. Even morality had very little to do with it. The rain fell on the just and the unjust, and only here and there could it be said that the unjust got the worse, a monitorial soaking. The just, on the other hand, sometimes got, not their deserts, which no one could assess, but what she now enjoyed. Peace, tranquil gratitude, affection; sometimes, as today, the gratification of still being of some small use.

"It's all so long ago now, and my Stephen has gone, and Jean is far away. I've got her Archie, so kind and good to me, and her granddaughter Jean, so nice and affectionate, if a little mysterious. I wonder what the young minx meant. Not Victor, surely? Well, if he's not after Eleanor-Eliza, he might be after Jean. A dear boy! It's all very well now, but that's not how I felt about it, forty . . . no, thirty-eight years ago to be exact . . . when I went home to empty little Laurel Cottage!" Stephen had only just managed it. The order to rejoin had come on the very morning of that hasty war-time wedding.

"No white satin or orange blossom, no wedding breakfast, no champagne! I could do with a glass of champagne now!" She smacked her lips faintly. The Old Meeting to which the Dormers traditionally belonged suited Jean well enough. It was not so very unlike the Kirk, and pleased her parents better than the secular bareness of the Registry Office. She had looked very nice in her sensible tailor-made, beside Stephen's well-brushed uniform. They had lunch together at the Station Buffet. A meagre war-time meal, but the "young couple" had to catch the afternoon train, Stephen to rejoin, Jean to travel with him, stay in the boarding-house adjacent to the mess for the day or two until the battalion left, and then go back to her teaching.

"The austerity of it. Already the Victorian way of life was gone and nearly out of sight. It doesn't seem to have done their descendants any harm! Is that the final verdict on the Victorians? We had so much that was superfluous? Whoever would have thought it? Not Doughty certainly. He was under the impression that he worked hard and thoroughly earned his indulgences, wine and social occasions, concerts and holidays abroad! And here is a whole generation . . . nay, two . . . doing very well without the things that he felt only a decent recompense. It all goes to show . . . what?"

Her imagination, always freer in musical expression than in any other medium, set her humming *Maritana* to herself:

"There is a flower that bloometh
When autumn leaves are shed,
With the silent moon it weepeth,
The spring and summer fled.

The early frost of winter
Scarce its brow hath overcast.
Oh, pluck it, ere it wither
'Tis the memory of the Past!"

She stopped and listened. Mustn't let anyone know she
indulged in such sentiments. How they would laugh! Or,
worse still, try not to laugh so as not to offend her. Rubbish:
she wasn't offended. That sort of sentiment might be utterly
inappropriate to their tough young lives, but to her . . . there
was something about it, a tenderness, a value put on manners,
gestures of mere politeness, of consideration for human
frailty.

And now, the Atom Bomb was going to obliterate
it all, and there wouldn't be any Past to be sentimental
about.

Wouldn't there? She was not so sure. There might be an
End of the World and a Judgment Day, somewhere and
somewhen, but she was obstinately sure it wouldn't come
about by the force of gadgets . . . did they call them? Chemi-
cals, explosives, silly ingeniousness and mischievousness.
And defiantly she hummed to herself the concluding verses
of the solo from *Maritana*:

"It wafteth perfume o'er us
Which few can e'er forget.
Of bright scenes gone before us,
Of sad tho' sweet regret."

She had to stop and laugh. It was a "caution" as old Wellowes
used to say, the way the Victorians went on: perfume always
wafted, Regret was sad and sweet. Pear drops!

> Let no heart have its power
>   By guilty thoughts o'ercast.
> For them, the poisoned flower
>   Is the memory of the Past!

There you were, a moral to everything, and poison even in the flower. Old Radolin had written in a verse that went differently.

> There is a flower that bloometh
> Than radiant stars more fair. . . .

She couldn't remember the rest, and the little trickle of melody died out in her memory as suddenly as it had come, and the main current of facts resumed its course.

"I'm a lucky old woman. No one has less to regret. My Past isn't poisoned. No guilty thought has o'ercast me! On the contrary."

Stephen had not been killed, miraculously. He had been hauled out of his depleted battalion and put to some administrative job, in the great new army Britain had so unexpectedly created, which was far more in need of clerks and storekeepers than of men marching in the ranks. He was still so punctilious that he wouldn't say where he was, but he came home on brief subsequent leaves without the mud, the smell and the half-washed look that had rather scared her the first time.

"Wait until I've had a bath," he had warded off her timid embraces, he looked so grim, so masculine, so different to the quiet inoffensive young man on whom she had lavished such care. On subsequent occasions, no. He was at least clean and had fairly regular hours. He never spoke of what he was doing, absorbed in Jean's approaching confinement.

That had given her some opportunity to show how she loved him, and approved of Jean, some outlet for the affection that couldn't span the miles or pierce the secrecy that now kept him away from her. Their child was the girl Janet, who had married a Canadian doctor and whose daughter, the younger Jean, was sleeping now in the third little bedroom from her own, in the long corridor of Cockle Hall.

"And who could want a better great granddaughter? Hardly a trace of Doughty or of me in her, but that's how family strains go, I suppose. Three-quarters Scots, the strongest element in her."

Stephen had come home, and returned to his job and taken a house in Eastwick. That was where Archie had been born. But the fatal break with all tradition that the war had made persisted and Archie had gone out to New Zealand, made an unhappy marriage and come home to be the engineer, and tenant of Cockle Hall.

Whoever would have guessed that this would be the long distance result of the Germans invading Belgium? How furious Doughty would have been: "You never told me my great grandson would be born in New Zealand," he would have said. That was where the Victorians were wrong. They thought they really did understand the designs of Providence.

Doughty was dead, these fifty years. Stephen, his son, died. That had been the bitterest blow of all, after going through the war. Some said that the gas the Germans used had got into his lungs. But she, a Dormer by marriage and not by heredity, thought otherwise. She believed that something in Stephen knew that the world no longer wanted the type of confidential clerk the Dormers had always been. Not that Stephen had ever said so. But returning, as nearly every member of the British Army had, not merely to the country in which they had been born, but to a way of life they thought they had defended successfully, he had discovered that the life of the old City, its institutions and outlook, had slipped away in the process. Girls with machines, very efficient and much cheaper, could do what one generation earlier only the sort of clerk the Dormers were could do.

"Not only Stephen. The whole family went, Janet to Canada, Archie to New Zealand. It was as though something overflowed. And now the younger generation comes flowing back. Not that I complain. I'm pleased enough to see them."

She began to feel drowsy. She had never discovered what it was that made it so difficult to sleep between midnight and two o'clock, and so easy, from two until six, when once again it became impossible. But so it was. Her bedside clock said a quarter to two. She put aside the book on which, as so often, she had been browsing, without turning the leaves, as her old, long memory turned for her the years that she had known, turned out the light, and settled herself. She soon fell into a dreamless sleep.

She awoke at her usual time, refreshed, or at least, as alert as people of her age ever are, when they can sleep no more for the moment, and are not ready to doze off, as they will a little later. Now she could read, and the book they had brought her from the County Library, all about the wonderful coloured fish that lived in the coral formations of the great barrier reef, held her attention.

"Wonderful," she kept on thinking, "and so brave of them. Fancy enduring all that heat, and seasickness and monotonous food, all in the pursuit of knowledge."

She belonged to a generation that just couldn't have too much knowledge. "Knowledge is power" was one of the saws on which she had been brought up. Knowledge made all the difference between the weak ineffective woman, the hindrance rather than the helpmeet of menfolk, and the sort of woman she had been, of whom Hannah had provided so fine an example. Hannah might very reasonably have been an incubus on her relatives and friends, one of those creatures who battened on the more hard-working members of society. But Hannah had driven her ailing body along the road to competence, success, even a mild local renown. Knowledge had been her tool and her material.

Equally Jean, her daughter-in-law, with her good Scots head, her sound Scots respect for knowledge, sheer hunger for what could be got out of books, had been a good wife, good mother, independent and helpful. Jean her grand-daughter would be the same.

"By the way, she's late with my tea. Unlike her! Isn't this the day they are all going back to their jobs, or their educational courses? Perhaps she's busy packing. It's not like her to forget!"

She waited another quarter of an hour. Sleep was now impossible. A feeling of compunction invaded her, as it will those who, elderly and cherished, cannot bear to be a burden. Finally, she pushed back the bedclothes, levered herself upright, and got into the nice warm dressing-gown and fur-lined slippers the various children and grandchildren had given her. She would go down and get her tea for herself. Opening her door with precaution, she had only taken a step along the passage when she stood rooted to the spot. The third door in the row of "cells" as the young people loved to call them was ajar. It was young Jean's room.

"What a shame. She's probably downstairs getting my tea. You're a suspicious old woman, Frances Dormer!" She was about to retreat, satisfied, when she heard, from that half-open door, another sound. A voice. A male voice. No! Not Jean. Unless she were ill. It was the voice of Victor. It was pleading.

"Let me, there's a dear!"

Then Jean's voice, "You can if you like!"

"Not if you don't want to."

She might have fled, she might have confronted them. There rose up in her a grandmother's anger at confidence betrayed, fighting against a warm-hearted woman's gratification when two young things come together. But the tones that reached her were not such as to justify apprehension. Victor's was urgent, but business-like, not bemused. Jean's was hoity-toity, Cock o' the North. Nor did she catch any hint of embarrassment in the next words.

"I expect she knows already!"

Who was this *she*? Was it Jean's adoring Gran'maman who was to be told something? This thought made her realise that she was eavesdropping. She never had and never would.

With greater precaution than she had exercised for years, she stealthily withdrew, reached her door which fortunately she had not completely closed. It rattled slightly in the fresh morning draught, and she gripped it firmly, slipped through and drew it close behind her. As she did so, she saw Victor drag himself across the passage to the stairhead. He made a fine figure, there was a taste and style about his dressing-gown a little too sumptuous to be English, a smouldering fire in his eyes, a little too dark for the descendant of the Dormers. As he went, Jean closed her door, hesitating a moment to give him a little peck of a kiss and a push with her hand. Her dressing-gown was far less impressive, but it fitted close to her neat little figure, while her smiling face showed a woman capable of strong passions, and always completely mistress of them.

Frances hurriedly resumed her bed, pulling the clothes round her, not so much for warmth, as to show no sign of their having been disturbed. "And now . . . what?" she asked herself, as people will who have suddenly thrust upon them a situation they feel they ought to have foreseen. "Presumably I shall get my tea. And some information! They say in East Anglia, 'It's no use getting old if you don't get artful!' I don't seem to have been very artful. The secrecy of that young Jean. Even more remarkable, the way Victor misled me. I began to think there must be something between him and Eliza-Eleanor!"

Then her real warmth of heart, the deep thankfulness for all the blessings she had received, broke over her in a wave.

"May they be happy, the whole lot of them. If I can believe that, I can go without a care."

Easy to say, not so easy to do. Tears came into her eyes, and she brushed them away.

"You old fool, you've had eighty years and more, and eighty good ones. And now you're not satisfied. You want another eighty to watch the young ones, and share their enjoyment. Well, you can't have what you want, that's plain English, isn't it?"

So she sat until sounds outside made her twitch the eiderdown straight and preen herself slightly. What was she going to hear with her morning tea?

There was a discreet tap at the door.

"Come in, dear."

Young Jean came in, that same unobtrusive dressing-gown belted tight round the firm young waist.

"Good morning, Gran'maman. Sorry I'm late."

An awful temptation to say, "You're not sorry a bit. Your assignation was thoroughly enjoyable, you little humbug!"

But she substituted: "My dear, I ought to apologise. I'm an old nuisance!"

"No you're not!" She got a kiss on her left cheekbone. Were those well-set lips the least suspicion softer than usual, as if they'd had a little extra use, not so long before?

"Oh, yes, I am. You'd like to go on sleeping, and you have to get up to look after this old bag of bones!"

"Nonsense, Gran'maman! It's a pleasure."

Again she nearly said, "That's not the pleasure that makes your eyes dance and your dimple come and go as you try not to smile." Once more she substituted:

"I wish you joy. Are the others up?"

"Some are, and some aren't."

Was she being regarded with amusement? She wouldn't have cheek, not even nice soft cheek.

"The men have gone to have a last look at your uncle's sea defences, I expect."

"Now, how did you know that?"

"It's their last chance, isn't it?"

"Yes, I suppose it is. They'll be able to go back to work reassured, won't they?"

In spite of herself she could not help twinkling, "It's nice to be reassured, isn't it?"

Young Jean, hands on hips, was regarding her.

"Are you being mysterious, Gran'maman?"

"Not more than most."

The young baggage shouldn't stand there, brazening it out, without reproof.

"Shut your eyes, and close your mouth, and see what the king will give you."

"You've got it wrong. Open your mouth, it should be."

"You do as you're told for once, you obstinate old dear."

"Very well, here goes."

She shut her eyes and closed her lips. She got what as children they had called a "butterfly kiss", a tickle of long eyelashes on her forehead, a whisk, a door softly shut and she was alone with her tea when she opened her eyes. Phenomenal! Jean had always been the one so grudging of kisses, with a strong Scottish distrust of exhibitions of emotion, even such mild ones as embraces between near relations. She must be deeply moved. But, characteristically, it hadn't made her hand shake. The tea was delicious. Either it, or the sense of young people's love bursting into flower around her, made her glow right down to her toes. She sat there, gazing out of the window at the uncertain East Anglian morning, the fitful breeze pushing great white clouds about, so that the bursts of sunshine and sudden shadow made a pattern on the wall. Only gradually did the first upsurge of emotion die out, the prosaic light of everyday return, household sounds, the scent of bacon being fried.

"Alas! Nothing can stand against it," she grunted. "I ought to be planning the children's future, years ahead, after I am gone, but what I really want is my breakfast, now, at once." She got up and dressed.

The big room downstairs had the unmistakable air of people having their last breakfast of the holidays together. Some had finished and some hadn't. Young Steve had gone out, Victor and Jean were nowhere to be seen. Nina Cresswell brought hers.

"Your family will decrease today, dear."

"It's all right, Gran'maman. Mrs. Kitchen has come."

There it was, the perpetual anxiety of the nineteen-fifties. First to obtain daily help, then to keep it. The domestic rhythm of Cockle Hall was never assured until that presence informed the atmosphere. Mrs. Kitchen didn't work for anyone. She "obliged" households of which she approved, at a price. But she was too efficient to be criticised in a world in which efficiency was precious and the willingness to oblige the cement that held the social fabric together.

"Victor's gone to fetch his car," Nina volunteered.

"Oh, that's where he's gone." She could hardly forbear a faint sarcasm. But Nina was serious.

"He's taking Eliza Triplet with him."

It made her laugh.

"Tell me, Nina, does she get out somewhere and change her name by the side of the road?"

"Something like that, I expect. They are dropping Steve at Cambridge and Jean in London."

"H'm. I wonder how far Victor will drop her?" But she didn't say it. She must pretend to be surprised when the time came. It was part of the game. But all this was put out of her head by the sound of singing, and good, not discordant, singing outside.

"That'll be Emil and his Scouts. Will you come and take leave of them?"

She pushed back her empty plate, levered herself up, hobbled to the door and faced the singing.

A great lorry stood there, panting, as it were. And well it might, for it was heaped with tents, bedding-rolls, clothes, kitbags, things she vaguely knew the names of, others that she had to guess at. On the top sprawled its human cargo, limber, intelligent-looking boys with something about them, a pallor, an experience that had stained them in infancy and which they would never entirely throw off. On the hood that overhung the driver Emil Tisch was seated, back to engine, conducting with his scout pole the student song they sang so well. Was it: "O, Jerum, Jerum!" She couldn't remember, but they sang well, and as the notes died away Emil turned to her. Good Heavens! He was going to make a speech. She was not quick enough, nowadays, for

flight, and she was intrigued. The Germans, clever, then
suddenly obtuse. Brave as lions, then suddenly cowed by
empty threats and foolish slogans. Sentimental to tears, and,
in a flash, brutal as any Asiatic nomad.

"The members of the . . ." she could never catch up with
those long allusive portmanteau words in which the German
language abounded, so that it seemed to grow them. She
heard: "*Volks*" and she heard ". . . *erei!*" but what came in
between, and what it all conveyed she was not sure.

". . . th . . . their best thanks to the lady over-presiding,
that so much kindness to our stay has added!"

They all pulled off their useful, sensible caps, waved
them three times round their heads, chanting in unison
"Hurrah! Hurrah! Hurrah!" Replacing their caps they began
clapping, but not in the shamefaced, thank-God-that's-over
way that any English party would have clapped, with an
earnest air of "Don't let's hurt the lecturer's feelings, he is
a bore, but if we clap he'll never know!" They clapped to
order, taking their time from Emil, "One-two-three, one-
two-three, one, one, one; two-two; three-ee-ee!"

She stood bowing and smiling, but as ill-luck would have
it, her gaze, which she had tried to turn towards all the four
corners of the lorry so that no one of them should feel that
his particular contribution to the noise had not been fully
appreciated, happened to rest on the driver from Palgrave's.
He had slewed round in his seat, with one hand on the wheel,
his roly-poly English face, visible through the little window
at the back of his driving cab, was at all times as professionally
bereft of all expression as his engine which gently purred,
as he held it braked and declutched. But as he watched the
graceful, premeditated and skilfully accomplished gestures of
the Central Europeans, there became visible on those blunt
features, the faint embodiment of what he thought. He did
not know he was observed, but when his eye caught hers, he
gave her something less than a smile, and far less than a
grimace. In the utterly impossible case of his finding words
for what he was thinking they might have been, "Well,

I'm . . . aren't you, mum?" Yet there was something else, the watchful cunning of one who has pushed forward a chair with a broken leg, or poised a bucket of water on the top of a half-opened door. And as the guests concluded their elaborate leave-taking with a flourish, he slipped in his clutch and the heavy vehicle lunged forward. He checked it in an instant, but not before every upraised hand was clawing the air, every taut body had rolled, every face had suddenly assumed a disconcerted look.

"Thank you very much. Good-bye!"

She raised one hand to wave, the driver gave her what, had it not been so respectful, might have been a wink, and the ponderous affair moved off.

She turned and fell into the arms of Nina, and they stifled their laughter on each other's shoulders.

"Oh, dear," she gasped. "It's a shame. Such nice boys. I shall tell Barney about his lorry driver!"

"No, you won't. You couldn't keep a straight face. It was so——"

"Very inconsiderate——"

"No. Apt. We're not clever. But we're not high-falutin. It's a virtue."

"I wonder. Or is it a fate?"

They had turned in at the wide porch between the banks of geraniums, and Nina led her to a chair.

"You must have a rest after all that!"

"Thank you, dear. So nice. So kind. So much emotion!" She stifled one final chuckle in her handkerchief as she dried her old eyes. Nina stood looking out of the window.

"I wonder what's going on in that sensible, kind and shapely head. I do wish Archie would . . . but he's been bitten once, poor boy. Surely he can see. . . ."

Nina, however, was not absorbed in herself, but in something else, outside in the yard. Now she was smiling and turned to give a thoughtful warning, "Here are some more farewells, Gran'maman——"

"My dear, that is now my vocation. Soon I shall take one

comprehensive farewell, and you'll have to find someone else . . . !''

She didn't say it, well aware that young and even youngish people don't like to be reminded that Life, which seems to them so real and solid, is fluent, running away all the time and bearing only an instant's impress, hardly more than a reflection on its surface. They feel obliged to say: "Oh, no! Nonsense. You'll live for years yet. We've never wished you away!" But they mean: "Don't darken the light that streams over us. We want to see, hear, taste. Don't tell us it's all coming to an end, however distant, when we're trying to build something that will last."

She closed her eyes for a moment. It had become rather a habit with her, rested her sight, gave her a chance to collect her thoughts and calm her nerves. For, like all the very old, she had lived so much that all impressions were slightly blurred by the endless allusions, likenesses to other impressions, memories, hopes and fears that, long fulfilled or dissipated, haunted their successors. When she opened her eyes again, she dropped her handkerchief on her knees with a start.

There entered two people, whom she knew perfectly well, but who behaved in an unaccountable fashion, not that which she expected of them, yet oddly reminiscent of something she had thought of in their connexion. Victor and Jean, holding each other's fingers by the tips, were making little mock-formal paces towards her. Victor with a face of pride, open and unashamed as he always had been, when, a nearly-spoiled schoolboy, he had cried out to her, "Look, Gran'-maman, how clever I am!" Jean, in contrast, lifted her skirt an inch, no more, with her free hand, while her demurely downcast eyes flashed for an instant through those long lashes, a gleam of unholy glee. When they were only a pace from her chair, they both dropped down on their knees, in carefully rehearsed unison.

"Blessing, please, Gran'maman!" cried Victor in exactly the same tone as, twenty years before, he had clamoured shrilly, "Ginger snaps, *pour goûter*, Gran'maman!"

That little Jean, her free hand released from her skirt, folded it, together with her other, and that of Victor, in simulated humility on her heart, but her shoulders shivered with the effort of controlling mirth.

What great-grandmother could resist? She reached out her old hand and touched the stubby, wiry short hair on the round skull, the hardly longer, but much finer, sweet-scented locks on the smaller one.

"Bless you, my dears!" She found it surprisingly difficult to utter, and hastily dabbed her eyes while they swung each other erect. Victor was still in his boyish "just look what I've found" mood.

"Isn't she wonderful, Gran'maman?"

"He's just daft!" his love commented tolerantly. "What shall I do with him, Gran'maman? He will show off!"

"Go along and love him all you possibly can, then you'll have something that can't be taken away from you, when you're left all alone in a corner as I am." But she didn't say it. That would have been yet another exposure of private feelings to which Jean was so averse, and which Victor took all too seriously. So she merely said:

"Well, this is a nice surprise."

"Didn't you guess?"

"No, dear." She wasn't going to say what she had at moments thought much more probable, adding, "And what do we do next, if I may venture to ask?"

"I know what I would like, but she won't!" Victor made a pretence *moue*.

"No, I won't," Jean retorted firmly. "I'm going to finish my course and take my degree. It's the only recommendation I've got."

"Just listen to her, Gran'maman, did you ever!"

"I think she's quite right, dear. I am rather proud of having set the fashion. I never had a degree, women didn't. But I had a profession. It's always something. You never know."

"There!" Jean faced him. "You wouldn't believe me, but you'll believe your sainted Gran'maman."

"*C'est dur, c'est triste!*" Victor made a gesture as if wringing his hands.

"When he talks French, you don't have to listen!"

"It's very becoming, all this impatience, Jean, but you're right. He'll wait."

"I shall not. I shall commit enormities."

"I shall strike attitudes, and disown him, Gran'maman. We shall be a spectacle."

"No you won't, dears, you'll be a very well-matched couple. Do you know the nicest thing I had said to me when I became engaged to be married?"

She could see them, in their mood of healthy, almost bodily excitement, trying to pierce back to the queer old times when Gran'maman had not been Gran'maman but a young woman, feeling, presumably, something that they were now feeling. But it wasn't very convincing. Grandmothers didn't have those feelings, they were old, they'd done with it all. And, much as she was loved, Gran'maman had married great-grandfather when he was already a widower with two nearly grown-up daughters. It was almost as fantastic as the whiskers and top-hats, the bustles and bonnets in which it had all been conducted some half-century ago. To the well-simulated interest that cloaked their dubiousness she spoke:

"A very experienced relative said to me, 'We think he has made a fascinating choice.' *He* was your great-grandfather!"

They murmured appropriately and did not giggle. It must seem rather rococo to them. She hurried on.

"One doesn't use such words now. But I will say to you both, I think you are very sensible, and I feel sure you'll be very happy," she concluded firmly, as if she were going to add, "There, is that modern enough for you," which of course she didn't, and there was an instant's silence, while Nina came in from the porch.

"Do you know what these young people have just told me, Nina?"

"Without being nosey, Gran'maman, it sticks out a mile, as the Yanks say."

Murmurs of thanks and handshakes all round. Perhaps only she, in her chair, felt she detected a tiny sigh of envy, and, once again was tempted to cry: "Oh, Archie, do hurry up. You'd be so happy!" But there was a little stir in the room.

"I suppose we ought to collect these love-birds and go. You know about Steve and Eleanor."

"Yes, dear, bless them too. What a car load of happy people you will make."

"It's all your doing," Nina said with a gust of impulsive warmth, as if begging her to do yet more for someone else. But no one would know that.

She held out her hands, and Nina helped her up. She stumped on her stick to express her excitement as she crossed to the porch. Sure enough, Steve had brought the car round, with Eliza Triplet, looking very smart and towny beside him, and beyond that was the Palgrave car, with Barney waving.

They packed the suitcases into the boot, young folks' badinage flew from lip to lip, but she stood there keeping her lips closed and her eyes dry with effort. It was just one more departure, and there couldn't possibly be many more for her. It was all right and just and proper, and she was ready to go and grateful for good health and affection and . . . and . . . she was just a human being and didn't want to. So she bravely hummed to herself:

> "Scenes that are brightest
> May charm awhile!"

and waved feebly until they turned the corner.

THE END